I

THE

INDIGO

PRESS

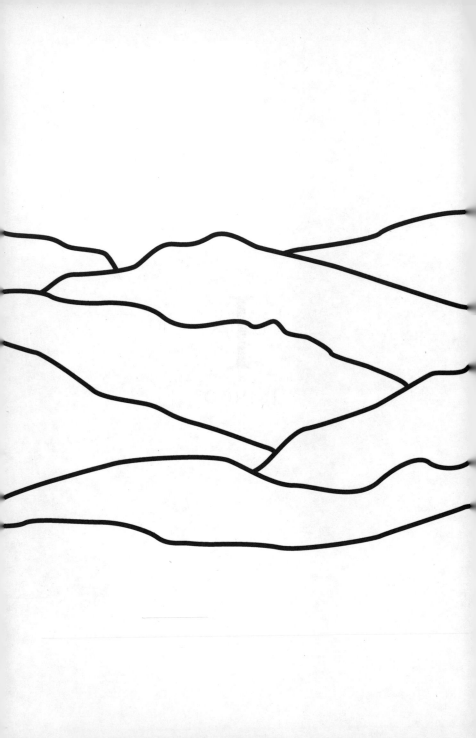

AN ACT
OF DEFIANCE

AN ACT
OF DEFIANCE

IRENE SABATINI

THE

INDIGO

PRESS

THE INDIGO PRESS
50 Albemarle Street
London W1S 4BD
www.theindigopress.com

The Indigo Press Publishing Limited Reg. No. 10995574
Registered Office: Wellesley House, Duke of Wellington Avenue
Royal Arsenal, London SE18 6SS

First published in Great Britain in 2020 by The Indigo Press

A CIP catalogue record for this book is available from the British Library

This is a work of fiction. Names, characters, places and incidents are products of the
author's imagination or are used fictitiously and are not to be construed as real. Any
resemblance to actual events, locales, organizations, or persons, living or dead, is entirely
coincidental.

ISBN 978-1-911648-04-8
eBook ISBN 978-1-911648-05-5

Design by www.salu.io
Typeset in Goudy Old Style by Tetragon, London
Printed and bound in Great Britain by TJ International, Padstow

To Family

PART ONE

Capture

1

Gabrielle Busisiwa Langa steps out from the darkness into the light. Her eyes are at first blind but then they see. Flashes of images stun her in the dizzying sunlight until her eyes stop blinking and settle. There, bearing down on her, a swollen, pitted face, glistening with sweat, a grubby Youth League T-shirt straining at the belly, thick fingers plucking at patches of wetness. A panga, its blade rusting, raised, slices through the air, once, twice. A movement on her left, metal scraping the ground, stones flying, a hoe swinging from one thin hand to the other and then back again. She looks up to see a khaki, military-style shirt, unbuttoned, exposing ribs, cheap sunglasses lying askew on a gaunt face, the lenses pitch-black. This one she knows. 'Hure,' she hears, the voice low and thick. Her eyes swoop to the right – a figure bent over, spitting. She registers the torn, dark green string vest hanging off the sloping shoulders, the tree branch sweeping the ground, the shaven head raised, spit dribbling, the eyes, bloodshot, bulging from their sockets, fixed on her. His lips form the word again. Huuureh. *Whore*.

There are others around Ben, who has been knocked to the ground. All she catches are snatches of him, fingers splayed, a foot shuffling in the dirt; a glint of metal in his palm, *the keys to the red car*.

'I'm – I'm – a diplomat. You're making—'

The words straggling out, as if his mouth might be full of blood, loose teeth – *the flurry of blows falling on him in the moments before she stepped out.*

'I – I – have my papers—'

He coughs, hawks up phlegm.

'Here, wait a—'

'Shut up!'

The men move so that in the shift of spaces and light she sees him there struggling to get up, his hand bloodied, reaching out, red seeping through the white and green of his shirt. It is the same shirt he wore the first time she set eyes on him, over a month ago now, when he'd strode breezily into that vet's surgery. 'Hello folks,' he'd said, his voice sonorous and foreign, 'I'm Ben, it's good to be here.'

'Idiot! Idiot! We know you are American. We are not interested.'

'Gabrielle . . . Ga— are you—?'

Shrill laughter slashes through his words. Her name is a cacophony of sounds in their mouths, mimicking his accent, taunting him. In an instant, her fear gives way to something else. She lifts her gaze, faces them, sets her eyes on the pitch-black lenses.

'Please, let us go. We—'

The slap sears through her cheek – the burning, stinging imprint of it is alive on her skin. It is so hard she staggers backwards. Stars zing around her as if she is a cartoon character.

'Hure.' A shove on her back fells her.

'Listen to me.' Ben, trying again to get through to them. 'The embassy—'

'Shut up!'

A boot-clad foot rising over him; shouts, dull thuds, slaps, a crack.

She feels the heavy prod of a hand on her elbow, and then rough metal against her chin. Her body – this is what she thinks, *her* body, as if what is happening is happening out of herself, to some other poor girl who finds herself in this particular horror – is dragged to the run-down Peugeot. Her feet trail the ground, kicking up stones, dust.

The boot is already open, a gaping mouth waiting to swallow her. She lets out a sound – a whimper, a strangulated cry, a choked shout. The hands are on her, gripping and pulling, pushing her inside. Her head shoved between her knees, her body, foetal, pressing tight against the metal floor; the stench of home-brew, sharp, pungent. The slam of the boot. The sputter and stutter of the engine misfiring. The smell of fuel making her gag, the fumes stinging her eyes. She shifts, tries to straighten her arms and legs, presses her feet up against the metal, gives a kick, ineffectual, her limbs cramped, weak, the boot solidly shut.

The car moves, the chassis vibrating wildly as if, at any moment, it will give way. Her head slams against an edge, the pulse and hum of something in her ears. A sharp turn, the wheels bumping along the dry scrub grass, the car rattling up the verge of the road, and then a screech, tyres on asphalt. She feels the trickle of blood from her arm. Her breathing is at first fast and deep, a wheezing that hurts her chest, and then ragged, spent, an effort, until all that seems to come out of her is the stillness of dead air. As the car speeds along, away, she pictures him there, left behind, lying on the hard earth, broken.

2

'Hello folks,' he said. 'I'm Ben, it's good to be here.'

Gabrielle looked up – the room, till then, had been a sludge of guttural Rhodie *good dogs, sits*. A tall, rangy figure, a brown-and-white dog on a leash behind him, stood in the middle of the circle of chairs, his back to her, and then he swivelled round and took a seat just opposite hers. The dog scrabbled up his legs, knees, onto his lap.

The woman next to him, a floral print dress hanging off her small shrunken frame, her hair, purple-rinsed, whipped up on her head like cotton candy, a teeny-tiny dog with legs thin and breakable as twigs asleep on her lap, whispered loudly in a dry, hollow voice, 'American.'

He turned and bowed in his chair.

'Yes, ma'am, but Rum here,' he said, stroking his dog, 'is one hundred per cent local.'

The white pensioners *oohed* and *aahed*.

The woman patted his leg. 'Well, welcome to Rhodesia, young man.'

'*Rho*—?' he said, running his hand over his close-cropped hair.

Gabrielle fiddled with Mawara's collar. He was a frisky, two-year-old Bouvier Terrier Cross.

'Thank you for the welcome, ma'am,' he said.

Gabrielle lifted her eyes to find him looking at her.

'*Zimbabwe*'s a beautiful country.'

As he settled his dog back down on the floor, Mawara strained at the leash and started barking. The American looked up, met her eyes.

She looked down, stroked Mawara's head, hushed him. The Dog Care and Grooming Open House began.

Afterwards, they were invited for 'drinks and nibbles' at the bar in the gazebo behind the glittering swimming pool in the back garden. She walked out into the blazing sunshine, blinking into the white light; the sky was a sheen of blue, no sense of the promised rain that was falling steadily next door, in Mozambique. She closed her eyes, felt the sun on her eyelids. She looked at her watch. Three o'clock. She had some work to catch up on but she was reluctant to take the walk back to the cottage in the heat, and plus, she was curious. She would have something to drink and then leave.

She sat down at a table furthest from the hub of the bar under a flamboyant, still-blooming red. She sipped her Sprite and, from her perch, saw him being waylaid, his limbs rising out from the throng of bent old ladies who were making a big fuss of his dog, Rum – a Jack Russell she had learnt, during the introductions.

Mawara was lying beside her chair, his head on his paws, nibbling away on a biscuit. Gabrielle heard a long, appreciative whistle and twisted in her chair.

'Tail fins.'

'Chrome finish, a beauty.'

Three men were standing by a brilliant red car – its exterior was punctuated by a white roof and gleaming metal fixtures. It was parked some distance from the other cars – the run-down Lasers, Datsuns and pickups – slightly askew, as though the driver had careened in and dashed out, leaving the door open in his haste. Or maybe the driver was just a brat. The vehicle seemed to her to be some crazy mix of sports car and pickup.

'Nineteen fifties, I reckon.'

The men were in their khaki shorts and thick long socks, feet in Veldskoens as if they had just stepped off farms, looking at the car reverently, too awed to touch it.

'Heck of a lot of hours to get it in this tip-top condition.'

'You're right, there.'

'Must have shipped the entire thing over.'

She turned again, saw that he had managed to clear a path through the ladies, and was now looking at the spectacle of his car. It could only be *his* car.

Unlike Giorgio, she found herself thinking, he did not give off that particular 'coming-to-save-the-Africans' humanitarian aid/NGO vibe, so, probably embassy.

The sprinklers went on, startling Mawara, who barked and tried to make a dash for it; she grabbed him by the collar. 'Sit,' she said, in the calm and authoritative voice the session leader had said was the most effective. After a bit of wriggling, Mawara sat down again. She patted him on the head. 'Good boy.' When she looked out again she saw that the American was still in the same spot, his hands deep in his pockets. He seemed undecided on his next move. Was he considering going over to the spectators, the 'folks', as he had addressed them, gamely chatting to them about the outlandish design and mechanics of the car?

His dog started yapping at the sprinklers.

She could not in a million years imagine Giorgio here, Giorgio with *that* car, *that* dog, *any* dog. There was nothing at all frivolous about Giorgio.

He shifted his head and looked right at her, and then he was striding across the lawn, dodging the sprinklers, coming in her direction, the dog skipping behind him.

He pulled out a chair, sat down. Rum scurried under his chair, her bottom to Mawara.

'Don't think that's quite the right move, Rum,' he said, putting his long arm under the chair. 'You want to be facing the enemy.'

He looked up at her.

'Ma – *wa* – *ra*, right?'

She nodded.

'Mawara,' he said. 'What does it mean?'

Mawara, hearing his name again, cocked his head, sniffed under the chair. Rum struggled to get to her feet, knocking her head on the seat. She let out a yelp. He picked her up, settling her on his thigh;

she stretched herself out as if she were a cat and looked down smugly at Mawara. Gabrielle put a restraining hand on Mawara's head, and fed him another biscuit.

'It means forward, as in, rushing full steam ahead without thought of consequences, reckless.'

Mawara tilted his head and looked up at her in an aggrieved way, as if he had been misrepresented. He barked and struggled up.

'Uh-huh,' he said. 'Good call.'

'Sit, Mawara.'

Mawara slumped down.

'He was already named. I got him from the SPCA shelter about three months ago. He's good company. And what about Rum?'

'She's also from the shelter.'

'Really? She looks too refined.'

Rum lifted her head, sniffed, then put it down again on his thigh.

'You're just putting on airs, aren't you, Rum?'

Rum licked his hand.

Gabrielle was willing to bet that that well-pedigreed dog had been abandoned by some white family fleeing the country, as The Old Man ratcheted up his 'we shall never be a colony again' rhetoric.

'Your car is a hit,' she said. 'You should go over there and introduce it to its fans. What is it exactly?'

'Nineteen fifty-nine El Camino, a coupé utility vehicle, good for town and country. A classic.'

He said it all as if he were reading from a brochure, but his boyish enthusiasm for it bubbled through; there was a story to the car.

'Well, you should take it down to Bulawayo, it's full of old cars, relics . . . I mean "classics".'

'Now you're mocking me, the clueless American.'

'No, no,' she said, laughing. 'They're actually skorokoros, the ones in Bulawayo, nothing like yours at all.'

'Skoro—'

'Koro. After the *about-to-come-apart* sound they make on the road – *skoro koro*.'

'Got it.'

'And the roads are really wide in Bulawayo,' she went on. 'You wouldn't have any problems.'

Bulawayo roads were legendary: built wide enough so that a wagon, spanning ten oxen, could easily make a U-turn on them. But Americans drove big cars, so maybe all roads were legendary there. Didn't they colonize the Wild West with wagons and guns, just like here?

They were alone now, his car left in its glory, the old-timers having stayed as long as they could, hoping that he would come over, probably too shy or star-struck to go and ask him about it. She spotted some figures wandering off across the road to the botanical gardens to exercise their limbs and their dogs. She should get moving, too. She had a stack of work to do. Perhaps she would even go to The Centre, pick up some files. Danika's case was worrying away at her. She wanted to make absolutely sure she had collected as much pertinent information as possible, that there was nothing vital she had missed that would jeopardize the hearing.

'So you're from down south, Gabrielle?'

Hearing him say her name sent a little shock wave through her.

'Bulawayo?'

'Yes.'

'I hear only good things about Bulawayo . . . *Skies?*'

She smiled and nodded, impressed that he knew one of Bulawayo's nicknames. There *was* something special about Bulawayo skies: so often cloudless because the rains had failed yet again, the purity and depth of the vast expanse of blue. A treasured memory of hers: once, while shelling peas with her mother under the jacaranda tree whose branches overhung the driveway, her mother had stopped mid-shell. She had looked up at the sweep of blue sky where a flock of birds flew way up high in a V. 'Make a wish,' her mother said. 'Quick, Gabrielle, a wish.' She had squeezed her eyes shut, tried and tried to pluck a wish out but nothing came, and when she had opened them the birds had disappeared, but her mother was still looking up at all that blue as if maybe she could just disappear into it.

'And that means you're . . . Nde . . . bele, right?'

She smiled at his pronunciation.

'Yes.'

It was a bit more complicated than that, but she wasn't going to go into all the details about how, when people looked at her, at her hair, they immediately classified her as 'coloured'. She knew that was a highly offensive word in America but here, it was supposed to be a neutral term – *Black, White, Coloured, Asian* – meaning that you had some white ancestry, in her case that of her unknown maternal grandfather. Growing up, her dense mass of corkscrew curls had caused her so much grief. At school she'd worn her hair bunched up at the back, tied with a ribbon: a clique of the coloured girls had pulled and tugged away at it, accusing her of perming her hair so that she could *pass* as one of them; the black girls had frozen her out because they too thought she was passing, perming her hair while everything else about her cried out 'black'. The white girls just ignored her. She had spent most of her school life flitting between groups, never really making any lasting friendships. And now, in the new political climate, she was not an *indigenous*-enough Zimbabwean: a real Zimbabwean not tainted by any white, colonial, imperialist, settler blood.

'And, um, which part of America are you from?'

'New Haven, Connecticut. Up on the East Coast.'

In Zimbabwe *he* might be considered coloured. That close-cropped hair of his? *Oh, it's because he doesn't wish for the African side of his ancestry, the mufushwa hair, to show through.* They called it *nappy* hair over there, didn't they?

'And how long have you been here?'

'Two months.'

Even less than she had thought. Giorgio had lived and worked in Africa for over ten years. He was twelve years older than her.

Her interrogation continued. 'You're *what* in the embassy?'

He raised his eyebrows as if to say, *good work* or, *it's that obvious, heh?*

'I'm the Assistant to the Assistant to the Cultural Attaché.'

He held up his hands, an amused look on his face – *There you have it; that's how far down the pecking order I am.*

His face was very pleasant to look at: symmetrically placed, regular features – eyes, nose, mouth, eyebrows all where they should be, nothing in their singularity that stood out, and yet . . .

Mawara barked and started lashing his tail against the seat.

'Well, Mr Assistant to the Assistant to the Cultural Attaché, I have to get going—'

'Wait, Gabrielle,' he said, holding out his hand.

'I, I have some work to do. Nice to have met you.'

She made to get up but the leg of her chair was stuck in the grass and she almost fell over backwards. Before she knew it his hand was on her arm, steadying her. She plonked her bottom back down on the seat.

'Work?'

'Yes, I, I have to go over some papers. Legal—'

'You're a lawyer?'

'Yes, I am.'

'*Really?*'

'Yes, really.'

She was looking at him with her arms crossed over her chest like a displeased headmistress, although, for the full effect, she should have been standing, all one metre and fifty-eight-and-a-half centimetres of her, and tapping her foot. She felt ridiculous, but she was now committed to her position, challenging him.

'Hey, I—'

'Well, I'm fully certified. In fact, I have a real live court date on Monday.'

She dropped her hands on her thighs, leaned her body forward, then back, put her hands on the edges of the table then dropped them again.

'I just had you down as a doctor, that's all.'

'Are you sure? Not a nurse?'

'Whoa, Gabrielle,' he said, holding up his hands, 'I just meant that the lawyers I know have a certain . . . umm . . . a hardness to them, they have a look, you—'

'Oh, lawyers as good-for-nothing, money-hungry scoundrels? It's different here, it's a highly respectable profession.'

'I've offended you. I apologize.'

He ran his hand over his hair. The way he kept doing that made her wonder if he was used to longer hair; if maybe, in university – college – whether he'd had something less schoolboyish.

'No, I'm not offended at all,' she said.

'The court case, what's it about?'

Gabrielle sighed.

'I'm sorry, I—'

'It's a private prosecution. We're hoping to not only win but to set a precedent. The Prosecutor General declined to prosecute.'

'Why?'

She considered his question. How much could she disclose? How much was lawyer–client privilege? *The Herald*, the government mouth-piece, was even covering the story: Danika's picture featured prominently in their lurid headlined pieces, but not the defendant's.

'Because, despite the witness statements, which fully corroborate our client's story, the defendant is a rising figure in the Party, so . . .'

'You're taking him on. That's awesome, Gabrielle.'

His was not the reaction she had received from Giorgio when she told him over the phone. *It is too big, Gabrielle. It is too political. Don't get involved.* Just like her father. 'Thanks for your support, as usual,' she had snapped at Giorgio.

'It's Constantina's case, I'm just assisting. She's the one who's awesome. She started The Centre . . . that's where I work. She takes on sensitive cases.'

The way he was looking at her made her feel shy, embarrassed. She started to get up again. This time she was successful in extricating herself from the chair.

He got up too.

'Gabrielle, there's a barbecue tomorrow, in Cheezy . . .'

He tapped his forehead with his fingers.

'Cheezy . . .'

'Chisipite,' she said.

'Yes, that's it. If you're not busy—'

She opened her mouth to interrupt him.

'Of course you'll be busy, your court case—'

'No, I mean yes, thank you,' she surprised herself. 'I'll come.'

Giorgio was no longer in Zimbabwe. She was supposed to have packed her bags and taken what all those Western backpackers so glibly took – a gap year – to Colombia, his new posting. But, she had answered that advertisement for The Centre and had got the job as a junior associate. She had sent him back the plane ticket.

'Great,' he said.

He wrote down her address on the back of one of the leaflets they had been given. She told him to hoot twice because the bell at the gate was for the main house, and she lived in the cottage.

'Is twelve-thirty good?' he asked her.

'Yes, yes, twelve-thirty, that's fine.'

'Great,' he said again. He stuffed the leaflet in his pocket.

'Do you want a ride . . . I mean now?'

'No, no, that's fine. I'll walk back.'

They stood there looking at each other.

'Tomorrow then, Gabrielle.'

'Yes,' she said.

She watched him walk up to that car, watched as he lifted Rum into the seat (the *passenger* seat she realized after a moment's confusion on her part as it was on the right-hand side), and then he turned round. The glare of the sun hid his expression from her. Was he smiling or mouthing something out to her? Finally, he got into the car and drove away.

She stood there alone with Mawara. Once again, she closed her eyes, and then opened them to the bright sunshiny day.

3

The blindfold is tight around her eyes. One moment, it is a clean, neat thing, black, adeptly tied; the next, it is a rag, something snatched in a hurry, a frenzy, a dirty thing blocking out the light. The duct tape (she heard the sound of its tearing) is wound tightly around her wrists and ankles; it seals her mouth.

She is in a room. She knows that this is so because a door has been opened and closed and she has been thrust here by the heavy blow of a hand.

Where in the room have they put her? She leans over backwards, almost falls over into the void. She shuffles on her bottom, trying to find an object, something, anything, the panic rising in her; she might be nowhere at all. But, before the lack of physical parameters overwhelms her a clarion sounds in her head, *I am in the middle of a room, that's right, that's why I can't feel any walls.*

She imagines the room that they have left her in and thinks of it as a small space with dark walls. There are no windows. It is hot in this room and in a moment of panic she cannot remember what she is wearing. Can she possibly have a jersey on? A jersey in February?

She tries to remember.

It was a work day. She had put on her viscose ivory-white 'court' blouse, the one with the high, frilly collar and pearl buttons; she sees it there on the hanger, hooked on the door handle – she remembers she had fallen behind with her washing and that it was the only clean blouse she had left – and then the navy-blue, polyester pinstriped suit, the skirt falling way below her knees, yes, there it is, there she is, tugging at the skirt.

She twists her neck, bends her chin down, touches fabric, yes, this must be her blouse, except she must have done the buttons up wrong in the cave, her neck has room to breathe; she tries to see it now, but her mind turns away from this, it cannot be white any longer, it must be stained with dirt, sweat . . . the marks that their hands have left behind.

She thinks of her hair, feels it as a thicket with things caught in it, bits of leaves, sticks, stones and, as she thinks this, an itch begins on her scalp, trails of ants marching, excavating. She shakes her head.

Slowly sounds come to her. They come from beyond the room, filtering through the walls to her. There are voices, children. A woman calling out. A car struggling to start. A truck backfiring. A dog yelping. A ball bouncing.

She is hungry and the hunger has a taste to it which plies its way through the duct tape, past her dry lips, into the pit of her stomach.

She is with Ben, sitting on the floor, a trail of pasta on her chin.

She feels herself move, her body rocking, tilting.

She presses her tongue against the bind, tastes the bitter stickiness of it. She pushes against it, hoping, but they have done their job well.

She is no longer certain of the time of day, if evening has passed, if it is now deep in the night. She does not trust the sounds she hears anymore: do they come from outside or are they just echoing in her head, imprints of things long gone?

The heat in the room agitates her. She feels it as some ploy, some trick, to confuse her.

Shouldn't her body tell her what time it is?

She imagines what can be done to her and stops herself. These are things that you read about in newspapers: mere squiggles in lead, ink on reporters' notepads. They are not her life. But here she is. And the words, pictures come. This is what can be done to her.

. . .

The hunger and fear carry her off into her childhood, the saliva gathering in her mouth as she smells koeksisters sizzling in hot oil – her mother's special Saturday-afternoon tea treat – but then that is swept away and she lurches into that gully in Magwegwe, the boy holding out the bubblegum, his friends waiting, wanting to see, touch; youths, too, bringing terror, trapping her with their hands and legs, angry voices lashing out at her, the feeling that had descended on her then, like now – she would never leave that place until they had what they wanted, until they had taken it from her. She is there, the boys' breath, hot on her face.

'Thula!'

'Wena, quiet!'

They are lined along the eroded earth, her back pressed against stone, hardened soil, roots of a long-dead tree.

She hurts all over but mostly the pain seems to come from the sides of her legs where she scraped her skin as she struggled to get into the place where the boys wanted her. Her bare feet are standing on something soft, perhaps old Madison, extra-strength cigarette packets, things the boys leave behind after their meetings.

'Thula!'

The voices come this way and that, full of different smells caught up in the dust.

'But, you are not hearing, huh?'

'Here is the chewgum.'

'Thatha.'

'You!'

She cannot move. The sound is coming again. Now, she hears it too. Here it is . . . *pff* . . . *pff*.

'Take.'

'Take you, come, come.'

She must stop. The boys will become angry. Maybe they are already angry. She must take the bubblegum. The boy is being kind. He is keeping his promise.

'It is getting too, too late. People are coming.'

The police are people.

There is a police camp just opposite the primary school; the policemen live there with their wives and children.

'It is black. Every hole is a black thing.'

'A hole is nothing, bhudi. It is not having a colour.'

They are talking about her, about what they will find *down there*.

'We shall see.'

Evelyn, the house-girl, has told her about the tokoloshi that the boys keep between their legs, how some of them are so big and so angry that when the boys release them they do bad, bad things to young girls; a girl will not even be able to walk after the tokoloshi is through with her, Evelyn says.

Why, oh why, did she follow the boy?

She had been sitting on the outcrop of rock, combing the hair of her one-eyed doll, Tracey, who was almost bald.

'Psst,' she had heard. She had looked up, towards the gate. The boy was standing there, his hand stretched out.

'Wena, I have something to show you. Buya, come. It is something good. Buya.'

She had slid off the rock and walked slowly to the gate. Her father had told her never to talk to the boys who walked up and down the lanes. Tsotsis-in-training, her father called them. This boy, though, did not look like all the other tsotsis-in-training. His hair was not dirty and uncombed. He was not wearing pitch-black sunglasses. He was not carrying a Lion Lager in his hand. The boy put his fist over the gate, opened his fingers and there she saw the pink bubblegum she was not allowed to have.

'Come,' the boy said. 'I will give you, soon soon.'

The boy helped her. He unlatched the gate, pulled it open.

He took her to the gully where the other boys were waiting.

'Phangisa, hurry! Lift your dress.'

Eyes crane to look, to see.

She cannot remember what colour underpants she has on, if she is still wearing the school royal-blue ones.

'We have to see.'

She feels fingers between her skin and cloth, a nail puckering at her flesh. She feels her skin released from the pressure of elastic, tug and pull, the underpants caught in the squeeze of her thighs, pressed so tight together that perhaps the boys might think that she wants to go to the toilet.

The fingers pinch her flesh and the underpants lie at her feet.

Eyes crane to look, see.

'It is nothing.'

Fingers push, pry.

'It is dry.'

'It is too small.'

'Anyways, this one is not a real Coloured, twenty per cent maximum possibility, from the mother's side.'

'Even less.'

'For sure.'

'It is only the hair that is fooling.'

'The nose, it is categorically bushman-type.'

'Default Coloured Number One.'

'Fact.'

'One time.'

'Times two, bhudi.'

The boys laugh. They leap out of the place, leaving her alone in the sudden quiet.

The rattle and whine of the door being opened startles her back into the room.

'Coloured, get up.'

Unknown hands are on her again, impatient, pulling her up, pushing her out.

'Heh, you shall see wonders.'

'Correct,' says another.

'Wonders of the Revolution.'

Who are these boys – men? What do they want from her? The answers to these questions come in fits – Danika's quiet voice, Danika's first words, rising and falling, dissolving into the fear.

4

That day when the car stopped on the road and reversed I, I was sitting on the wall just chatting with my best friends, Rose and Petronella.

The driver pointed to me and said, 'You, come.'

Rose and Petronella looked at me and Rose gave me a dig with her elbow. 'Go,' she whispered.

But I just kept sitting on the wall wishing that the car would go away. Then the door of the passenger seat opened and I could see him sitting there.

'We are lost,' the man said. 'We are looking for the secondary school. We need a guide.'

The man was looking at me. 'I am a VIP in the government. Surely, you will respond,' he said.

The man's voice was very smooth.

'Go,' said Petronella this time.

I jumped down from the wall. I was so shy when my skirt flew up a bit. I opened the front door but the driver said, 'Back.'

The car was very nice. I sat very still, right against the door.

'There are so many beautiful girls here,' the man said, 'but you are the most special one.'

I knew that these were sweet words, but his voice was so smooth; it made me feel like smiling and saying thank you.

'Why are you so far away?' he said, and he moved a little bit closer to me. 'A girl so special needs a special uncle,' he said. 'Someone who can appreciate such speciality.'

And then his hand was just there, on my knee. I could not move.
My breathing was something that made me ashamed. He did not ask
me any directions. He was not going to any school at all. He dropped
me in town after he told me where I should meet him in one day's
time. He gave me thirty dollars.

Gabrielle stopped the tape. She lifted the recorder from the couch.
It was the first time she had played the tape at home, heard Danika's
voice here. She could imagine Danika sitting on this battered
yellow-and-blue striped couch, the couch she had transported all
the way from Bulawayo, because it was where her mother always sat,
in the little room just off the lounge, sewing, reading, listening to
the radio.

Five months ago, Danika and her father had come to The Centre,
finding her, the only lawyer, on the premises. Danika's father, in black
trousers and a checked jacket which looked, both in wear and style,
like hold-outs from the 1970s, kept asking when Mrs Maderera would
be back. He was obviously uncomfortable with Gabrielle's age. He had
stepped outside while she interviewed Danika.

Danika, dressed in her school uniform, sat down and spoke, her
hands on her lap, her head bent down, her voice so soft at times that
Gabrielle had to lean over to catch her words. Now and again Danika
had looked up at her. Those big brown eyes searching her to see if she
was going to be judged, blamed.

She pressed play again.

Everything happened so fast. I did not tell anyone about it. I went to
the place where I promised to meet him in one day's time. I took the
money with me. I wanted to give it back. But, when I tried, he said
that the money had accumulated interest. It was now one hundred
dollars and that I could pay it in kind.

Just as during that first interview, Gabrielle felt a surge of anger. This
man was well into his fifties. A father of five, if not a grandfather already.

He said that he was proposing love to me; out of all the many girls who were asking for his love he was choosing me. He was giving me a great gift. He laughed. You will enjoy, he said. He asked me if I had been touched before. I said no, and he said that he knew I was a good girl. He, he told me to undress. I was afraid.

Danika had stopped here. Gabrielle had given her a glass of water and waited until she was ready to go on.

He, he started . . . he started touching my breast . . . it happened fast. I dressed and he said that we would meet every week.

Gabrielle had gently asked her questions, probing, picking through the story – *when, where, how many times* – while trying to reassure her, as best as she could, that it was not a case of her being doubted or accused. Her questioning was informed by what had been drummed into her head at university as the fundamentals of criminal-law prosecution: isolating *actus reus* (the physical elements of the crime) and *mens rea* (the mental elements of the crime) which were to do with the intent and capacity of the accused. A private prosecution would mean that they would have to prove beyond reasonable doubt each of the essential elements of the crime that constituted *unlawful carnal knowledge of a young girl* (statutory rape) under the law.

She had called Danika's father back into the room; Danika had excused herself to use the toilet. She had asked Mr Dube when and how he had become aware of what had happened – *it was being said around the school by students and some teachers, one of the parents informed Danika's mother, and Danika confessed everything to us.* They had also noted her change of behaviour: Danika had become very quiet and withdrawn over some time but they had thought it was just the pressure of exams. They had discovered it about three months ago. She asked him if he had had any dealings with the accused. *No, not at all*, he had spat out. *Never.* Anger and determination were seething in the thin line of his lips and in the hands holding tightly to the brim of his old-fashioned hat. He was outraged at what had befallen his favourite child, the smart daughter he hoped would complete her education and perhaps even go on to university. That the State refused to go through with a prosecution had further inflamed him. A friend had told him about private prosecutions.

Constantina had filled in the gaps Gabrielle's questioning had missed. Were condoms used? When did Danika first become sexually active? Did she have a boyfriend? Boyfriends? 'You cannot be squeamish about these things, Gabrielle,' Constantina had chided her. 'She will be on trial here. We have to be prepared for any tactic, for everything the defence may throw at us under Mistake of Facts arguments.'

Constantina had warned Danika and Mr Dube that the process would be long and hard. There was no guarantee that they would even get the Certificate of Private Prosecution that the Prosecutor General needed to sign off on before they could proceed. If the case did go to court, well, magistrates, in general, did not look favourably on private prosecutions; the court could declare the prosecution an abuse of power and throw it out.

'I want this animal to be exposed,' Mr Dube had said, undeterred. 'He must go to jail. There must be justice. She is a good girl. He has spoilt her.'

Well, finally, court summons had been served, and that only after Constantina had secured a court order to get the police to help them.

Gabrielle checked her watch, put all her paperwork and the tape back into her satchel, ready for the morning. She had written some notes for Constantina. She buckled the satchel, gave it a pat. She stood up, carried it by its handle, took a look in the mirror. Yes, it was beautiful, well made, but, more importantly, it gave her heft and confidence.

The satchel, of tooled leather, was a recent acquisition. Trinity, her best friend since university, had taken her to Mbare Musika last week. It was her first time in Mbare, the notorious township, and she was shocked by the throngs of people and the market's immense size, which made child's play of Makokoba Market in Bulawayo. At first sight it seemed to be just an assorted cram and jumble of activity of no discernible order (and the smell!) but then, wandering through its warren of dirt paths, mindful of the pickpocket gangs, the mess turned out to be somewhat organized and full of surprises. There were vendors selling their wares either on the dusty ground or on crates, everything available, from dried caterpillars, pigs' ears, herbs, car parts ('reconditioned', 'recycled', 'stolen'), second-hand clothes, most of them sent by European and American charities for the poor and somehow diverted here, to curios, which explained the scattering of backpackers. She bought the satchel from a man with no teeth except for two incisors, who sat on a low stool, next to his leather goods, working. The briefcases she had tried out in town had made her feel ridiculous, like a businessman fraud (her father?), but the satchel just *worked*.

She put the satchel on the couch, then took a critical look at herself in the mirror, fiddled with her top, tried to smooth down her hair which was, as ever, intent on doing its own thing. She had made the mistake of combing it out instead of letting it air-dry into its corkscrew curls. It was now in full-blown afro mode, Diana Ross-style, circa 1970s. She resorted to a rubber band. She thought about changing – maybe she should but, too late. There was a hoot and then another one, just as she had instructed. She took a deep breath and stepped outside.

He was leaning on the gate, his arms swung over it, Mawara, good guard dog he obviously was not, already all over him, licking, Gabrielle supposed, as much of Rum as he could get.

She walked as naturally as she could.

Relax. Relax.

She was aware of his eyes, lifted away from her dog, to her, watching her every move.

'Hi,' she said, doing a funny, jerky thing with her hand that was supposed to be a wave.

'Hello, Gabrielle.'

'We'll have to be quick,' she said. 'We have to coordinate our movements. Good dog, Mawara. Stay.'

Ben gave her a mock salute.

'Lift the latch and I'll dart through.'

Mawara started whimpering.

'Good dog, Mawara. You stay. I'll be back soon. Good, good dog.'

She kept patting Mawara's head, while manoeuvring herself towards the gate. 'Good dog.'

'Now,' she said to Ben. She pushed her way through the gap. Mawara's paws slapped on the iron.

'Good dog, Mawara. Stay. Good dog.'

Mawara whimpered and barked and whimpered. He ran and jumped and lay down, rolled himself over as if he were showing her his carnival tricks.

'Good dog, Mawara. Good dog.'

She automatically went round to what was the passenger side in normal cars and then, realizing her mistake, she went to the other side where he was already standing, holding the door open for her.

'I keep getting stopped by Harare's finest,' he said, as she was getting inside. 'They think the car's contravening some by-law, *the steering wheel's on the wrong side, sir*. I haven't been given a ticket yet, though.'

He closed the door gently behind her.

She didn't ask him if the police wanted him to give them a little something, but perhaps the diplomatic number plates stopped them from soliciting a bribe.

She was taken aback by the modesty of the interior – just plain black vinyl seat covers; she had expected the red-and-white explosion to continue inside. She was struck by the original fixtures: the spare, metal steering wheel that looked surprisingly flimsy, and the gauges on the dashboard, which belonged on a plane somehow, she thought. Everything felt as if it had been made by human hands, not machines.

'Nice place,' he said, once he'd settled into his seat.

The old Cape Dutch with its wraparound verandah did look impressive in the sunshine. The garden would be glorious in October with the jacarandas in full bloom.

'I used to work, during my first and second years at university, as a waitress in Mr and Mrs Papadopoulos's restaurant, The Athena, just off First Street. They own the house and when they heard I was looking for a place they offered me the cottage.'

'So, you were decked out in that wide skirt with the bells at the bottom, and the frilly apron?'

She laughed. 'You've eaten there!'

'Yes, I have, and I've been serenaded by Mr Papadopoulos himself.'

'It's quite an experience, isn't it? That's one of my favourite places. The other one is The Italian Bakery, just round the corner from here. I go there early in the mornings before the rush sets in, do some work and—'

She felt out of breath, and was suddenly embarrassed by her volubility.

'Charles makes a damn good espresso,' he said, 'and he's working on my Shona: Zvakanaka.'

'Zvakanaka to you, too.'

'And to think I haven't run into you there before, Gabrielle.'

The way he was looking at her made her feel self-conscious. She looked away, caught sight of two boys, one of them manoeuvring a wire car, with its steering wheel suspended on a long piece of wire. They were pointing at the marvel of steel and chrome before them.

'You have fans,' she said. They looked about six, seven, and were most likely the children of the gardeners and maids who worked in the houses here.

Ben motioned for them to come, and then he got out of the car.

'Hey, guys—'

One of the boys yelped 'Murungu!' They spun on their heels and ran, the wire car hurtling in their wake. Ben turned round and mouthed, 'What?'

'It's your accent,' she told him when he got back in the car. 'It makes you an honorary white man.'

'That's . . .'

She watched him process his new place in the world. How would he describe it?

'That's just *whack*, as we say in the streets.'

'Oh, which streets may those be?'

'Oh, the mean streets of the black murungu, Gabrielle.'

As they made their way she plied him with questions, filling in the details of his life. He had gone to Yale.

'Wow, you must be very intelligent,' she teased. 'Isn't Yale what you guys call the Ivy League?'

He nodded. 'Yes, to the Ivy League part but I did have an advantage in admissions. My mom's a professor there.'

'Really? What does she teach?'

'Math. Pure Math.'

She was embarrassed by her surprise. It suddenly came to her that, just like those pensioners at the vet's surgery, everything she knew about America came via television.

'She was actually the first female African American professor in the faculty.'

This time she kept the 'wow' to herself.

He had studied Hebrew and Arabic and he had no idea why the State Department had placed him here, but, he said, smiling at her, in retrospect, he was very happy that they had. His father was an engineer. He designed and built boats. 'Is he white?' was on the tip of her tongue but, fortunately, she caught herself; she could just imagine the look on his face – shock? Disgust? Incomprehension that such a question could even enter her head, at the supposition that might lie behind it?

'Well, Gabrielle,' he said, as they passed the vet's surgery and turned into Borrowdale Road, 'I've been to one, two, three, *five*, diplomatic parties since I arrived, and I just have a hunch that this one will be a lot more fun.'

The words leapt out of her. 'Yes, Giorgio would drag me—'

'Giorgio?'

'He's a . . . a friend.'

Pathetic. The stutter, the tremor. All of it. And his eyes moving from the road to her. *Boyfriend.* The word seemed so light, young and breezy. Not Giorgio at all. What then? My friend? My partner? No matter. All in the past now. *My ex.*

An emergency taxi had decided to make an 'emergency' stop in the middle of the intersection to offload some passengers, and load new ones.

'So, you and he—?'

Someone hooted behind him; the emergency taxi had moved on. They turned into Churchill Avenue.

'He's in Colombia.'

What she should have said was that, back then, he was the pro-gramme coordinator for the High Commission for Refugees . . . imply-ing what? That the relationship was strictly business, above board?

She looked away from his enquiring gaze.

She had first set eyes on Giorgio Fiori at the university library. He was wearing a rumpled white shirt, cargo pants and desert boots. She was standing impatiently behind him while he went through the drawer of index cards. When he turned round, he bumped into her. 'Excuse me,' he mumbled and walked off. But, so-called fate (or circumstance) was working in threes, intent on their meeting again.

The second time she bumped into him, figuratively speaking, was at the bakery, later the same day, where she was whiling away time before the movie started. She was having a cappuccino at the bar because the tables were all taken. He stood next to her, said 'ciao' to the Ethiopian-Italian owner and ordered an espresso. He put his books on the counter, fished out a packet of cigarettes from his shirt pocket, tapped a cigarette out on the counter and then took out a lighter, was about to light it when he looked at her.

'Do you mind?' he asked her.

She was astonished that he even asked. People smoked in Zimbabwe all the time, everywhere. This was tobacco country. As they were standing there, thousands of tonnes of tobacco were curing in barns, up and down the country.

And, yes, she did mind, but she didn't say that to him.

She said instead, 'I'm almost finished.'

He put the cigarette back in the packet.

'Thank you,' she said.

He smelled slightly of smoke, sweat and dust; he had sunburn on his nose, cheeks and forehead; his hair was damp at the edges and he had stubble, as if he had been on a long trip, out in the bush. It turned out that he had just come back from a refugee camp, along the Mozambique border.

She picked up her cup.

'Buonissimo,' he said. 'The cappuccino here, it's very good. But in Italy, cappuccino is only for the morning.'

'Oh, I'm sorry,' she blurted out, putting the cup down, without taking a sip.

'But this is not Italy,' he said, 'so you can have cappuccino in the evening.'

He sounded tired and irritated. She looked over at his books. He picked one up. The title was something about migration.

'Research. I am thinking of doing a doctorate.' He put it back down. 'It is a matter of finding time and wanting, how can I say it – the distraction.'

He didn't have a stereotypical 'Mamma Mia' Italian accent when speaking English. He spoke in a measured way and, in the beginning, she thought that was because of the language, not that it was who he was.

The third time was at the cinema entrance. He was going to see the same movie, *Amistad*, also alone. Trinity had refused point-blank to go and watch a 'slave movie'. They ended up sitting together in the near-empty cinema, the most uncomfortable experience she had ever had watching a movie. They were not strangers, but not yet even acquaintances and they were in this intimate space, their arms intermittently brushing against each other, sharing a moment, for over two hours. She was pretty squeamish, and had to check herself from hiding her face against his shoulder during the mutiny scenes.

He gave her a lift, in his beige Land Cruiser, back to her hall of residence.

It became a kind of routine that they settled into. Meeting at the library, coffee at the bakery and perhaps a movie or, if there wasn't anything interesting showing, they would get a pizza at St Elmo's in the shopping centre downstairs or a dinner at the newly opened La Dolce Vita on the mezzanine level. For some time it was just an unlikely friendship. They didn't touch until, one day, she made the first move: they were seated in his car, saying their goodbyes and she leaned over and kissed him. It was the most daring thing she had ever done; in truth she was teased and goaded into it by Trinity. 'What's wrong with him?' her friend had chortled when she had unwisely revealed the chasteness of their encounters. 'Is he gay?'

'Grazie,' he said, when they separated.

For what? The kiss? Or was it for something else? What did she give him that warranted that 'thank you'? His words puzzled, unsettled her. But he soon took charge. And sometimes she felt it was a 'thank you' for giving him the permission to go ahead.

They were together, on and off, for almost two years, although they did not do that grown-up thing of actually living together.

'Mengistu lives in this suburb,' she said as they were passing Gun Hill.

'Yes, I know.'

He was distracted, not biting into that juicy morsel. Was he trying to work out exactly what this Giorgio business was all about? Perhaps she should try and clarify things.

'He's been here for about ten years now, I mean Mengistu. Everyone is fed up with him.'

The student leaders at the UZ, who were self-avowed Marxists, had been conflicted about the former Ethiopian dictator, the 'Stalin of Africa' who had fled Ethiopia and was now living in a plush villa, with police and army guards, all paid for out of the pockets of cash-strapped Zimbabweans.

She opened her mouth again, this time to say something about Giorgio but hesitated. Clarifying things might be construed to be a reckless act of presumption, that she thought that *this* was something, the start of—

'Hey, what's going on?'

For a moment Gabrielle thought he was talking about her and Giorgio, but it was the goings-on in the street before them that had caught his attention. The cars had come to a standstill at the round-about and drivers were getting out to watch a huge banner being tied high up on the street lamp posts, spanning from one side of the road to the other. VOTE YES. A tick and an AK47 superimposed on it. She thought the sign might as well say, OR ELSE.

'Democracy,' she said. 'Well, a variety thereof. I'm a volunteer with the Constitutional Referendum Action Group, and every time *we* try to stick a poster up we get a police order to remove it.'

'You're an activist.'

'No, no, nothing like that,' she said, waving off the idea. 'What? We're just a bunch of recent graduates explaining to people exactly what they're being asked to vote on.'

'And that makes you an activist in any book, including the official CIA handbook,' he said, playfully wagging his finger.

The banner up, the cars started moving again. Turning into Enterprise Road, they had to slow down because some members of a Vapostori sect were crossing the road at a leisurely pace. She watched the prophet, tall and lean, long black beard twisted to a point, a shiny bald head, a staff in his hand, trailed by the women, some of them, no doubt, his wives, in their long white gowns and headscarves, and the babies bundled tightly on backs with towels and blankets, despite the heat. They were making their way to some open land where they would spend the day worshipping under a thorn tree, one of many, many groups that had mushroomed since food prices had gone up and primary education and healthcare were no longer free. There were rumours that The Old Man was courting them, putting the blame for the bad times on the white man, Britain and homosexuals who were trespassing against God's laws.

Ben looked away from them to her.

'You marched.'

'We all marched, an occupational hazard, par for the course at the University of Zimbabwe, especially if you're a member of the Law Faculty. Our student leader was in the year above mine, and he was always ready to rumble.'

'I thought that kind of thing was dangerous around here.'

'Only if you're a certified activist.'

She remembered their last demo back in '97, which was to protest the looting of the War Veterans' Compensation Fund. She was mortified, days later, when one of her friends showed her a Joseph Bernard Langa on the list of claimants, and asked if they were related. Her father had received one hundred thousand dollars for a disabled foot. He, who had never set foot in the bush during the war (he'd boasted to her) had somehow reinvented himself. Genuinely disabled veterans were indigent while fully able government ministers and their cronies, some of them having been declared to be 117 per cent disabled, helped themselves to the fund.

They had tried to get out of campus, to make their way to Africa Unity Square where there were going to be speeches, but they were sealed in by riot police for two days. Jeremiah, the Student Union President, was detained and he came back to campus laughing the whole thing off, but there was talk that he had become an informant, which she didn't believe. They were made to sign a document renouncing violence; anyone who refused to sign was expelled.

They turned into a leafy cul-de-sac.

'I'm ashamed to admit, Gabrielle, that the closest we ever came to protest at Yale was when they threatened to raise the price of lobster rolls in the Commons dining hall.'

She couldn't tell if he was serious. Was this American deadpan humour? The stakes here were very high. It was no laughing matter.

'Well, we Zimbos are about to do the impossible. We have just survived the millennium bug and now we're going to give our esteemed leader a black eye. We're going to say *No No No* to yet more powers for the Executive, including the right to summarily confiscate land.'

'That's some fighting talk, Gabrielle. I'll make a report to my superiors.'

'Don't smile. We mean business. Enough is enough.'

The only person who thought differently in her circle was Trinity, who worked for *The Herald*. In her book, The Old Man already had the votes in his pocket, like always; they were all on a fool's errand, actually making the tyrant look good because he was 'allowing' this democratic exercise to take place. *The Herald* was packed with full-page advertisements of the dangers of the 'No' vote, and who the puppet master behind it all was: *not-so-great* Britain.

In true fashion her father had gone berserk when he'd found out about her involvement in the education drive . . . *The president knows what's best for the country; if he decides he needs more power . . . you young people . . .*

They swung to a stop in front of a pair of wide black electric-controlled gates. Ben leaned out of the window and spoke into the intercom. As they drove in she felt compelled to add, as if for her own peace of mind, 'And anyway, Ben, for your information, Articles Twenty and Twenty-One of the Constitution currently guarantee the freedom of expression and the right of assembly and association for all Zimbabweans.'

He opened her door and held out his hand. 'In that case, let's get out there and exercise these constitutionally guaranteed rights. After you, Gabrielle.'

'Ah, Ben, Ben, welcome, welcome,' said the beaming, exuberant host, enveloping Ben in an almighty hug. He was dressed in a heavily embroidered white gown.

'Come, come, let me show you around . . . and who is this lovely lady you have graced us with, my friend?'

'Adebayo, this is Gabrielle, she's a lawyer.'

'Welcome, welcome, come, come, let me introduce you around.'

The garden was filled with young African diplomats. Gabrielle heard English, French, Zulu and possibly Swahili, and other languages she couldn't name. There were elaborate hairstyles and headgear on display; outfits in vibrant colours and designs – African shirts, boubous, dashikis, caftans, agbadas, kente, the names of which she knew from some of Giorgio's books. She was the only woman wearing jeans. She was embarrassed for not having made an effort; if only she had known that this was an African gathering and not some American affair. But even if she had 'dressed up', she would still have stood out in her sober European-style dress. Zimbabwe didn't have a national dress; as one of the student activists at university put it, *we Zimbabweans were thoroughly colonized by the British.*

Above the voices there was music, *highlife,* she thought it was called, from Nigeria. Once Adebayo left them, Ben was pulled and tugged in every direction – *Ah, Ben, Ben, did you hear, Ben, good to see you . . .* He was swept up in hearty hugs, wallops on his back, vigorous handshakes and kisses, even attempts at high fives, which he took all in good stride, soliciting jovial laughter. Once he was released he would introduce her. *You're Zimbabwean!* they exclaimed. It felt as though Zimbabweans were, for whatever reason (aloofness? Shyness? Haughtiness?) a rarity among them.

She found herself standing in front of four long tables overflowing with food: rice dishes, fried plantain, the waft of coconut and curries, fish . . . all of it exotic to her, to accompany whatever came off the barbecues. The dishes were so fragrant that her mouth watered; much, *much* more flavoursome than Zimbabwean's own stodgy cuisine, which owed its debt to the British, who had stayed much longer and sunk deeper roots here than in other parts of Africa. In a way she felt herself to be more foreign than Ben.

'Let's get started,' he said, picking up a plate, handing it to her, reaching out for one for himself.

She could imagine him back in the States, among friends, relaxed. And here he was, a long way from home and yet, seemingly, at home.

'I had a great time,' she told him as they were sitting in the car, in front of her gate. 'Just what the doctor ordered.'

Mawara was still doing acrobatic tumbles.

'Thank you,' she said.

'I had a great time, too.'

'I'd better go. Mawara might inflict grievous bodily harm upon his person.'

'Wait,' he said. He went round and opened the door for her.

'Is that a New Haven thing?'

'It is now.'

He was leaning against the door frame, looking down at her, talking to her as she sat there in his car.

She should move, get out, but it was so good to have him like that, as if they were teenagers in a movie.

He opened the car door wide and he bent down and kissed her. It was a soft, gentle kiss, barely there on her lips, but it sent her heart doing the equivalent of Mawara's frantic antics. She held herself still and then she placed her hand gently on his chest. He drew away from her, traced her hairline with his finger.

'I'll be seeing you, Gabrielle,' he said.

5

Eyes open and the darkness pours in.

In the distance, pinpricks of light moving, until floating heads appear, garlanded in light.

'Comrade,' she hears, and the lights burn, making the cold air hiss and cackle, sending out sparks.

A hyena howls.

'Special Anti-Revolutionary Consignment,' the hyena says, and howls into the agitated night.

'Cockroaches, rats,' the hyena says, her chin clenched between claws, twisted this way and that.

'Coloured,' the hyena says, the flames burning bright and hot against her skin. 'Move.'

She is somewhere in the bush, ekhaya, 'back home', far, far away from the city. Her feet rising and falling in the dark, trampling grass, her breath coming in and out, in out, eyes opening and closing, opening, closing, heart beating, beating, beating.

'Coloured, you are very beautiful.'

The words smell: home-brew, dagga and want, spilling into her, hungry, greedy.

'*Heh*, you will be seeing much. I will be your extra-special tour guide. No charge. You are going to a good, good place, believe me.'

.   .   .

'You must see this like a vacation like the murungus are having. You are vacating. Wild-Life Safari. Five Star. You will enjoy.'

The hyena howls and howls.

'I will be your tour guide. I will be your teacher.'

She looks up and cannot find the moon, not even a sliver of her. She has flown away. Disappeared into the night.

She thinks of a hot night delirious with malaria, her body strewn on the hard ground, the sound of drumbeat and chanting about her. A hot night and someone lifting her from the ground, the moon swooning, dipping into the earth and up again and her words against a neck, her breath hot on his skin, *look, look, the moon is flying. She's flying.*

She thinks of the long ride back. The car jumping away on the dirt road and there, from out of the night, a white horse caught in the lights, springing up and away into the dark. Did you see that? She turned to ask.

She thinks of the long night, the room frantic with flight and words, it's okay, you are just dreaming, words like a lullaby, 'you are fine, you are fine'.

She walks in the night, on this day, in the company of lights.

The silence falls away.

Words, first slow, then fast, become the night.

As though her head is emerging from water, from sleep, from a drugged state, stupor, the babble of sounds discern themselves, become understood. The language of the Revolution seizes the night, pounds away at it, holds it tight and fast in its grasp.

6

'Is everything all right?' Gabrielle asked Ronald, who was scrubbing away at The Centre's very own skorokoro Laser, which looked as though it had taken up permanent residence on the scraggly patch of grass in the yard.

Ronald, a jack of all trades in the neighbourhood, chuckled and nodded his head vigorously.

'Really, Ronald, you're quite sure it will make it to Rotten Row today, without something falling off?'

Ronald scratched his thickly matted hair, a faraway look in his eyes as if he was envisioning the journey that the car would have to make, its many hazards.

Leafy Prince Edward Street, in the upmarket side of central Harare, intersected with Samora Machel Avenue, and came out the other side as Rotten Row, discarding its leisurely suburban character, winding its way down the kopje to its final destination, the dirt tracks of Mbare. Along its length it was a swarm of activity emanating from the banks, the offices, the boutiques, the Harare City Library, the tuck shops, the emergency taxis, the commuter omnibuses, the vendors, hustlers. Further down, at the Magistrate's Court, legal practitioners, law-abiding citizens, criminals, defendants and complainants intermingled with newly-wed couples. It could be argued that the court was called Rotten Row not only because of its location, but also due to its general dilapidated state (crumbling floors and ceiling, condemned lifts, blocked-up toilets), and because of all the stench that rose from the corruption of the courts. Being in Rotten Row was a trial in more ways than one.

'They gave her a tune-up at the garage,' he said at last, 'but you know those people can be crooks, crooks, but I stayed there all the time just to make sure there was no funny business with parts.'

She nodded, waved him goodbye and walked gingerly up the concrete steps. Ronald had applied liberal quantities of Cobra Wax Polish (extra-shine) in an attempt to spruce them up and, as a result, the steps were even more hazardous than usual to navigate in her heels. This dingy-looking house with its peeling white paint and rusting gutters was The Centre. She walked down the narrow passageway, straight into her office, the second on the right, with a window overlooking the crop of maize that was being grown illegally on council land.

'Why can't you be a high-flyer?' her father demanded, the one time he came to Harare to see her set-up for himself. He was en route to Party headquarters to hand in his credentials. 'Instead of all this non-paying charity nonsense? You could have beautiful offices in Borrowdale. What is such an intelligent girl like you doing down here in Hatfield with these people? I can set you up in some smart offices. They can even build it from scratch at Borrowdale Brooke.'

His business empire in Matabeleland now incorporated a clothing and shoe factory, and he had just recently won a government tender for school uniforms.

He hadn't donated a single cent to The Centre, despite her pleas.

'Principles,' he declared, when she swallowed her pride and asked him for some funds. 'Charity begins at home. Do you want to make me a poor man? The problem with you is that you have been spared the harsh realities of poverty.'

He was obviously hoping that a couple of pinches of it would bring her to her senses. And yes, he had spared her a lot of things by putting her in that convent mere weeks after her mother's death, not even discussing it with her until she had found herself there, on that wet January morning, in front of that forbidding, heavy door, the cardboard suitcase in her hand, the black trunk at his side. What had he said as they waited for the nun to open the door?

'You're embarking on an adventure. This is the best solution.'

Yes, right.

He had chased away her aunts and uncles, his own brothers and sisters, anyone who might have an opinion on what should happen to her. His reasoning? He didn't want her to grow up with illiterates, learning bush ways.

A man of many paradoxes.

And what did she say to him in reply?

'It's okay, Daddy. I will be fine.'

Always the good girl. Trying to make it somehow easy for him, despite everything. He should have been a better husband. He should never have paraded his underage girlfriends all over Bulawayo so that her mother was an easy target for her pious church choir friends:

'Naka Gabrielle,' they would say, feigning innocence, as they sat in the living room, Bibles and hymn books at hand, tea cups on the side tables. 'We saw your husband with a very young lady, dressed in a very revealing manner . . . maybe she is a relative of yours?'

Yes, her father's affairs had brought shame and ridicule to her ever-stoic mother. There was that one time when the Lyons Maid ice-cream vendor had abandoned his red-and-white trolley in the middle of the road and jumped over their fence, rushed into the kitchen and chased the house-girl round the property with a sjambok screaming that someone would die this day: it turned out that the house-girl had been promised in marriage to the vendor – lobola had been negotiated, but word had got round to him of her father's nocturnal visits to her room.

Gabrielle shook her head. There was work to do; no sense in wallowing in the past – her father was what he was. He would never change. It was just that he was breathing down her neck, leaving messages on her answer machine about family loyalty, him of all people. He accused her of prejudicing his chances in the Party by going after one of its rising stars. Never mind that she was only assisting in the case, doing the legwork.

She sat down at her desk, which was a simple, unvarnished pine affair bought from one of the carpenters who'd set up stalls along the Airport Road.

She was expecting Danika and her father soon. She would drive them to court where they would meet up with lead counsel, Constantina, who was already there, on another case.

She popped a spearmint in her mouth, rubbed her back and neck. Every time she bent over, her neck was throttled by the high neckline of her blouse. In her final year at university a brilliant female lecturer had held a working breakfast with five selected female students. She had told them that one of the harshest lessons she had learnt in the courtroom was about dress. The men could do virtually no wrong in this department. But for women, the courtroom was a minefield, and each courtroom with its own magistrate or judge was a law unto itself. On her first day as a fully-fledged lawyer the lecturer had arrived in court wearing a smart pencil skirt, a fitted white shirt and jacket. 'Well, ladies,' she said, 'it was like I was another type of working woman on the prowl. Even my own client propositioned me. I lost the case. The magistrate called me into chambers and told me that I was too beautiful to be a lawyer, what with my becoming figure.' The lecturer had concluded: 'The guiding principle in my court attire is, would a prospective mother-in-law in the rural areas approve? I dress for her.'

A knock at the door jolted her. She stood up, called, 'Come in.'

She smiled at Danika standing there in the doorway and thought, not for the first time, how very young she was, with the four rows of neatly twined hair, the whiff of coconut oil, her small, slender body, her smooth, round face gleaming with Vaseline, and the expressive eyes resting just for a moment on her and then away to the floor. She was wearing a short-sleeved plain yellow dress that just skimmed her knees, modest but not, Gabrielle feared, modest enough. She hated herself for thinking that, but that was the reality that would face Danika in court, every exposed bit of skin, her arms, her legs, would be taken as evidence against her. The fact that she was pretty was yet another negative. She was just fourteen when she had been approached by the defendant, seven months short of her fifteenth birthday.

'Hello, Danika, how are you? Come and take a seat, we have some time before we have to leave.'

Danika walked into the room, her movements hesitant as if every step required thought, a commitment.

'Sit down, Danika.'

Gabrielle showed her the chair, the same chair Danika had sat in before, but today, still, it was as if the room, its furnishings, were new to her. Her eyes were fixed on her hands that were folded on her lap.

'Is your father here, Danika?'

'No, Miss Langa, he will be here soon. He had to check some documents.'

Danika was talking into her lap, her hands cupping each other, one moving over the other.

'Danika, are you all right?'

Of course she wasn't all right. Gabrielle couldn't begin to imagine what must be going through the girl's head. What nerves, what fears.

'Danika, do you want me to explain again what will happen in the courtroom today?'

She waited, watched the hands restlessly moving. The silence between them was shattered only by the traffic outside, and a stray shout, someone calling out, *iwe!* and then the sound of laughter and chatter.

Gabrielle got up, closed the window.

'Danika, today—'

'I – I – have missed my period, Miss Langa. It's not . . .'

Her voice quavered, the hands suddenly stilled.

Gabrielle tried to quickly process this information. What was Danika telling her? That the defendant was still abusing her, and hence her pregnancy? That she was being abused by someone else? Had this case exposed her to other predators?

'Have you told your mother, Danika?'

Danika jumped up.

'I – I can't. I—'

There was a knock at the door.

Danika clutched Gabrielle's arm. 'Miss Langa, please don't tell anyone, please—'

'Danika—' Gabrielle said, but she was interrupted by another, more persistent, knock.

'It is my father. We must go, Miss Langa. We must go.'

7

'Inside!' shouts the youth, gesticulating wildly with his panga, smashing it on the corrugated iron, the sound of it ratcheting through the air, sending a flock of birds scattering from an overhead power line.

She stands before the long building in the clearing, her legs trembling and threatening to buckle, her mouth full of sick that she swallows down. The youths have made them walk, run, jump and once crawl, at their whim and pleasure. Her legs are aching, covered in cuts and bites. The youths have stopped now here, now there, dragged sleeping villagers out of huts, jolted them awake with threats and insults, accused them of harbouring sell-out children from the city.

'Inside, idiots!'

The youths herd them into the building, its metal doors open, big enough for a tractor to drive through. It smells of animal. Cows or pigs or even horses have been here. Her feet step on mud or waste, human, animal. Overhead, on the metal roof, a single light bulb gives off a diffuse light, full of shadows.

The crescendo of slogans that assaulted them in the dark has given way to a charged silence, broken by a smattering of pamberis and pasis, the voices, despite their effort, weary. Her straining eyes fall on the huddle of bodies in a corner, limp fists raised and a youth jutting out his hand, screaming out his commands, hurling some missile – a stone, a stick – into the huddle.

'Eh, comrade, we are here.'

The youth turns mid-scream, hurries to them, his mission forgotten, discarded, greets his comrades with high fives and fist bumps. As they exchange news – word of the others up at the farmhouse feasting – she feels a breath on her, familiar in its mix of home-brew and dagga.

'Coloured, we are taking back our land. We have chased the white man. We have taken his farm. We have taken his ploughs, his tractors, his workers. We have taken his crops, his animals. We have taken. You think your little opposition can stop the taking? Watch. Now we will take from you. We will take. This is our court of law. Welcome.'

8

Gabrielle took out the docket and the supporting documents from her satchel and placed them on the table. She also had a copy of the *Criminal Law Amendment Act: Chapter 9:05, Section 3. Unlawful carnal knowledge of young girl,* under which the case fell. She was always struck by the problematic language of the statute.

If any person:

   (a) unlawfully and carnally knows or attempts to have unlawful carnal knowledge of any girl under the age of sixteen years; or
   (b) commits or attempts to commit with any such girl any immoral or indecent act; or
   (c) solicits or entices any such girl to have unlawful carnal connection with him or to commit any immoral or indecent act;

he shall be guilty of an offence and liable to a fine not exceeding one thousand dollars or to imprisonment for a period not exceeding five years or to both such fine and such imprisonment;

provided that:

   (i) it shall be a sufficient defence to any charge under paragraph (a), (b) or (c) if the accused satisfies the court that:

    (a) the girl at the time of the commission of the offence was a
       prostitute; or
    (b) the accused was at such time under the age of sixteen years;
       or
    (c) the accused had reasonable cause to believe that the girl was
       of or above the age of sixteen years;
  (ii) nothing in this section shall be taken to alter or limit the law in
     regard to rape.

At university, Gabrielle had been shaken by the attitude and views of many of the male students, when it came to discussing this particular section of criminal law: during lectures even the quiet ones became vociferous and emotional; they ranted about *culture, good girls, virgins* and *so-called rape* which they claimed, in many cases, was actually just *seduction* and should be settled in family and traditional courts under customary law, where (male) elders would judge on the matter and damages would be paid to the father if anyone was considered to have been damaged. She was sure it was the *carnal knowledge* terminology instead of the more explicit *statutory rape* term that made them feel it was not really a crime at all. Case in point, during one lecture: *These girls are very well developed, why should a man be punished for being used? Once they start bleeding they are ready.*

And, in actuality, magistrates did veer far and wide (*willy-nilly*, as one of her lecturers had put it) in their interpretation of *reasonable cause*. The girl was wearing make-up – reasonable cause. The girl was wearing a miniskirt – reasonable cause. The girl was tall and carried herself like a woman or, as per one magistrate in his acquittal verdict, *she knew what she wanted* – reasonable cause. And so on. Misogyny could take full, prejudicial flight. Constantina had joined a group of lawyers and human rights activists campaigning to have this Act repealed and replaced with a Sexual Offences Act that really protected women and young girls from sexual abuse and which would make marital rape a crime. She had told Gabrielle that most of their presentation in court would be aimed at shaming the magistrate into not acting on his biases.

. . .

Danika, who was sitting in the row behind, next to her father, was trembling. Gabrielle was about to say something when a flurry of activity by the door stopped her. A group of youths were calling out crudely to each other as they jostled their way into the room. Passing, the youths cut their eyes at them. Gabrielle noticed at least two wearing Party T-shirts and wondered if that was permissible in court. Mr Dube's demeanour did not change. He sat calmly, waiting for the court proceedings to begin. Constantina was looking over the documentation, she too seemingly oblivious or immune to the youths' appearance and behaviour.

Witnesses had suddenly retracted their previous statements. It was clear that someone had got to them – not least of all, she thought, by using threats of eviction from the government flats, one of which the defendant kept (Flat 501), the same one that several witnesses had said they had seen the defendant and Danika in her school uniform (positively identified from photographs) enter on multiple occasions, and two of them had gone on further to say that they had seen other girls in the company of the defendant. Gabrielle had gone door to door with no luck. Petronella's parents had threatened to give Gabrielle a beating if she ever tried to contact their daughter again about such nonsense; their daughter was only interested in studying and not being led astray by loose girls. Rose's parents had allowed her to be interviewed but refused to have her as a trial witness. At some moments, she felt as if the case was a non-starter, the law was just not on their side; it was a classic case of *he said-she said*, and it would all depend on whom the magistrates believed, or chose to believe in. As she sat there, a sudden realization dawned on her. Could it be that Constantina was using this case simply as a lightning rod – win or lose, they were going to highlight the injustices and contradictions of the law? For weeks now, Gabrielle had been writing letters to donor governments and agencies talking about The Centre's work. Emphasize this case, Constantina had told her. Make sure to include a copy of the law. So it was not only to get funding then but also to solicit support – especially from the Swedes and Norwegians, who were very sensitive about gender-equality issues; they could bring pressure to bear on the government. Looking at it like that, Danika was just a pawn in Constantina's grand scheme of things. Gabrielle felt culpable. But this was not the way she should be thinking. Their job was to represent Danika to the best of their ability. Did this make her a bad lawyer? Or did all lawyers have moments of doubt when representing their clients on the solidity of their case? Or was that what separated the winners from the losers? The winners never entertained anything other than winning. One lecturer had told her outright that it didn't matter whether you believed your client or not; what mattered was getting the courts to believe them.

Gabrielle reached out for their one bit of corroborating evidence (if the magistrate would permit its submission): the picture that had been splashed on the front cover of the notorious weekly tabloid, under the caption SWEET SUGAR DADDY O, which showed the defendant getting out of his BMW while a girl (to be later identified as Danika Dube) stood to the side. In his bombastic statements on camera, in which he threatened to sue the tabloid and otherwise deal with the photographer, the defendant had unwittingly acknowledged knowing the girl in the picture and had alluded to the nature of their relationship.

Gabrielle looked over to the opposing counsel's table – still no one there.

'What's going on?' she whispered to Constantina.

Constantina shrugged. 'We shall see soon. We are prepared.'

Constantina was short and solidly built and, in the courtroom, she looked – in her wide-pleated skirts, broad-collared blouses, sensible, white nurse's-style rubber-soled shoes, her hair neatly plaited in concentric circles with twine, which she would give a pat every now and then – like a beloved great-aunt who had just stepped off a rural bus. She would begin her address to the court with a seemingly timid, almost apologetic, 'Your Worship', her hands clasped together in the traditional manner of respectful greeting, and then the legal arguments would gather force in her quiet, commanding voice; that was her power, how she appeared so non-threatening and yet threatened with every squeak of her shoes.

The youths, who were occupying the back row, were making themselves seen and heard. She knew just enough Shona to pick out their vulgar sexual expressions and to know to whom they were directed. She looked over at Danika. Her head was bent down; she was chewing on her lip. Mr. Dube's father was looking solidly ahead at the magistrate's chair. He was unshakeable. She could only imagine what must be going through his head, hearing the obscenities that the youths were casually throwing about the courtroom. It was always a surprise to her how small and strangely intimate the courtrooms were, especially when the door was shut. The benches had been wiped down with Dettol and the medicinal smell added to the claustrophobic, unsettling nature of the room. She supposed better the smell of Dettol than the odour coming from the sewers and blocked toilets that would assault them when they left the room.

The defendant's lawyer finally made his appearance. He seemed to have come to the courtroom with no documents and was exuding a self-satisfied, almost bored air. His client was nowhere in sight. Gabrielle's alarm was growing. Had something been decided in chambers? Without Constantina? Was that—?

'All rise,' shouted the orderly.

The magistrate, a small, portly fellow came into the room, theatrically clutching the gavel. The magistrate settled himself down, nodded to the defence table.

'Mr Mukhosi, what do you have for us today?' The magistrate chuckled as if he had shared some private joke with counsel. This was highly irregular: Constantina, as the prosecution, should have been addressed first so that she could lay out their case.

'Your Worship, as you can see my client is not present.'

'Ah, that I can see.'

'Yes, Your Worship, it is of great importune unfortunance that my esteemed client has been taken ill for many days now.'

'That is indeed extremely unfortunate,' concurred the magistrate.

Gabrielle's heart was thumping. Was the magistrate just going to dismiss the case outright with – *no, just calm down*, she chided herself. She couldn't show, by any nervous gesture, that this was her first court appearance on a truly substantive matter. She couldn't let Danika sense something was amiss. She stopped herself from fidgeting with her papers. This magistrate, she was sure, was one of the many rumoured to be practising in Zimbabwean courts without even five O levels – a possibility, given that the only written constitutional qualification to be appointed a magistrate was that they be a 'fit and proper' person. Constantina showed not a hint of perturbation. She was waiting for whatever farce was going on to play itself out, for the government to show its hand.

'We respectfully ask for an adjournment, Your Worship.'

Constantina stood up.

'Yes, Mrs Maderera,' said the magistrate, his hand already on his beloved gavel. Gabrielle felt the irritation on Constantina's behalf. Constantina, who was in her fifties, was not married – a fact the magistrate knew very well from previous court interactions.

'Your Worship, given that the defence has offered no certificate of ill health and so, in effect, the defendant can be judged to be in contempt of—'

The gavel went down. Not once but twice. 'Mrs Maderera, sit down, sit down.'

'Your—'

Down went the gavel again. 'Sit down, Mrs Maderera, or else *you* will be judged in contempt of court.'

Constantina sat down.

'The law must not only be seen but must be seen to be done. To this end I adjourn the proceedings.'

Constantina stood up again.

'Yes, Mrs Maderera.'

'Adjourned, till when?'

'Next week. We shall meet here next week, same day, same time. That is all. Court adjourned.' Down went the gavel.

Gabrielle stepped out of the courtroom into the courtyard. The stench coming from the uncleaned toilets had her flinging her forearm over her mouth. Danika was some steps away from her. Two youths were accosting Mr Dube and Constantina, at the far side of the courtyard, near the exit. The khaki-shirted one suddenly looked towards Danika and Gabrielle, said something to the other, spat on the ground and then the two of them wandered off along the corridor, perhaps to another room. Mr Dube stood still for a moment watching them, hand clenched in a fist. Constantina said something to him and he shook his head. Danika had started walking towards her father.

'Danika—'

Danika turned, her hand resting, unconsciously, on her stomach.

'I would like to talk about what happened in there. What adjournment means.'

'I have to go, Miss Langa, my father is waiting. Goodbye, Miss Langa.'

The defence was playing a cat-and-mouse game, she had wanted to tell Danika, trying to wear them out with delays upon delays. They were afraid of even the preliminaries. That was a good sign.

'What did those youths want?' she asked Constantina.

Constantina patted her head.

'Just the usual tactics. Trying to intimidate. Can you believe it, right here in the esteemed corridors of justice?'

Constantina waved her short arm around at the dingy courtyard.

'I told them to mind their language, calling an old woman a so-and-so is just not acceptable in our culture. I have some other business to attend to here, Gabrielle. I'll talk to you tomorrow. We have to rework our strategy.'

She watched Constantina make her way to another courtroom, and wondered again at her boss's resilience, her always-upbeat nature, her absolute, unshakeable belief in words like *truth* and *justice*, even after so many years of practice and seeing how much the process mangled truth, justice. She herself, after only a year, was already getting jaded—

A tap on her shoulder snapped her out of her reverie.

'Godfrey! What are you doing here . . .? Oh, what a stupid question to ask a reporter.'

Godfrey, who had a camera slung over his neck and was carrying a sketch pad, shrugged his shoulders. 'Oh, just searching for this and that. I'm heading back to the office.'

'Can I give you a lift?'

'That would be very generous of you.'

'Gabrielle, those youths, they mean business,' Godfrey said, as she manoeuvred the car out of the tight parking spot.

'Constantina doesn't seem too worried.'

'Constantina is a legend in these parts. As a matter of fact, I was speaking to her before the proceedings and she gave me some potentially explosive news.'

'Really?'

'Yes, something about a possible ring among the powers that be, underage girls being procured and groomed.'

Rework our strategy. Is this what Constantina meant, stirring the waters, seeing what debris rose to the surface, what they could throw around, make stick? Or maybe Constantina really did know something?

'This is the first I've heard of it, Godfrey. Did she give you names?'

'Nothing, this was all off the record.'

She suddenly felt as though she *had* jumped into water too deep. Her father's warnings to stay out of political matters flickered, Giorgio's too.

'Those youths, Gabrielle, they were watching.'

And again she felt that clenching in her chest, and then she opened her mouth, exhaled.

'They can watch,' she said. 'Maybe they will learn something.'

9

The day is beautiful. The day has not revolted. The skies have not darkened. The sun has not shrivelled and died.

She does not know how the night has turned itself into this day and how she has come to lie on this ground, undercurrents of pain in the limbs of her body, waiting, it seems, for her to pay full attention to their suffering. Was she placed here or did her body give up the struggle, succumb to its weariness despite the consequences and simply fall to the ground?

She does not know what has happened between then and now. If she has spent the entire night singing and chanting, clapping and stamping the ground, raising her hands in a fist, shoving that same fist to the ground in disgust, shouting streams of words. She does not know if she has eaten, if she has been fed, if water has passed through her lips. Her body, once preoccupied with its hunger, seems to be building up its resources, its case, for the bruising of its parts.

Has she been beaten?

Thought seems to her, as she lies there, to be a wisp of smoke floating over her; if she can only reach out and grasp it, but there it goes, dissipating in the light.

And now, her body cries out.

She is afraid to open her eyes. Not so much because of what she might see but for the pain that might hurtle out of them, the pain that she feels shut in, zigzagging desperately beneath the lids. If she just lies there, her eyes closed tight, the day, this day, might just vanish and, waking up, she might find herself on a morning lying on a warm bed, a dog called Mawara scratching at the door, the day itself a promise. She can lie here. The ground warm and hard, a casement for wretched flesh and bone.

'Get up.' A voice pressed against her ear. The voice, so soft and hard, seems to her a trick in her hearing. She has not heard it.

'Did you not hear? Get up.' A hand against her face, digging into her skin.

If her eyes remain shut, the day, this day, does not exist and she, her true self, lies on a warm bed, listening to a dog called Mawara scratching on a door.

'Get up!' Spittle on her face, on the edges of her mouth she feels it there, tiny crusts caught in the droplets.

She must open her eyes. She must do this. But the pain wrestling in them stops her.

'Are you playing with me?' Fingers, harsh and strong, prise open her lids, and her fright is the fright she sees in the other eyes. Afraid of what? That she might be dead? Do they not then intend to go that far?

The man's smell enters her. There is sweat and dirt. And something else. Something that lies encrusted on the man's body. Sex. It is a hungry, angry sex. Where has he taken it from?

'Get up,' he says and, as though the command would be incomplete, unable to stand on its own merits, tosses, 'Bitch.'

Around her, silence. Around her, eyes watching. Fearful. For her. For themselves.

She must get up. She must turn away from the warm bed. She must ignore the scratching of a dog called Mawara on a door. She must enter this day. She must cloak herself with a new self, and here is this man handing her one.

She gets up.

And falls.

'Down with imperialist sympathizers! Down with imperialist tea boys! Down with imperialist madams! Down with imperialist saboteurs and their paymasters! Down with land hoarders! Down with economic prostitutes!'

Their voices are shrill. The hysteria, histrionics of forced conviction.

She lifts her body from the ground, from its warmth, its hardiness, its casement of flesh and bones, and she, too, stands among them. Her voice, at first tentative as though not quite believing in itself but soon, it too reaches its pitch.

'Pamberi ne land acquisition! Forward with land distribution! Forward with land grab!'

The sun, its heat, curdles the voices, the words.

The man (the comrade, the youth) in front of them opens and shuts his mouth. Silence falls.

'Do you think we are playing here? Is that what you are thinking! Do you think we are here for games! Eh, if your mouths cannot work properly for the revolution they do not need food! Food cannot be wasted!'

'Pasi ne BBC! Down with Britain! Down with Gay Gangsters! Pasi ne referendums! Pamberi ne ZBC! Pamberi ne *Herald* news!'

10

The guard waved Gabrielle into the building.

A cloud of smoke was hovering over Trinity's desk. Gabrielle rapped gently on the cubicle partition and her friend, cigarette tightly clenched in the side of her mouth, braids falling over her small, earnest face, looked up from the story she'd been busy at work on.

Gabrielle gave her usual greeting. 'Haven't you heard? Smoking kills.'

Trinity drew a deep drag, blew smoke upwards and then snatched the cigarette from her mouth and stubbed it out on a copper ashtray.

'And how many times do I have to tell you that the Holy Trinity in these parts manifests itself as Beef, Spirits and Tobacco?'

Smoking, drinking straight from the bottle, the pierced nose (now sans stud), the butterfly tattoo on her wrist (obtained in Jo'burg), and a penchant for miniskirts were some of the things that had set Trinity apart at university.

'Give me two minutes, Gabrielle, my creative juices are flowing.'

Trinity bent down into her work again, her copper bangles jangling as she typed.

Gabrielle looked around at the newsroom. The atmosphere was rather subdued in the government-run daily, no hustling or bustling. Who knew what 'news' was being concocted at the far end where the editor's office lay, what directives had been issued by the Minister of Information? The vibrant *Daily News* where Godfrey worked was giving *The Herald* a thorough run for its money.

'Done.'

Trinity looked up, stretched, reached for the copper tray, frowned at the dead cigarette.

'Do you know what the title of this piece is, Gabrielle, straight from our dear editor's mouth? BRITISH PIRATES OPERATING IN MOZAMBICAN WATERS PREVENTING OIL FROM GETTING TO ZIMBABWE. I had to realize a 'fact'-based story from that, complete with witness accounts and unnamed but reliable sources. All in a good day's work.'

'Why don't you join your boyfriend at the *Daily News*? They're making waves there,' Gabrielle teased.

'What? Godfrey, that daydreamer with his cartoons? I'm a realist. That outfit is not going to last long. The powers that be are going to shut them down: it looks like I'll have to pay for my own roora. Did I tell you that Patrick is following after his father? You should see his drawings Gabrielle, masterpieces.'

Gabrielle was always amazed at Trinity's lack of bitterness at the exorbitant bride price – ten, no twenty, no *fifty* head of cattle, necklaces, costumes, even a trip to Botswana – her family had put up, and Godfrey's relatives' reluctance to pay it because of Patrick. Godfrey had already paid damages for impregnating her without having first secured marriage. Trinity had become pregnant in her second year and she and Godfrey lived together in a one-bedroom flat in Tatenda Place on Josiah Chinamano Street. Trinity never left her son in the care of Godfrey's people because she was certain that they would kill him as they considered his cleft palate to be a bad omen. Their attitude hadn't changed even after Patrick had undergone the operation.

'So, dish, my friend, how's Mister Big Ben?'

'I knew I shouldn't have said anything.' Definitely not given her a head-to-toe description over the phone – too much ammunition.

Trinity nudged her with an elbow and laughed. She was enjoying herself. She had never really cared much for Giorgio Fiori. She couldn't understand what Gabrielle saw in that dry murungu who had virtually made a recluse of her best friend: no more raucous, brandy-and-Coca-Cola-fuelled Friday, Saturday nights, hopping from one party to another, unless Giorgio was away on a mission.

'So, what else is on the grapevine, Trinity? What is tomorrow's news?'

'Deflection, I see.'

'Just want to know what's on the cards.'

'We're in for a bumpy ride, my friend, uncharted territory, who knows what The Old Man will do with *absolute* absolute power? *The Herald*, of course, will be there to misreport it.'

Gabrielle looked uneasily about her, but the other reporters were not paying them any attention. Trinity had told her that only the editor was an ideologue: *the rest of us are just wage earners. And even the editor, do you think he believes half of the nonsense he sends out? Please!*

'Excuse me, Gabs, I have to give this superlative piece of "non-fiction" writing to the copy desk.'

She watched Trinity with that efficient walk of hers, slapping the papers against her thigh.

The two of them had met during a Student Union General Assembly. Sitting at the back of the Great Hall, they'd collapsed into fits of laughter when someone, not hearing one of the speeches clearly, had shouted out, 'Can you come again?' followed by other voices, 'Yes, come again, come again.' Trinity had whispered, 'And there goes a thousand and one ejaculations.'

Gabrielle's stomach sounded off a series of growls. She looked around, embarrassed.

Tobias, the sports reporter, doffed his fisherman's cap and gave her a wave from his cubicle; she waved back. He'd been very generous in giving her and Trinity VIP tickets to Dynamos–Highlanders matches. That was another thing which had kept her and Trinity friends: their passion for football, despite their being in opposing camps of the most virulent of rivalries. Dynamos versus Highlanders, the Clash of the Titans, was a historic battle: conquest, defeat, Shona versus Ndebele; the Glamour Boys from Harare stalking their home territory at Rufaro Stadium, or 'Bosso Bosso' from Bulawayo, flaunting their stuff at

Barbourfields Stadium . . . and someone always emerged bloody-nosed from these encounters.

'So, Gabs, do you think you'll succeed, get that child rapist to pay?' said Trinity, when she came back.

She thought of Danika that morning standing in her office, pregnant.

'Constantina is in fighting mode.'

'And you?'

That was a pertinent question. What was she exactly? All fire and systems go? The truth was that she was riddled with doubts, and this fact took her completely by surprise. Dealing with a living, breathing person who could be hurt, scarred by court rulings and judgments, was a long way off from all her high-minded, student-level principles and ideals.

'Well, as one of my learned professors used to say, "The law's an ass but it's all we've got."'

Trinity quickly scribbled something on the pad on her desk.

'Hey, don't quote me!'

'Don't worry, you'll be one of my unnamed but oh-so-reliable sources. Come on, Gabs, I need some Sunshine City air, and a drink to go with this,' Trinity said, brandishing a fresh cigarette.

11

The youth says, 'Heh, you dogs, if you are being thirsty drink your own water.' He spits on the ground.

Crusts of bread are thrown on the ground and they, like pigeons, flurry around, picking away at the bits.

She looks at the crust of bread resting in her hand like a wounded bird. Around her she hears mouths working. The crust of bread seems to her heavy with improbable meaning.

She remembers as a child fiddling with a piece of bread, tearing away at the crust and her mother, her beautiful mother, slapping her hand away.

It is a simple thing, to bring this crust of bread to her lips, to open her mouth and take it in, to revel in its staleness. But she is afraid of what chewing this bread, working it in her mouth like the others, swallowing it, will unleash in her body.

The hunger that had claimed her has, like some dejected beast, retreated. The piece of food in her hand seems to her to be like some bait, some treacherous entity, that will release the marauding beast. And if her body is so attacked, what else might be susceptible?

She thinks that she is coping quite well. By which she means she is functioning. She is able to see, to hear. To think. Should her body collapse, might not her – what is she to call it – reason, spirit, follow? Would it be better simply not to let the morsel into her body, not to let it violate the uneasy peace there?

She looks at the crust of bread in the hollow of her hand, the wounded bird. She feels her mother's slap. She brings it to her lips, opens her mouth and swallows the bitterness into her and, for a dizzying moment, she feels as though time is sweeping through her, rushing through every cell in her body until she is and she is not, she exists, she does not, she is here and she is not, and she opens her eyes, her gaze tilting and wavering, the past and the present surging and receding until they are one. Here.

12

'Sorry to keep you waiting,' Gabrielle said, getting in the car.
She had been on the phone with Constantina; she wanted Gabrielle to come in early on Monday. There was physical evidence, a game changer.

'Red, white and blue,' he said, once she was seated.

She was wearing jeans, a white T-shirt, a red plastic belt.

'In your honour.'

'Thank you, I'm definitely honoured.'

She looked outside to where Mawara was jumping away.

'I think you're going to have to put that dog on sedatives, Gabrielle.'

'He's getting better, but he really makes me feel guilty every time I leave him.'

He looked at her. 'Softie,' he said.

'I'm a lawyer,' she said. 'I'm tough when I need to be.'

'Notice is duly served.'

She liked sitting in this crazy car, watching the world whizz by. As he drove, she could see him breezing along a country road in America driving his American car with not a care in the world, whistling along to something.

'What is New Haven like?'

'New Haven,' he said, 'located in the Nutmeg State of Connecticut, birthplace of the lollipop and the hamburger.'

'I'm impressed, go on.'

'It's a small city, but it being a college town—' Her confused look stopped him. 'Yale's in New Haven—'

'Oh,' she said, factoring this into what she knew about him: he had gone to university in his hometown, a university where his mother taught.

'So for most folk New Haven is just the downtown area, you know, around the campus, which is pretty run-down, but, I mean, you have the Yale University Art Gallery there, which has Picasso, Miró, Degas and Van Gogh's *Night Café*, no entry charge, so you can just stroll in and take a look as many times as you like – that's pretty special.'

She had no idea what Van Gogh's *Night Café* looked like. She was intrigued that he would choose this to tell her about his hometown. An art gallery. A painting. Did he go there often? Why did he pick that painting? Was it just because it was the most famous, or was it something more personal to him? She was trying to decipher who he was by the little clues he dropped. A quiver of agitation passed through her: the realization that he too might be engaged in the very same task, trying to figure her out by her pronouncements, what she chose to reveal.

'The *Amistad*, the slave ship—'

'Yes, I know, I watched the movie.'

She felt like an imbecile as soon as the words came out of her mouth but, fortunately, he was too busy trying to manoeuvre the car round a couple of potholes to have paid full attention to her answer. It had started to drizzle, perhaps the effects of Cyclone Eline that was building up over the Indian Ocean and was heading towards Mozambique, growing stronger and stronger in force.

'Well, that all actually happened in New Haven. There's a memorial where the jailhouse used to be, where the slaves from the ship were imprisoned while they awaited trial.'

After the movie Giorgio had said it was too Hollywood. She didn't understand what the issue was. Weren't all movies made in Hollywood, so what was the point of his comment? She understood enough from his tone that 'too Hollywood' meant that it was deficient in something. Something essential. She didn't tell Giorgio that she had enjoyed it, if enjoyment was the right thing to say about that kind of film. It had engrossed and appalled her.

'I have an invitation to visit Ghana. I'd like to see the Cape Coast Castle, the Door of No Return.'

He talked as though she should know these places. The only thing she knew about Ghana was that the beloved and popular first wife of The Old Man had come from Ghana. At this exact moment she could not quite locate Ghana on a map of Africa. She did not know any Ghanaians. At university she had met no other Africans – she had heard of a medical student from the Seychelles. She did not know what the Cape Coast Castle was and what the Door of No Return signified. Her befuddlement must have been clear as day.

'You didn't learn any of this at school?'

'No,' she said. 'Only British and European History, and the American War of Independence.'

Even her knowledge of pre-colonial Zimbabwean history – the time before David Livingstone 'discovered' the Victoria Falls, before the Pioneer Column formed by Cecil John Rhodes and the British South African Company conquered Matabeleland and Mashonaland, before the Great Indaba where the Ndebele King, Lobengula, signed away land and mineral wealth with an X – was woeful. Exhibit A: until pretty recently, all she knew about Great Zimbabwe was that it had once been called the Zimbabwe Ruins, and that before independence the white government had claimed that it was not built by the African population but by Arabs or Phoenicians.

It was embarrassing to admit that it was Giorgio, with all his anthropological books (he'd studied at the School of Oriental and African Studies in London), who'd broadened her knowledge a bit – all those tomes he had in his house about African Cultures and Civilizations, Shona and Ndebele Peoples, their Religions, their Gods, their Mythologies . . .

'British History, without the slave trade?'

'Yes.'

'Hmm.'

She couldn't even definitively claim that Zimbabwe was not on the slave-trade route: what if the traders *had* come this far south, inland, their ships docked in Cape Town, Durban? And didn't South Africa actually import slaves from India?

'The slaves were kept there,' he said. 'The Cape Coast Castle, in the dungeons. It was a trading centre, slaves and gold for cloth, timber, spices . . . and the door is where they stepped out to get to the slave ships.'

They drove in silence up Borrowdale Road. The moment passed when she felt she should apologize for her ignorance. He was probably irritated, put out by what he must think was unforgivable. She hoped he would turn on the radio but he just kept on driving, lost, it seemed, in his own thoughts. Maybe he was regretting having her in the car. Maybe she should make up some excuse, not feeling well, and ask him to take her back home. Maybe this would be the last she would see of him.

'Hoops,' he said, out of the blue. The car was stationary at the traffic lights. She followed his gaze. There were a couple of basketball nets attached to the walls of the houses of the new development that was going up, just opposite the racecourse.

'Do you play?' she asked him.

'Nope.'

Was her question offensive? 'I – I meant, well, here it's football and you're tall, so I just thou—'

'I play a bit of tennis, badly, and I sail when I get the chance.'

'Really? I've never been on a boat. Have you been to Kariba?'

'No, not yet.'

'Rhodies – white Zimbabweans – they take their boats out there for fishing and camping.'

'Weekends, as a kid, we'd go out on my dad's latest boat. He designed this incredible schooner.'

'Schooner?'

'They're – no, you'll just have to come to New Haven and I'll show you. Have you ever been camping?'

As a way of answer she said, 'There are hippos and crocodiles in the lake.'

Like her, Giorgio was not a hiking, camping, fishing guy. When they went to Nyanga they eschewed the National Park cabins deep in the pine forests for the stuffy colonial-era Rhodes Nyanga Hotel. And during the day they didn't climb mountains or do trails. They ate, read, ate, slept.

'Well, not in Connecticut.'

'So, you fish and camp?'

'Yep. We have a cabin in the mountains, pretty basic, but it's beautiful out there. And in winter there's skiing.'

'You ski?'

'Yes, I do.'

'Don't you get cold? I mean in Zimbabwe, fourteen degrees and we're coming to work with blankets. You'll see what I mean in June.'

He smiled. 'That's what thermals were invented for, but yes, sure, it does get pretty cold. Sometimes so cold we have ice storms, when the rain freezes; it makes for great pictures, icicles hanging from lamp posts . . . but, yes, there's good skiing there.'

She wanted to ask him if those were normal things that a black man, an African American from New Haven, Connecticut, did, or if it was just him, but, once again, she was afraid of causing offence. He was just telling her the facts of his life, nothing more.

'Now, come on, Gabrielle, your turn: childhood, growing up in Bulawayo . . .'

She was relieved to see that his mood was lightening up. It was a pity that he had chosen to go down this path which she had no wish to travel on, but he was waiting for her to say something. She would keep it short and simple.

'My father's a businessman, and an office bearer in the Party. And my mother, she died in a road accident when I was thirteen.'

He looked at her but said nothing. And she liked him for that.

'The bus she was in had a burst tyre. It careened off a bridge into a flooded river.'

As a child she'd blamed her father; she'd always believed that her mother was on that bus fleeing him.

She knew nothing of her mother's relatives, only that her grandmother had had a fling with a European working on the construction of the Kariba dam in the 1950s – Spanish, Portuguese, maybe even an Italian. Ostracized, her grandmother had found her way to Bulawayo where she raised the coloured child alone.

She looked out at the road. The rain was falling steadily now. Perhaps there would be no market today. She would have loved to stay in the coolness of this vehicle, in the comfortable silence they had now fallen into. But, here they were, the car coming to a stop at the turning to the parking lot. A scotch-cart suddenly appeared out from the bushes bordering the road. An old man sat, bent over, inside the cart. He was wearing a tattered hat and a shirt, the right sleeve torn from its seam; he looked up, gave them a wide toothless smile in the rain.

They sprinted from the car, their feet splashing into puddles, and huddled under an awning, waiting for the rain to subside.

'Made to measure, sah!'

'What the—?' exclaimed Ben.

An apparition had materialized in front of them. It was dressed, head to toe, in black plastic bin liners and it was shaking a clutch of bin liners at them.

'Strictly made to measure, sah!'

'I think he's selling them,' Gabrielle said, trying hard not to laugh.

'Trash bags?'

'For the rain. Raincoats.'

Ben looked at her and then at the apparition again.

'Recycling, Ben, African-style. Although I hope they're new ones, at least.'

'Okay then,' he said. 'Let's do this.'

They bought the 'raincoats' for an exorbitant two dollars, whittled down from the sky-high price of four dollars each. The bags on, they looked at each other and burst out laughing. She was drowning in hers and his was way too small, stopping just above his hips; he looked, with his long arms sticking out of the armholes, like a scarecrow. So much for "made to measure".

They rustled over to the other parking lot behind the supermarket. On Sunday mornings the space was converted into little stalls: rows and rows of trestle tables crowded each other, brimming with second-hand clothes, books, knick-knacks, all kinds of idiosyncratic objects.

The vendors were braving the rain, their wares protected by make-shift plastic sheeting held down by stones. They passed a couple of tables with second-hand books, another one with vintage jeans (*old and used*, was Trinity's usual comment) and then a table with Rhodesian memorabilia: shoeboxes with stamps, postcards, coins, notes, bullets, badges and medals from the Rhodesian army, copper plaques with flame lilies and the Rhodesian flag, a *Rhodesia is Lekker* T-shirt, a small gas canister and stove, a chipped beer mug with an elephant, its trunk curled over a flag with *Rhodesia* and, on its body, *is Super*.

'Hey, howzit. Hey you two, come have a look, it's all genuine.'

The man who had the reddened, bloated look of a heavy drinker, a network of spider veins radiating from his nose to his cheeks, was already taking away the stones holding down the plastic. Luckily his table was in a nook, just behind the entrance to the supermarket so it had some protection from the rain.

'Check this beauty.'

He was holding out the beer mug, but Ben had wandered off to the far side of the table where a turntable sat, beside it a crate full of LPs. He was going through the records, lifting the albums out. He looked like a real aficionado.

'Hundred dollars for the lot,' said the man.

'Hundred?' said Ben.

'Jeez luck, you're American, thought so. Yah, one hundred for the records. The turntable, that's different.'

'This isn't a shakedown, is it?'

'No, man, no. Two hundred for the turntable, final offer. Really good quality. Teak. As good as new. Okay, man, I'll give you a discount. Two-fifty for the lot. Turntable, albums. Ask your chick, it's a blimming good deal, man.'

Ben forked out the bills, without conferring with *his chick*. Thirteen crisp Zimbabwean twenties, letting the vendor keep the ten. For a moment she thought the man might have been really trying his luck, expecting newly minted American dollars, but he took the notes without even looking at them, already smelling the booze-up he was going to have.

Ben carried the crate, she, the turntable, going through the supermarket entrance to avoid the rain as much as they could. They were obviously quite a sight because she saw a couple of people do a double-take.

'So, that was interesting,' he said when they were sitting in the car. He was wiping his face dry with a tissue.

'You could have had it for less than half the price, Ben. As soon as you opened your mouth. I mean, if you had kept your mouth closed and just—'

'Is this the hard-nosed lawyer talking?'

'Well, be duly advised, as soon as you opened your mouth, dollar signs started blinking in that man's eyes. You were quoted freshly delivered murungu prices.'

He laughed. 'So, even to the sexist white guy I'm a murungu.'

'Yes, most definitely so.'

'Five dollars for everything, Gabrielle, what can I say?'

She wanted to tell him it was even less on the black market but he was probably aware of that, the Zimdollar was going south fast.

'Nineteen sixties Motown classics, forties jazz, someone had great taste.'

'Or maybe his chick did.'

'Now that's just *crazytalk*, girl.'

They were still in their bin liners and she was dripping water everywhere.

'Umm, we should maybe get out of these,' she said. 'I'm making a mess of your car.'

She could just imagine what her hair looked like.

'It's vinyl, Gabrielle, I don't think wet trash bags will do it much harm.'

The rain had petered out, reduced to a soft drizzle once again.

Ben opened his door. 'We have to find something for you, Gabrielle, let's go.'

What she found was a tiny silver brooch of a lizard in a box full of ribbons and threads and badges.

'Nice,' he said when she pinned it on her T-shirt. 'But I didn't hear much bargaining.'

'Only because my Shona's worse than my Ndebele,' she said sheepishly.

Giorgio would have bargained it down to a third of its price in his heavily accented English, leaving her standing embarrassed by his side while the vendor would steal her hostile looks, blaming her.

'We have to celebrate,' he said when they were standing at the entrance of the shopping complex, his arm across the open, wrought iron gate.

'That would be nice,' she said, like some ladylike character who should be twirling a parasol in the sun. In fact, the rain had stopped, so they dumped their raincoats into the nearest dustbin.

'How about Mimi's?' she said. 'They have a wonderful apple strudel.'

They ordered their strudels (with cream), a cappuccino for her, a Coke for him, at the counter and, because the sun had come out again, they sat outside, first wiping the seats of the wet wrought iron chairs with serviettes.

'Those guys calling out *hey, sister, sister* had the same feeling as some sidewalks in New York. You don't mind it?'

'No, why? Do they mind it in America?'

'Some do.'

With Giorgio, those same vendors would have addressed her as 'madam'.

She watched him, his long legs stretched out in the strip of sunlight that had broken through the clouds, his eyes moving from her and along the square with its paved stones and benches under palm trees, its wooden crates of geraniums and sweet peas on the low walls, along the exposed brick facades of shop fronts with their colourful awnings dripping water, a photo studio, a shoe shop, a saddler, an angler supply shop, hardware, a pharmacy, newsagent, some dress shops, its lamp posts and iron gates, further along, the pub tucked into a little corner. She suddenly realized that she could imagine him on a boat, out on the water, his long, lean frame standing there on the deck, his hands fiddling with the sails, doing whatever it was that you did to keep the boat going.

'It's pretty quiet here, Gabrielle, compared to downtown.'

'Yes, no street kids, hawkers, beggars, touts – all kept away by those guys over there with their plastic batons, and look, Ben, there's one pulling down *Vote No* posters on that wall.'

They watched the rather small guard leaping to reach the posters that had been craftily placed some way up.

'I guess they don't want the Youth Brigade toi-toing through here.'

To think, next Saturday there would be a polling booth over at Borrowdale School. Would the youths be deployed, the riot police?

The waitress came with their bill, placed it by his side. She opened her bag, but he beat her to it, putting the notes on the silver dish.

'Thank you,' she said. 'I owe you.'

'In that case, you can come with me to the art gallery next week. There's an exhibition of Shona sculpture. Have you been to Domboshawa? You must have been, it's just outside Harare?'

She shook her head.

'Well, we're working on a cultural exchange with a couple of artists from around there. They're going to be showing some works at the gallery. I went to see one of them in his home village.'

If she had heard this from any other foreigner she probably would have rolled her eyes. It was a statement usually accompanied by the strong smell of proprietary and bragging rights – *I went to an African village . . . my African village.*

'It's quite something out there: these fantastic boulders on this hilly terrain, thorn trees, and the sound of stone being worked on, and the singing, Gabrielle, just one voice lifting off, others coming in. I'm being corny, I know, but the place just feels spiritual.'

'Ah, the American has a soul.'

He lifted her hand from the table, clasped it dramatically.

'Yes, he sure does.'

And then he was serious again, still holding her hand.

'I'll take you there, to see for yourself, that's a promise.'

13

The comrades are bored.

They are sick and tired of their captives' voices. Of their fear. Of their incompetence.

She does as the man says. She is thirsty. She swallows her spit. She swallows and swallows until her body is filled with spit. Her body rebels and, bent over, she watches the crusts of bread mashed up in the spit leave a trail on the ground. She wipes her mouth with her hand. She looks up and the sky is so blue that if she closes her eyes she could delve into all that blueness, disappear right into it.

The blueness of the sky hurts her eyes; she turns away from it.

On the ground the trail of spit has died.

She sees a woman, an old woman, lifting her dress, her head trapped in the cloth, her breasts shrunken and shrivelled.

She sees men – no, boys, youths, comrades – laughing, pointing at the old woman.

She sees girls huddled together. She sees men – no, boys, youths, comrades – watching the girls, twirling sticks in their mouths, making signs with their hands.

From far-off, she hears the yelping of dogs.

The comrades are bored.

Dangerous.

14

Mr Dube had given Constantina, sealed in a brown envelope, a pair of royal-blue school underpants, stiffened with what Constantina said was almost surely semen. Where had Danika hidden them? Who had found them? Her father? Her mother? Win or lose, would Danika survive the brutalities of this case?

She and Constantina had spent the week in a frenzy of activity, trying to find ways to get the evidence examined in the country; and then ultimately they decided that the best, safest bet was to send it to South Africa, to a private laboratory. That required funds, of course, and so she'd also been writing begging letters to donors. Come Friday, it felt as if the week had gone by in a blur of frustrating non-achievement. Saturday, she was ready to take her mind off the case, happy to hear those two hoots.

'Oh my, Miss Langa,' Ben said, flashing her a wide grin, not shielding his eyes from the glare of her bright yellow sundress. 'You're a vision.'

As they walked among the sculptures in the gallery he talked about art in a way which was knowledgeable but didn't sound at all pretentious. He told her about Picasso and Modigliani and how they were inspired by African masks and clay, and that he was keen to go to this artist commune in Guruve (he was sure he wasn't pronouncing it right) in the north of Zimbabwe which had been apparently started by a friend of Matisse and Picasso. He showed her the three sculptures the artist he'd visited had done, and she liked one in particular. It was a greenish serpentine titled, *An Ant Eating a Woman* and when she went round it she couldn't decide why the artist had called it that but somehow the name seemed to fit. Was this too inspired by Shona mythology? As a lawyer she was used to dealing with practical facts, but here she was, surprised to be moved by some of the works, the art.

'This is my first time in here,' she said. She was standing beside *An Ant Eating a Woman*.

'Really?'

'I've passed this place so many times and I've never once been inclined to go inside. I'm ashamed and embarrassed.'

'Your dress, as soon as I saw it, Van Gogh's sunflowers came to mind.'

'Okay, you will have to educate me. Leonardo da Vinci's *Mona Lisa* is just about the only world-class painting I know.'

'Van Gogh, Vincent Van Gogh, he was a Dutch painter. He started off painting in the Dutch style of that time, these very heavy, dark paintings, and then he went to Provence, in France. He was just blown away by the colours, the quality of light there, so he started experimenting, mixing pigments to capture all those vibrant yellows, in the sunflowers, the cornfields.'

Hearing him talk was entering a new world. She, who had never been out of Zimbabwe or been much of a reader or even thought of the possibility of being an art aficionado.

'Have you seen them, the sunflowers, the paintings?'

'Yes, the ones in Amsterdam, London and Munich. I'm afraid we Americans destroyed one when we bombed Japan. And I think the other one is in a private collection.'

'Did you go to all those places just to see them?'

He laughed.

'No, I went to Europe for the summer, in my sophomore year.'

'You know, one of our mayors came back from Amsterdam with this brilliant idea that he would build a canal system in Harare.'

'Really? How would that work?'

'Don't ask. He saw the canals, loved them, wanted them, was going to build them brick by brick . . .'

She bent down, looked at the price tag.

'Wow, six thousand dollars. That's a lot of money I know it's art but—'

'That's about a hundred dollars.'

'I wasn't converting, and even if I was it's still a lot of money for Zimbabweans.'

Her tone stopped him in his tracks.

'I'm sorry. I'm an idiot.'

'I wouldn't go that far,' she said.

They walked around the gardens, stopped to watch a large wedding party, all purple satin and extravagant frills, have its pictures taken. There was a marimba band at the bandstand packing up. Just off the footpath, a municipal policeman was thrashing away with his baton at the branches and trees that made an alcove, hoping to ferret out a couple engaging in 'indecent behaviour'.

They went over to the bar at the Monomotapa Hotel and sat at a table outside. A couple of the patrons were wearing *Vote No* T-shirts and there was a good-natured debate going on across three tables about what the outcome of next weekend's referendum would be. There were also posters tacked on the trees in the park; from what she could see, more Nos were on the trees than had been ripped to the ground. Progress or determination or foolhardiness? Something was in the air, and just as if her thoughts were being read, Tracy Chapman's 'Talkin' Bout a Revolution' came on the sound system.

She spotted Trinity with Patrick cutting through the park on their way to the playground at the back and called out to her. Trinity's eyes widened when she saw who her friend was with, and the thought slipped through Gabrielle's head that maybe she should have let Trinity go uninterrupted on her way, more so when she saw that mischief-making twist on her lips.

'Trinity, Ben.'

'Ben, Trinity.'

They exchanged 'hi's', Trinity with a dash of over-enthusiasm, a sharp contrast to Trinity's first meeting with Giorgio, which had taken place in his office. With his suit and tie, his document-littered desk, tired out and irritable after a long day of meetings with government officials, he had looked every inch the uptight global do-gooder bureaucrat that Trinity would forever peg him as.

'And this handsome young man is Patrick,' Gabrielle said to Ben.

Patrick shuffled behind Trinity, poking his head between her legs, but then his curiosity got the better of him and he gave Ben a toothy smile.

They walked to the playground together, Ben scoring major points for how easily Patrick took to him, Ben letting him clamber onto his shoulders, the two of them exploring the playground on their own.

'So, that's Big, Beautiful Ben,' Trinity said. 'Not bad, sha, not bad at all. Kudos to you, sistren.'

'I'm glad you approve.'

Trinity's verdict after meeting Giorgio: 'For an Italian, he is very dry.'

'That is what I call an upgrade of the highest order. All the way to First Class since he is an *African* American.'

'Honestly Trinity, you're shameless.'

'*What?* You know I'm speaking the unvarnished truth. You were always so sad with that Giorgio of yours. This is a new Gabs I'm seeing, shining like a diamond.'

'Okay, Trinity.'

'Gabs, that guy couldn't even act like a proper expat, no gifts, no overseas trips—'

'Trinity, I am not—'

'And then, when he finally asks you to go overseas, where does he pick? London? Paris? New York? No, Mister-Save-the-Worlder . . .'

'Trinity!'

' . . . Wants you to pack your bags and go to Bogotá! *Bogotá?* Drug capital of the universe. I mean, if you want that kind of adventure you can just take a one-way ticket to Lagos, or hitch a ride to Jo'burg.'

'Are you quite finished?'

'You know I'm right. Now tell me about the sex.'

'Okay, Trinity, not this again. Our friendship might be officially over, bye.'

'Touchy, touchy. I'm sure it's good. You're blooming *sexual healing*. And you've got bags under your eyes, too—'

'Trinity, I'm a lawyer. I work very long hours. And I've been doing referendum—'

'Which reminds me, Gabs, I spotted some youths on First Street, so steer clear. I think the powers that be are suddenly waking up to the fact that this referendum thing might not be such a walkover after all – just look at those ones over there by the fence.'

Gabrielle looked to where Trinity was nodding. Five youths, three with their backs turned to her, were heckling passers-by along the footpath, raising their fists and barking out slogans; the other two were slouched, smoking, dagga from the smell of it.

Gabrielle felt an uneasy tremor of recognition.

15

'Coloured,' he says to her, 'this is your rubbish.'

The leather bag is hooked on his finger. Her satchel. He drops it on the ground. He watches her. She could, should, scramble for it, reveal its secrets, its life, give the man the pleasure of her dishevelment. She does nothing.

'Coloured,' he says. 'Pick up that bag.'

She holds the bag in her hand, an uncomfortable thing, how did she hold it before?

'Open,' he says.

She is clumsy with the straps. Danger circles her and the man's voice seems so close, so intimate, it could be, must be, her own breath. He snatches the bag from her, tips it over her head, shakes, shakes the contents out.

A notebook.

Pamphlets from the Constitutional Referendum Action Group.

Pages from the Daily News.

The youth picks up the notebook, slaps her face with it, once, twice, pushes it against her chest until she takes it.

'Coloured, read.'

Around her, silence. She sees the old woman lying on the ground, her legs splayed, her dress over her head, her breasts, shrunken and shrivelled. She sees the young girls, their eyes wide and uncomprehending, their arms always pressed at their breasts, protecting them. She sees the man, watching her.

She opens the notebook.

Danika's transcribed interview . . .

Notes . . .

Observations . . .

That other life.

'Read!'

When he has had enough of her voice he snatches the book from her hands, tears out pages, rips them into ribbons. He dangles a piece, a long worm before her and says, 'Coloured, let us see you do something very special. Open your mouth.'

All that blueness she could delve into, disappear. She would only have to close her eyes.

'Coloured, mouth.'

His nails dig deep into her skin, scratching there. Her mouth, squeezed open, the paper resting on the tip of her tongue.

She bites into the paper, chews and swallows, chews and swallows, feels the words, the treacherous words, dissolve in the cells of her body, nourishing her.

He looks at her, his face contorted in fury, his eyes boring into her, as if to peer through her body, to scour the cells of her being, to find out where the words have gone, and if they hold any more power. Unsatisfied, he snatches up one of the referendum pamphlets, crunches it in his fist, forces her mouth open and shoves it in.

16

She set out from the house just after seven o'clock thinking she was being over-zealous. She would, she was certain, most likely be one of the few early birds at the polling station that was set up in a tent just across the Avondale Shopping Centre parking lot.

Turning the corner, she stood for a moment, shocked and pulsating with exhilaration. The storm clouds had momentarily cleared – there has been lightning, thunder and rain through the night – and, before her, was a line snaking across the parking lot all the way beyond the post office, all along King George Road.

At the rate it was going they would be here for most of the day, maybe well into the night, yet people were chatting away. Some entrepreneurial spirits were setting up barbecue stands, thankful for the break in the rain. Vendors were doing a brisk trade in Cokes and buns. She had gone up to The Italian Bakery and found it closed. Everyone was off to vote. Her stomach was already starting to grumble. She would have to buy a mealie cob soon.

'Gabrielle, there you are. I bought you supplies.'

Ben.

He lifted his hand to show her a brown bag. He opened it; the smell of croissants was deliciously tormenting. Her stomach rumbled.

'How did you get these? The bakery's closed.'

'Connections. Connections.'

She laughed at this quintessential local expression.

'You mean Charles?'

She put her hand in the bag and brought out a buttery croissant. She was actually drooling.

'Thanks, Ben.'

'Looks like this is going to take a while.'

'Yes, I didn't think people would turn out in these numbers.'

'Not only here, Gabrielle. I've been around Mount Pleasant, Borrowdale, Highlands, Chisipite, lines everywhere, people trekking to get to the booths with chairs on their heads, babies on their backs; I sound like a CNN broadcast, don't I, but it's really humbling to see.'

'I just hope the Youth League don't make an appearance, so far so good.'

'Too many cameras. They should've banned the international media.'

Said like an old hand.

'But in the rural areas,' she said, 'no cameras there, so maybe, as usual, this is just a city thing, this turnout.'

She thought that was probably it. The Old Man letting the city folk get on with their delusions of Western democracy, care of CNN, BBC, while down in the bush where most of the population lived they were wearily casting their votes in the same old depressing way, but still, seeing all these people, black, white, a tiny spark of hope, maybe . . .

'So, Gabrielle, should I take Mawara out to the gardens, seeing as you're all tied up here?'

'Umm, what about Rum?'

'Rum will cope.'

Him taking her dog out for a walk seemed to be a step, another step.

'Thanks, Ben, that would be great. Just ring the bell. Mister Papadopoulos knows you by now.'

He gave her the bag and produced a bottle of water, too.

'You came prepared,' she said, and then laughed awkwardly.

'I'll be back with lunch,' he said and then, looking up and down the line, he added, 'probably dinner, too.' With that he turned, and she watched him until he disappeared round the corner.

.   .   .

When the results were announced over the radio, two days later, she witnessed the spontaneous revelries on First Street: people cheering and dancing and someone handing out red 'referee' cards because this time The Old Man had been given a yellow card, a warning, but, come the presidential elections, he was going to get a red expulsion card, for sure.

Trinity was there with pen and pad in hand.

'If the riot police show up I'll just flash my *Herald* ID, tell them I'm working on a story on how these imperialist lackeys are defacing the Greatness that is Zimbabwe,' she said, beaming. She shook her head at the spectacle before them: the impromptu dance routine that had broken out to an Oliver Mtukudzi number, a group of students toi-toing to 'Chinja, Chinja' and an old man blowing on a cow horn while somebody was enthusiastically beating a drum.

'You look very amused, Trinity, what's so funny?'

'This. Us, the citizens of this most wonderful country.'

Godfrey came over to tell them that there was a seismic shift in national politics. In his exuberance he even planted a kiss on Trinity's lips. Trinity rolled her eyes.

Unlike Trinity, who was city born and bred, Godfrey had been raised in the countryside. He had herded cattle since he was six, went to a mission school deep in the bush – Gabrielle could imagine his angular frame leaning against an anthill, his thoughtful, deep-set eyes surveying the land before him, his thin fingers sketching on some old cardboard, the cattle, the goats, the birds, thorn trees. He had done some incredible portraits of Trinity. There was also a courtliness about him; Trinity always joked that it was she who had corrupted him.

As soon as he left to snap more pictures, Trinity turned to Gabrielle. 'Cometh the man, cometh the hour – everyone thinks it's plain sailing from now on. Don't they know that The Old Man has been long at this game?'

Gabrielle slapped her friend on the arm. 'Come on, Trinity, we won. We actually won. Enjoy it. Tell your *Herald* readers the sights and sounds of Harare on this day.'

Trinity shook her head.

'I'm a hard-nosed realist, my friend. The Old Man now knows the nature and strength of his enemy. He won't make the same mistake twice. I'm telling you, this is just an interlude. Hokoyo! Watch out. Judgment Day will soon be upon us.'

17

The comrades hold her in their eyes.

She looks at the old woman: in time, will she too not lift her dress, lie on the ground, her feet splayed, her breasts shrunken and shrivelled? A sight to make the boys laugh. She looks and sees that the schoolgirls have scattered. Where are their wide-open eyes, their plump legs, their protected breasts?

She thinks of the paper in her body, the flimsy weight of it, sodden in fluid, a pulpy mess.

She wills a memory – an act of defiance – something whole and true that the comrades cannot take, touch. *There is the snatch of sun on her fingertips. His face against the window, watching her. A smile, a whisper, her face upturned, a graze of a kiss—*

'Coloured, we have your friend. You must be happy. You must say thank you.'

She looks up at them, thinking *Ben.*

'Here she is.'

Danika stands there, her hand against her stomach, fingers splayed, her eyes cast down.

'Are you not happy to see your friend, eh? Iwe, respond.'

His finger is on Danika's chin, lifting it. 'We have brought you here to keep Miss Lawyer company, what do you say?'

His finger drops from the chin, taps one cheek, then the other, then tap tap on the forehead, tap tap again.

'You will enjoy. Heh! We will enjoy.'

18

Jeremiah stood up, yawned and then swore. 'He is doing this on purpose. Why can he not just come out and say whatever he wants to say. Some of us have jobs.' He slumped down on the sofa again, and reached out for another beer.

The eight of them, friends from university, were crowded round Trinity's old TV set, waiting for The Old Man to give his verdict on the results. He was supposed to come on straight after the news but, as usual, there were technical difficulties at ZBC. What was his response going to be? Fifty-five per cent of the population had dared to dream, to hope. And now, with parliamentary elections only four months away and presidential ones in two years, and should the wild card, the former trade unionist leader, derisively termed 'that tea boy' by The Old Man, decide to stand, who knew what these cheeky Zimbabweans might now be capable of. *Chinja! Change!*

The small coffee table was littered with beer bottles, packets of crisps and peanuts and the conversation, which had been loud and jocular, was now muted. Nerves had taken hold.

'What about that performance from that fool, the Minister of *Dis*information?' said Trinity. 'I don't think it can be topped. I'm sure that's the technical difficulty. The Old Man is scratching his head wondering what to say, what to do to match that.'

There was a general outburst of cursing at that, most of it to do with the deficiencies and abnormalities of the Minister's manhood until Trinity cried out for order, in case they had forgotten there was a child in the next room. They could hear Godfrey's snoring coming from the bedroom; he had gone to put Patrick to bed.

The Minister (former eloquent anti-government professor, reincarnated within a few short years into vitriolic, adjective-riddled presidential right-hand man), with his egg-shaped head bobbing up and down the TV screen, had come out swinging the day before. Apparently, they had all 'shot themselves in the foot' and he warned of 'dire consequences', as if shooting oneself in the foot wasn't a dire enough consequence.

Jeremiah took to the floor again with a beer bottle swinging from his hand.

'Fellow patriots, let us be clear, the Party is in an acute state of shock and suspended animation. It has been dealt a body blow. We shall now witness the heinous beast that will arise from this injury.'

'Come on, Jeremiah, I don't think—'

'Shuu—'

'It's starting—'

'Look at those killer eyes, this is going to be—'

'Shuu—'

There he was, grimly filling up the screen. Dressed impeccably in one of his Savile Row suits, the hair gleaming black despite pushing eighty, the face smooth and taut, the cleft above his lips filled with black hair, giving him a startling resemblance to a certain European madman, hands poised on the desk, the gold watch glinting in the studio lights.

His eyes lifted from his hands and he looked directly at his subjects.

His mouth opened.

He acknowledged defeat.

But before they had an opportunity to exhale, to punch the air in delight, they took in how the words were coming out from those prim lips. Gabrielle could practically taste the bitterness and bile in that mouth. The rejection was personal. Deeply so. He was not going to take it lying down, that was for sure.

19

'Ah, that is good,' the youth says, rubbing the swell of his belly. He cradles the black pot in the crook of his arm, its long handle sticking out. On its rim and side, white crusts. He dips his hand in the pot, leaves it there for a while. He looks up at them, his mouth smeared with grease, straggly bits of green leaking from his lips, runs his tongue over his lips, takes the hand from the pot, shoves the clump of white into his mouth. He does this over and over until the pot is empty; he tosses it onto the ground where it cries *chink chink* as it hits a stone. The silence is full of legs rushing in, hands, clambering and knocking about, the pot scraping, scraping the ground, crying *chink chink*. For the best part of maize meal is the burnt bit stuck at the bottom which has to be scraped and scraped, worked hard at.

'Now, we have just been listening to a very interesting story. But I am thinking that not everyone can understand it. The language of the whites is very difficult sometimes. Too difficult for honourable *pee zants* and such like. So let us ask the lawyer to tell us the story in our indigenous language. Yes, let us do that.'

She hears his words, the darts of poison embedded there.

'Lawyer, forward!'

She sheds the layers of her cloak, finds herself naked. The sun burning through her.

'Forward! One, two, three!'

She feels her lips part, waits to hear herself speak.

'Forward please!' His screech shocks the air, charges it with violence.

She looks about her but the faces have become as one. Closed to her.

She opens her mouth, but cannot find the words in Shona.

'Speak!'

She wants to pick up the cloak, gather it about her. Whatever cloth it is made of, she needs to hide this self, stave off the cold, the heat.

'Mistress of the Colonizers.'

He savours the words. She watches him run them through his head, pop them into his mouth again.

'Down with Mistress of Colonizers.'

'Down with Mistress of Colonizers!'

The voices pound at the air, pound at the ground, battering her cloak, making holes.

'Down with prostitutes!'

'Prostitutes who fornicate with colonizers, imperialists.'

The schoolgirls' arms hang by their sides, their breasts unprotected. For, now, they are thankful to her.

'We will teach prostitutes how to behave.'

20

'Oh, madam,' Charles called out from behind the bar. 'Do you want another cappuccino?'

Gabrielle shook her head. After two and a half cappuccinos she was feeling much less bleary than when she had walked in. She had left Trinity's flat at about twelve o'clock last night. In the emergency taxi ride back home her fellow commuters were very quiet, unusually so, and one of them, a young man who was wearing an opposition T-shirt, had grimly taken it off and thrown it out of the window of the moving car: who knew what would be unleashed and when. Charles had told her that people in the township were expecting the worst now. He had seen some army trucks, so it was not just the overwrought imagination of her university revolutionary buddies.

She sipped her cappuccino. Looking outside, she could see this part of the city stirring. The emergency taxis were churning out people by the kerb: shop assistants who worked in Bon Marché Supermarket at one end, TM at the other and in all the little knick-knack shops in between which comprised Avondale Shopping Centre. There were also the Nando's and St Elmo's Pizza restaurant staff, the Standard Chartered bank workers. Some cars were getting washed in the parking lot and the newspaper vendors were dashing about, calling out the day's headlines. The *Daily News* was probably already sold out (if the poor vendor hadn't been hijacked by Youth League Members). The flea market stalls were already set up in the lane between the supermarket and the bank; among the old clothes and pirate videos there would soon be a brisk black market in 'money change'. The queue for the morning's fresh bread was well under way outside the bakery. It was time to get moving, but here was Ben bounding up the steps and, even before he crossed the threshold, he was calling out to her.

'Gabrielle, great, are you done?'

He seemed so much at one with the world.

'Hey, good morning, Charles, what's up?'

'Good morning, sir.'

'*Ben*, sir.'

Charles veritably giggled.

'The usual order sir, ah, sorry, sorry, sir, Ben, the croissants?'

Sir Ben was standing there, leaning against the door frame, head and shoulders slightly bent over, giving a thumbs up to Charles and then splaying his fingers to a 'five'. Charles went to the kitchen to pick up the freshly baked croissants.

She watched Ben stride across the room to her table, his legs covering ground in no time. And here he was now, leaning against the bar counter, fingers tapping away on the marble, a smile playing on his lips.

She started putting her papers away, fixing her eyes on the task at hand.

'Rum and I had the whole gardens to ourselves this morning,' he said.

'Ummm, how is she? Has she recovered?'

'You and your mutt owe us, Gabrielle. After the stunt your dog pulled I think she's going to require life-long psychiatric care.'

'I told you he would be a handful.'

'Handful? I get that, Gabrielle, but that extra-heavy weight of yours sitting on top of Rum, doing whatever it is he thought he was doing – I don't think he knew what himself. And, I've never smelled so much gas, what are you feeding him?'

'Just Zimbabwe's finest T-bone steaks, Ben,' she said, laughing. 'With some sadza and relish on the side.'

Charles came bearing the bag of fresh croissants. Ben paid, over-paid, got into a back-and-forth exchange with Charles about 'tipping' and 'The American Way', an exclamation of 'zvakanaka' from Ben, another giggle from Charles.

Walking down the steps behind Ben she took a quick look at her watch: seven forty-five. The sun was on her face and, as Ben opened the passenger door for her, she felt a burst of joy, confidence. It would be a good day.

He started the car, reversed out of the parking lot, the car washers and street vendors giving the startling American vehicle a merry send-off, whistling, rags slapping on the shiny red metal. They were off and away.

'Now, Gabrielle,' he said as they were waiting at the traffic lights, 'vis-à-vis the current political climate—'

'That's good, you sound just like a Zimbabwean Permanent Secretary.'

The light changed to green and he turned into Second Street Extension, almost hit a commuter omnibus that veered into his lane and suddenly stopped, as was their style. Ben calmly swerved with not a single curse word leaving his lips.

He slowed down at the traffic light. Opposite them was the Coca-Cola Bottle Company. *Have a Coke and a Smile,* the sign on the brick wall read in the familiar script of the drink that would bring the whole world together in perfect harmony. She actually started humming the song in her head.

'There was a meeting at Party HQ, late into the night. Gabrielle, they're after anyone they think was behind that No vote: teachers, lawyers . . .'

Despite herself she felt a quickening in her pulse, a tightening in her chest. She shook her head. She was getting infected by everyone's paranoia.

'We were just educating people about the referendum. We weren't telling people to vote No.'

She felt his eyes on her but she couldn't look at him, couldn't let him see how touched she was that he should be worried about her, but really, she was nobody. She was *not* an activist.

'Seriously now, Gabrielle. They're up to something. Comrade Hitler—' He shook his head. 'I still can't get to grips with that name – well, his war vets are in the frame.'

'Ben, you'll get arrested for spreading information likely to cause despondency. We have a newly inaugurated law, for your info.'

'I have that handy thing called Diplomatic Immunity.'

An army truck whizzed past, then another, packed tight with soldiers, obviously on their way to the barracks located near the airport. She had been told that there was an interrogation centre there.

'Comrade Hitler and Company were over at Headquarters last night to get dispatch orders. They've got their green outfits, Made in China. Word is, the youths are going to go by the name of the Green Bombers. It's not looking good, Gabrielle.'

He swung the car over to the little parking bay by The Centre and then he turned to face her.

'Just be careful.'

She was holding onto the door handle, trying to scoop up her satchel with the other hand.

'I'm fine,' she said, suddenly irritated by his insistence that things were going to be bad, that she herself might be in some danger. He was being overly dramatic. But the weight of the satchel was incriminating; she still had some leftover pamphlets from the Constitutional Referendum Action Group in there – she really should get rid of them.

'Our usual date at the Gardens, Gabrielle? Five-thirty?'

'Yes,' she said, liking very much, despite her annoyance, the sound of 'our usual date'.

21

The youth snaps a branch from a tree, stops in front of an old man. The old man's head is bent and the sun beats on the grisly patches of hair.

'Sekuru, begin the lesson.'

The old man lifts his head wearily, looks at the outstretched hand with its stick. She watches him slowly shake his head.

She hears, 'Sekuru, is this your daughter? Are you a coward? Come on, teach her a lesson. The honour begins with the old. That is our culture.'

The old man looks at the stick and slowly shakes his head again.

She hears the small, tired voice, resolute. 'I am too old for this game, my son.'

The stick seems to hang in the air of its own accord as though the hand holding it were merely an illusion, the mind filling in what it cannot otherwise believe. The stick could do many things. It might come crashing down on the grisly head in wrath. It might fling itself on the ground in disgust. It might turn its attentions elsewhere, offer itself to some other hand. The stick pauses in the air, considering its options. The stick looks elsewhere and finds a girl. Danika.

She watches Danika feel the weight of the stick on her shoulder, the burden of its anointing.

'Iwe! Teach this prostitute a lesson.'

She watches Danika stand, her hands at her side, quivering.

'Can you not hear? Take.'

Danika lifts a shaking hand.

The stick lies there on the open palm. Danika's fingers fold around it, claiming it.

'Start, mistress. Start.'

She watches Danika's hand raise the stick. So slowly it goes, up, up as though the hand is weighted by a thousand sorrows.

'Come on, come on. We are waiting.'

The stick surprises her with its gentle thump on the cushion of her hair.

'Are you playing? Shit. Do you also need a good lesson? Come on!'

The stick shocks her with its crack on the side of her shoulder.

'Yes, yes, continue, continue.'

The stick is raised and, watching its journey to her body, Gabrielle turns away from it, from all the damage it will do and looks up, way way up, and she delves into all that blueness, into all that space, so deep she goes, deeper still, gives herself up to it. She laughs, long and hard, the pain and fear dissolving in her breath, into the blue.

22

The youths were in the courtroom. Gabrielle noticed them as she turned from Danika to ask Mr Dube if he was quite comfortable, if perhaps he needed a glass of water. It was the same two youths from the gardens. There was no doubt about it. The khaki shirt, the belligerent air about them. She watched as the one wearing the khaki shirt dug into his pockets and pulled out a pair of sunglasses. He peered at his face in the lenses, snorted and put the glasses on. The lenses were pitch-black, cheap plastic frames, probably bought or stolen from the vendors who sold them at fuel stations or by traffic lights. The other one slid onto the bench and placed his head down, between his knees. His body convulsed and Gabrielle wondered if he was throwing up.

The magistrate stepped into the room. Behind him was the defendant. Gabrielle looked at Constantina, who shrugged her shoulders in response. The defendant was a tall and imposing figure with the shiniest forehead she had ever seen. He was wearing a three-piece suit, with a pink satin bow tie sitting on his wide neck, and he had what seemed to be a cosmetics bag tucked under his arm. He looked as if he was on his way to a wedding, the bag probably stashed with banknotes. He raised his hand in a fist, flashes of a gold cufflink, and there was a whoop in response. The defendant sat down with his lawyers; not in the dock. Gabrielle and Constantina exchanged looks. It was the first time that Gabrielle had seen the defendant in person and she was shocked by his cavalier attitude. Surely, even for a man like him, this was shameful, that he was being dragged into a courtroom to answer such a charge. He seemed to share a joke with one of his team because he let out a guffaw. He was looking directly at her.

Mr Dube muttered something. Danika was steadfastly looking at her lap.

Gabrielle heard a noise behind her, turned to see the khaki-shirted youth hawking and spitting on the floor. She waited for the magistrate to say something but no admonishment came.

'You may commence,' said the magistrate, pointing his gavel at their table.

Constantina stood up. She turned to Danika, gave her a reassuring smile and then turned again to the magistrate.

'Your Worship, we would like to present the court with fresh—'

The magistrate banged his gavel.

'A moment, please.'

'Your Worship—'

'Mrs Maderera, please take a seat, madam.'

'Your Worship, if I could begin—'

'Madam, please.' The gavel went down again. 'I do not want to find you in contempt, sit down. It is my prerogative to exercise due care and diligence here.'

Constantina sat down, her head shaking, fuming at the irregularity in proceedings even before they had actually started. It was clear that the appointed magistrate was grossly incompetent, or something else was going on.

'Good, good, quite excellent.' The magistrate banged the gavel again, as if it were a new toy he had come upon. 'Good. Now, I want to correctly suggest if it is not better, for all parties concerned, but particularly for Mr Dube, in order to duly maintain the honour of his daughter, if this matter should not be handled in a more discreet fashion, that is to say, in the traditional manner, by the elders.'

There was some clapping and whistling from the back. Gabrielle did not have to turn round to know that it was the youths.

Constantina shot up. 'Your Worship—'

The magistrate raised his gavel to silence her.

'Mrs Maderera, your client should be made aware of their options and I am not so sure that this is the case.'

'Your Worship, that is indeed the case. The complainant has chosen this legal process in an informed manner.'

The magistrate turned to Mr Dube.

'Is that true, Mr Dube? You understand exactly what will happen in this courtroom, what questions your child will be required to answer, and under what penalties she will be made to do so?'

Mr Dube shook his head.

'Ah, so you don't understand, after all.' The magistrate looked triumphantly at Constantina.

'No, sir, I understand,' said Mr Dube. 'I am just not understanding why you want to frighten me. We will not drop this case. My daughter has already been damaged. Now I want to get justice.'

The magistrate sighed.

'Be that as it may, I'm adjourning the case for a week to give you proper time to consider my suggestion and the implications of going forward with this business. Court adjourned!'

'Your Worship,' protested Constantina, but the magistrate had already left.

Gabrielle clasped a tissue against her nose and mouth. The stench was more pronounced than usual because of the rains that had caused the septic tanks down in the courtyard to overflow. She was standing on the balcony, trying to absorb what had just happened in the courtroom. She looked down at the courtyard. She saw the magistrate, behind him the youths, the khaki-shirted one slapping him heartily on the back.

Walking out of the yard – already dreading the emergency taxi ride back to the office; the Laser had refused to start this morning – she spotted the red Chevrolet and Ben leaning against it, playing court to the little crowd of street children who had gathered round.

'Well, hello there,' he said, when he saw her, shading his eyes with his hand. His sunglasses were hooked into the 'v' of his shirt. She liked the fact of his having taken them off while he was there with the children. Had he been wearing them she probably would have thought 'poser' or 'arrogant jerk'.

'Hello, there,' mimicked the street children, trying on their American accents.

Ben flashed them a grin and a thumbs up.

He opened the door for her.

'What are you doing here, Ben?'

'An appointment.'

'Here?'

'Nope. Hop in.'

'Hop in,' shouted the street children, hooting and whistling.

She climbed in, watched him pay for the 'parking' services the children provided.

'You're popular,' she said.

'The car is. So, Gabrielle, now that we've run into each other like this, I'm thinking lunch, oh, I don't know, a home-cooked something or other.'

'Thanks for the invitation, Ben but—'

'Come on, you look like you could use a meal.'

'Thanks.'

'Um, that didn't come out right. What I meant to say is, I could use a meal, with you.'

She felt the heat on her face. She looked down at her watch. 'Okay,' she said. 'Thank you.'

'So, what were you doing, this side of town?'

'I had a meeting with some street performers, just across from the magistrates.'

'You do good work, as an Assistant of the Assistant to the Cultural Attaché.'

'One tries.'

'Where did you get "one tries" from? The British Attaché?'

'As a matter of fact, yes, one says that all the time.'

She put her elbow on the ledge of the open window, her chin in her hand, looked out at the passing cars.

'You look sad, Gabrielle.'

'Do I?' she said, turning to him.

'Yes.'

She sighed and felt a kind of relief that she could talk, say what was in her head out aloud to someone.

'The hearing didn't go well today. Actually, it didn't go anywhere, yet again.'

'That happens quite often?'

'Yes, it does. I don't know, this is sacrilegious for me to say, but I keep having these second thoughts about the whole thing. Sorry, you don't want to hear about this stuff.'

'Yes, I do, if it's making you sad I want to hear it.'

It was the most beautiful thing he could have said at that moment.

'It's just that she's so young, our client. It's frustrating how the whole thing is loaded against her. She essentially has to prove her innocence, no matter what the law says. And whatever happens, in this culture she is soiled goods.'

She didn't tell him about the youths, their intimidating presence at the back. The way they had looked at Danika as she walked in the room. Or that she was now certain that the magistrate was under some political pressure.

'That's the same back home, Gabrielle. Most rape trials end up being an assassination of the victim's character.'

'I know, I know. We have some potentially very damaging physical evidence, but it's going to be a huge struggle to get it admitted. She's so young, that's all.'

Constantina was going to South Africa to try and expedite the processing of the evidence with the laboratory. Without it, the case was doomed. What was also worrying away at her was Danika's pregnancy.

She hadn't told Constantina about it, and she didn't know if she was doing the right thing.

They came to a stop behind a broken-down Peugeot, its hood open. The disgruntled passengers of the emergency taxi were arguing with the driver, who was fanning a cloth over the steaming engine. Seeing Ben, some of the commuters broke away, gesticulating for a lift. A youth standing on the pavement was looking at her. He raised his hand and stuck his thumb between his fingers, the sexual sign boys make. She looked away from him. Ben filtered into the next lane.

'Maybe I *am* too soft.'

'You care about your client as a person. That makes you an exceptional lawyer to have.'

She shook her head. 'A good person, maybe, but I don't think that's necessarily compatible with being a good lawyer, exceptional or otherwise.'

She looked out at the long perimeter wall of State House on the opposite side of the road, topped with razor-coiled barbed wire. Somewhere in the depths of those grounds perhaps The Old Man was plotting his next move, rubbing his hands in glee.

Ben turned right just before Dead End Drive, so called because several innocent people had been shot dead over the years while driving by the soldiers manning its exit points. The road was closed between 6 p.m. and 6 a.m, but sometimes the soldiers forgot to put down the barrier, or they were drunk and shot first, asked questions later.

He drove by the security cabin post of his building. The guard leapt up, gave him a snappy salute and a wave to boot. And a Colgate extra-strength white smile. It seemed the American had quite a way with the locals.

His building was a futuristic cascade of glass and limestone.

'Very impressive, Ben, and right opposite our dear leader, I see.'

'Couldn't resist.'

.   .   .

Four, five steps and she was in a huge room, its walls alive, saturated with colour – three large paintings, one on each wall – making her feel, even though she had never been in the sea, that she was in it, carried by tidal waves of colour, which swept her from one painting into another.

'Wow, Ben, are these yours?'

'Uh-huh.'

'I mean, *you* painted them?'

'Uh-huh.'

'What do you mean, "uh-huh", they're, they're . . . wow.'

'Uh-huh.'

'Ben, you really are an International Man of Mystery. You're an artist.'

He was just standing there, leaning against the wall, as cool as could be, as though all this wasn't a big deal.

'And these are what you call abstracts?'

He nodded. 'I'm working on some other—' He stopped himself; he was actually blushing.

'And to think I was teasing you about "ethnic stuff" at the gallery. I feel so foolish. There's not a single piece of Shona sculpture around.'

'Yes, there is. Follow me.'

He took her to a corner where a teak bookshelf lined the wall.

'There she is,' he said.

She looked at the sculpture and then up at Ben. Her hand was on her chest. She bent down and touched the stone, the cold seeping into her palm. She moved her hands over its curves as she had done in the gallery. *Ant Eating a Woman.*

'It's beautiful,' she said.

'Yes, she is.'

She quickly looked about her. 'Oh, there's the record player also.'

Their find from the flea market was against the other wall, on the floor, the crate of albums next to it.

'So,' he said, rubbing his hands, 'I'm thinking, pasta alle vongole.

Clams fresh from Cape Town, the many delights of the diplomatic pouch.'

'Don't tell me, Ben, you're a gastronomic maestro too.'

'Not quite,' he said.

'Can I, can I take a look around, unless you need help in the kitchen?'

'I think I'll manage.'

But she couldn't quite move from the wide space of the lounge, with its French windows, which opened out on to a deep verandah. There was so much light in the room; the paintings seemed to vibrate with it. She spied the easel at the far end of the room, turned to the wall, a sketch pad on a table. What was he working on now? She was too shy to take a look.

She walked across the room and stepped outside. The view was magnificent. An expanse of green and blue. Below her, a swimming pool, four women in bikinis lying on deck chairs. The scene was so incongruous with downtown Harare, just blocks away, that she rubbed her eyes. Yes, the women were still there.

She turned round to find him tucking an apron into his waistband, waiter-style. She felt a surge of something, and she quickly turned away from him, pinned her eyes on the scene outside.

He stepped out onto the verandah. She was aware of every bit of his presence, his slightest movement. From downstairs there was the sound of a dog barking and she was glad for the relief of finding something to say.

'Where are you hiding Rum, Ben?'

'At the embassy compound. She has friends there.'

'Mawara will be very jealous to hear that.'

'Don't tell him. She gets cranky when I leave her here.'

Their hands were on the railing, fingers almost touching.

'Umm, growing up, I wanted to live in a flat. I thought it would be really cool, like in a book. And I also wanted to go to boarding school, which I eventually did.'

'Really?'

'Yes, after my mother died. My father had too much going on.'

Too many girls. Too much hustling and bustling with his enterprises. She would have cramped his style.

'He shipped me off to the nuns.'

'The nuns? How was that?'

'It was okay. Actually, in retrospect, it was the best decision he made, for me.'

He let go of the railing, clapped and rubbed his hands. 'So, wine, beer, Gabrielle? But since it's actually my birthday—'

'No, it isn't!'

'Yes, it is.'

'And, and how many years are you, if you don't mind me asking.'

'Twenty-six.'

'Well, happy birthday to you and, in your honour, yes, I'll have some wine.'

He brought out the two glasses.

'Mazel tov,' she said, clinking hers with his.

He raised his eyebrows.

'Don't get too excited. That's all I know, from the movies, Woody Allen.'

She didn't tell him that she had seen these Woody Allen movies with Giorgio.

Here he was now, bearing the two plates like an accomplished waiter. She had never had pasta with clams before, being squeamish about seafood. She looked at the pasta with the shells scattered on top of it. It looked pretty. How was she supposed to eat it? Were the shells there just for decoration, and should she just put them to one side of the plate and get on with the pasta? She hoped so. She didn't think that she could stomach picking out the fleshy bit inside the open shells.

'Dig in,' he said.

He wound the pasta expertly on his fork, speared the meat from inside a shell and then put it all in his mouth.

Because he was looking at her, she followed his lead. She was quite adept at rolling the pasta on her fork, but she steered clear of the shells.

'It's so savoury,' she said.

'Avoiding the clams, I see,' he said mischievously.

'No, no, I'm getting to them.'

She picked one up, looked suspiciously at the orangey flesh.

Ben laughed. 'Oh Gabrielle, you should see your face. You don't have to eat them.'

'No, no, I'm going to try it.'

She speared the meat with her fork and made a conscious effort not to close her eyes or grimace when she put the meat inside her mouth and swallowed without chewing.

'It's good,' she said. And to prove her point to him she picked up another shell.

He lifted his finger and slipped the strand of spaghetti on her chin into her mouth. The gesture was intimate, unexpected.

While he was busy making coffee she went over to the record player, sat down, cross-legged; she undid the first two buttons of her court blouse. She turned the record player on, picked up the arm and placed the needle on the album. She liked the sound of the record going round and round, the needle searching for its entry point, the expectation of the first catch, beat of music. It was 'I Love You Porgy'. She heard his footsteps. She didn't know what she looked like to him but she was happy to be here, in this room with him, listening to Billie Holiday.

They were sitting on his living room floor, looking at each other, words stilled, nothing but the music and the sound of the needle picking up the voice and the notes.

He lifted his hand and smoothed it over her hair, grazing her ear, neck with his fingertips.

He leaned away, looked at her, put his finger gently on her lips, traced them.

Everything was happening in a delicious slow motion. She knew that she should get up, go back to work, but she was here now.

He leaned in. The music came to a stop, the needle tracking the grooves of the album. The chanting came to them through the open windows.

Looking out, they could see a stream of war vets and Party Youths on Josiah Tongogara Avenue, gathering themselves around State House. Traffic had come to a standstill. Several cars were surrounded. Branches were pelting bonnets, a white man was being dragged out of an old Peugeot.

'Damn.' Ben was talking into a satellite phone. She'd seen them used on TV by CNN journalists in Kuwait during the Gulf War.

A fraction of the mob had broken away and seemed to be heading towards the building.

Ben was already at the front door, turning the key. She felt a fierce trembling pass through her legs as she stood rooted to the spot in the room. Her neck twisted back to the window and with horror she registered the fact that the bulk of the mob had disappeared out of view while at the same time there was an almighty noise storming the building. Ben darted to the French windows, pulled them closed. The shouting was close now; something metallic was being rapped on the stair railings, against doors.

Ben was moving quickly around the room, pulling down the blinds.

'You don't have burglar bars.' She heard a falsetto of panic, accusation, in her voice. 'They can just smash the windows.'

'I don't think they'll stay long. This is obviously orchestrated, as soon as they've made their little point they'll – shuuu.'

He was standing a metre or so from the door, looking, as she was, at the handle jerking up and down, the wood shuttering and rattling with pounding fists and crashing metal.

The floor reverberated with the stomping feet.

Shouts of *We Shall Never Be a Colony Again* were shot through with *Pamberi*s and *Pasi*s.

And then suddenly it was quiet and she heard the shuffling of the mob withdrawing.

She watched him pack the satellite phone away, put it behind the couch.

'All quiet on the Western Front,' he said.

23

Her laugh enrages the youth.

He snatches the stick from Danika, hurls it at the laughing prostitute.

'Heh, you are laughing, bitch.'

Her laugh bores into him; it sneers at him, at his stick, at his manhood, at his revolution. Again and again he hits her. She is laughing, laughing all the time as though he is giving her a good, good time. All around him he hears voices, whispers. The stick falls from his hand, clatters to the ground, lies forlorn there. The laughing is no more, also the voices, the whispers.

She lies still and quiet on the ground.

The first thing she is aware of is the dark. Has night fallen, she asks herself? How long, then, has she been elsewhere? Which night is this? She knows somehow, senses it, that she is no longer outside. The air seems more closed in and there's a smell, waiting in the wings to attack her bloodied nostrils. She purses her lips. Tastes blood. Who has carried her body here?

'I did not want to hit you. I was afraid. I am sorry, Miss Langa.'

The voice seems to wash over her. She moves her head with its pain so that her eyes look up. But there is only darkness.

'Miss Langa, Miss Langa, I am here.'

Here lies the voice that knows her name. Here it is. Sitting at her side.

'Miss Langa, are you . . .? I I am very sorry, I . . .'

The feel of her tears, the sting of the salt on her cut cheek, the balm of the water on the blood. She tries to remember the girl's face, Danika. To let the voice guide her memory. She sees a face with wide slopes, round, round eyes, a flick of a scar on an eyebrow. Is this the girl's face?

'They have gone to the farmhouse, Miss Langa. They have locked the door. I am very sorry.'

She knows that the girl, Danika, has been crying. While she has been elsewhere the girl has crept up to her body, watched over it in tears. She wants to tell the girl that it is all right, she understands, but her voice remains trapped in her breath which in turn struggles to leave her body. Will she be able to get up? She longs for a shard of glass, a mirror. She has a need to see her face, to register the attacks it has absorbed, to look at herself, to see who she is, what she has become.

'They have come to the school, Miss Langa.'

The girl's voice takes her out of herself.

'They have taken me from the classroom. They have beaten the teacher when he tried to protest. They have said I am causing problems for a big man and they will teach me how to repent. They are saying that if I do not learn and stop my nonsense my father will be the late. Miss Langa, we must be strong. You are my lawyer.'

'Danika, I'm so—' A fit of coughing stops her, pummelling her, her breath ricocheting out of her body, digging into the hurt at her side.

'I, I have some water, Miss Langa.'

Water.

'Here, drink, Miss Langa.'

She feels the steel cup pressed against her lips. She struggles to part them, to work through the pain. The water slips through her lips into her mouth where it lies there, cool and extravagant, until she is brave enough to swallow.

'They will come back, Miss Langa. They are drinking and drinking.'

She hears what the girl is saying, what the girl means.

24

'Hello, hello . . .'
     The phone was ringing when Gabrielle dashed inside, out of the rain that had come in a flash. Mawara, not one for getting wet, had taken shelter in his kennel, on the verandah of the main house. It has been a week since Cyclone Eline finally hit Mozambique. The rain started there, and went on for so long it seemed as if God was intent on flooding the entire earth once again. It was biblical – the coming of the New Millennium – banks of rivers breaking, the roads of Maputo turned into surging rivers and babies born in trees. The cyclone's reach had extended to the eastern and southern parts of Zimbabwe, Mashonaland largely spared the catastrophic downpours. Strong winds had swept away crops, bridges and homesteads, leaving over a million displaced, homeless.

'Gabrielle . . .'

His voice, so out of the blue.

'Oh, Giorgio, wait a moment, I'm drenched.'

She put the receiver down and hurried to the bathroom where she took a towel and rubbed her hair, her face. She shed her clothes and wrapped herself in a dressing gown. She went back into the lounge, desperate for a cup of hot tea. She picked up the receiver.

'Sorry about that, it just started—'

'Gabrielle, I have to be quick. I'm coming to Zimbabwe.'

For a moment she thought she hadn't heard him right.

'Here?' she said like a fool, as if Zimbabwe had somehow changed its geographic location.

'Yes, I've been temporarily seconded by head office to help in the emergency relief efforts.'

Of course, given his knowledge of the country, the region, its logistics, that made perfect sense.

'When, when are you arriving?'

'Tomorrow evening. I'm staying at the Monomotapa. They're calling my flight, I have to go. I'll see you tomorrow.'

She opened her mouth to get a word in but all she heard was the static on the other side.

He was going to be here tomorrow. Giorgio. He spoke as though they were still an item. Tomorrow, face to face, she would have to do the deed, make him understand it was well and truly over.

She made herself that tea, switched on the TV, put it on mute when she heard the ZBC news drums.

It has been two weeks since that Address to the Nation, and the nation seems to be going on as before, nothing more, nothing less. Perhaps, despite the feeling of foreboding his speech had cast, Zimbabwe was showing the rest of Africa what true democracy was. Perhaps, after the initial shock, The Old Man was being the statesman, and he had called his youths to heel.

The exhaustion hit her as she sat there watching the pictures of youths and war veterans gathered outside the *shake-shake* building of the Party's headquarters.

It has been days of long nights, working on Danika's case, trying to get a court order that would force the defendant to give a sample for DNA testing. Without it, the results from the underwear would be useless. They had secured it late this afternoon. Constantina took her out to celebrate, milkshakes and hamburgers at Wimpy. That man, the defendant, was surely in a state of panic now. He had to produce a sample of blood or a swab from his cheek or a piece of his well-coiffed hair. Failure to do so would render him in defiance of a court order, and the penalty for that was jail. The tide was turning.

Danika would get justice. The next court date had been set for the following week, Wednesday.

The phone rang. She leapt up, certain it was Giorgio again.

'Hello, Gio—'

'Gabrielle—'

'Ben! Hi!'

'Hey, are you free tomorrow?'

'Tomorrow I . . .'

'Lunchtime, I was thinking of a picnic.'

'Ben, tomorrow's Friday, it's a workda—'

'Come on, I have it on good authority it's going to be the brightest, sunniest day in the calendar and I've a ton of diplomatic pouch edibles in my hamper. You eat during your lunch break, don't you?'

She looked up at the TV screen. Youths and war veterans were sitting on some tractors in a farm pretending to be driving them, gleefully hamming it up for the cameras.

'How about next wee—'

'You'll love this place when you see it, Gabrielle.'

'Okay,' she said, 'lunchtime, one o'clock. But if anything turns up at the office, I'll have to cancel.'

'I got you.'

25

'Down, down with imperialist sympathizers.'
'Shut up!'
'Keep quiet!'
'Down with tea boys.'
'You, shut up!'
'He is right. We must speak.'
'Down with prostitutes.'

All about her bodies become men, women, girls, boys. The light, sudden and warm, shocks the bodies, embarrasses them. They have been lying like sheep entangled together and now, awakened, each gathers their limbs, claims them as separate, as their own. She does not move. The girl looks at her, a face suspended in the light. Through swollen eyes she sees: the wide slopes, the round eyes, the flick of a scar on an eyebrow.

'Can you stand, Miss Langa?'
'Leave that witch, you.'
'Down with prostitutes.'
'Shut up!'
'Who are you telling . . .?'
'Shuu . . .'
'Shuu . . .'
'They are coming.'

26

'So, Ben, where is this hamper of yours, or was that just big talk?' she asks.

'Ouch, that hurts, Gabrielle. It's at the back.'

'So, that's the "utility" part of your vehicle. And where exactly are you are taking me?'

'Top-secret, classified information.'

'Shouldn't I be blindfolded, bundled into the back?'

'Damn, you're morbid, Gabrielle.'

They drive past the plush houses and gardens of Borrowdale, Highlands. At the traffic lights, on a patch of land opposite the shopping centre, she looks out at a flourishing crop of choumoellier. A woman, a baby tied on her back, is plucking off some leaves and putting them in a zinc dish, probably to sell by the bus stand later.

'There's a lot of kale out here.'

'Kale?'

'Yes, they'd make a killing in Whole Foods.'

'Oh, you mean choumoellier.'

'Cho—?'

'Choumoellier,' she laughs. 'I think it's Afrikaans-English. It's my least favourite vegetable. It's tough and, boy, does it stink up the place when it's boiling.'

'Well, it's a thing back home.'

'A thing?'

'Yes, among certain folk. Vitamin-rich. It's a specialty vegetable.'

So, it turns out that the humble choumoellier, most common and scorned of all local vegetables, is some kind of culinary wonder overseas.

She looks slyly at him. 'Umm, are you one of these "folk", Ben?'

He chuckles. 'Yep, I'm partial to a bit of kale!'

'You know what my mother would have done, with all this kale? She would have planted it smack in the middle of a flower garden. When we moved into Khumalo, which was full of Rhodies back then, she caused quite a ruckus in the beginning with her gardening. They were scared she was bringing standards down.'

Her family had moved into the house in Khumalo when she was ten. Her mother did away with the fussy flower beds and created an open space that fused what she called 'African beauty' with the formal aesthetics of an English garden: rockeries and cacti alongside sweet peas, roses, lawn and hedges, and, controversially, vegetables and maize crops. The garden was so enchanting that the white neighbours could not resist it, dropping by unannounced to 'just take a look' and sipping Five Roses tea with her mother's home-made biscuits. Sometimes there would be a surprise gathering outside: the white ladies crossing paths and mingling with her mother's prayer circle or sewing group friends. She helped her mother serve them tea, with whichever girl had come from the rural areas. Her mother's garden was featured in *Look and Listen* and, in *Mahogany*, her mother was photographed sitting on one of those 1970s-style wicker peacock chairs, wearing a maxi patchwork skirt and a broad-brimmed straw hat, looking very much like a glamorous model.

'Your mother was on to something. I think they do that kind of thing in California.'

'She was gifted in so many things. My father used to stock her dresses, the ones she designed and sewed, and they would sell out in no time.'

She could never understand how her father had been able to woo her mother; and then, when she was eighteen or so she had stumbled on her birth certificate. Doing the maths, she saw that her mother was already pregnant before she was married. The banality of it had winded her.

'Once, this crow flew into the garden and he got entangled in the phone cables, and he just fell down on the lawn, wing broken. The gardener was all for finishing it off with a hoe, you know, crows are thought to be harbingers of bad luck, deep witchcraft, or the actual carriers of bad spirits, but my mother wouldn't let him. She took the bird, she was very gentle with it, she put it in a cardboard box and drove to the vet. I remember sitting in the car with this bird struggling in the box, terrified, and my mother saying that the bird was someone's mother too and deserved a chance at life.'

'She sounds like an incredible person.'

'Yes, she was. The vet had never nursed a crow before. I think people just kill them. But he bandaged the wing and we took it back home. She fed it, nursed it. The gardener thought she was mad.'

Her father was terrified of the bird, accusing her mother of wanting to bring harm to his household and threatening to kill it himself, but he never did.

'In a couple of weeks it was fine. I remember standing in the garden with her, my hand in hers, watching that bird wriggle out of the box and struggle to lift itself up . . . and then it did, it flapped its wings and flew.'

When her mother died two years later, her father had circled all the way back to that crow, convinced that his wife had fallen prey to witchcraft. He had everything that belonged to her burnt – her clothes, her beauty products, her sewing, pictures of her; the garden was dug up and everything thrown out. Thinking now, she wondered if that's why her father sent her away. She had stumbled upon that crow on the lawn, and she was the one who came running to her mother to show her, who brought it into their lives.

'I miss her.'

She cannot believe she has said that. And having said that, she sees it is true. She has said it to him, given him this truth about herself.

They drive on and on, all the way until Borrowdale Road becomes Domboshawa Road, and then they are no longer on the tarmac but on a dirt track, bush and thorn trees for as far as the eye can see.

'We're almost there,' he says.

They rattle on for a bit longer and then he comes to a stop under a thorn tree. Outside, he reaches into the 'pickup' and lifts out a basket.

'Ah, the famous hamper,' she says.

They walk up a gentle slope. She has left her jacket and bag in the car. It is very hot and whatever rain has fallen here has long been absorbed into the ground.

'This is it.'

He takes her hand and she climbs up onto a rock. Standing there, she gasps. A wide clearing, a meadow almost, but it's what looms over it that awes her. Great slabs of rock coming right out from the ground in mighty sweeps. It's as if she might have landed on the moon, a new land, hard to believe that they are just outside the city limits. Then she hears the sound of water trickling. She sees it now, caught in the sun's rays, running down the steep gradient of the stone, as if it were weeping.

'It's breathtaking, Ben. I, I can't believe I've never been here,' she says.

'Remember those sculptors I told you about?'

She nods.

'Well, on the way back, I have to stop by their village to pick up a piece for the embassy.'

'Oh,' she says, 'thank you, Ben, for bringing me here.'

She leans against a boulder, looks at the expanse of bush and rock, takes in the quiet, and suddenly he has both his hands on either side of her, and he is looking down at her as if she is the only thing in all this landscape. He leans in, kisses her.

'You're shaking,' he says.

'I'm, I'm nervous . . .'

He kisses her again, his fingers, his hand moving on her face, on her neck, underneath her blouse, on her bare shoulder, the shock and feel of him.

'Ben, I . . .'

He stops, waits for her to say what is in her head, but she just breathes into the silence. His hand moves on her bra, under the straps.

Her mouth gives in to him, her lips opening and taking his lips, his tongue in. She has never been kissed, touched like this. She has never felt this much desire of her own. And suddenly there is no shyness to her wanting of him. She moves her body against his, her hands on him, impatient for the touch and feel of his bare skin, under his shirt, his skin warm and taut, smooth. His hand is under her skirt, moving up along her thigh, slowly, and then on her underwear and she lets out a sound, he stops, his hand still on her, his fingers on the lace. He looks at her, kisses her. She presses herself tight against him, his fingers slipping through the lace, touching her.

The clouds shift and suddenly they are in the sun's full glare. He takes her hand and, after a few steps, they come to a stop at two enormous slates of rocks angled against each other, a cave.

All is quiet and still save for them, hand in hand.

27

The bottle smashes on the wall. The comrades stagger in, falling and shouting, calling everybody's mother a so-and-so. She smells the beer, the fine wine, the hard liquor and tries to imagine the farmhouse with its bounty, the wreck of it. She tries to imagine the comrades in the farmhouse drinking, drinking, drinking. Is this what The Old Man means by *The Third Revolution*?

'Try and stand, please, Miss Langa,' Danika says. 'It will be better that way.'

There is so much noise in the silence, it roars through Gabrielle's ears, through her body.

On her head the casual press of a heel. This is the heel that might slam her into the floor of the barn. This is where her head might be split open, brain sliding along animal waste, entrails of thought smudged on the floor. A laugh above her and then the heel is gone.

The comrades are here.

28

Gabrielle wakes up with a start, her head on his chest, his fingertips grazing her forehead.

Her back hurts and she has cramps in her left leg, which has been bent under his.

She is suddenly conscious of the two of them alone and is, all at once, gripped by panic. What has she done? What is she doing? She picks up her blouse, turns away from him, puts it on, fumbling with the buttons. She feels his fingers on her neck.

'Gabrielle,' he says.

She turns to face him. She raises her hand, puts her hand on his chest, traces her finger on the thin line of hair there. There is the sound of their breathing. And then something else.

'Do you hear that?' he says, scrambling to his feet.

She is seized with the one thing, the horror of it: *something bad is happening* as the voices grow louder, closer and then a silence that tells her they are there, right there, upon them.

'Stay,' he says, not looking back at her, 'I'll see what—'

And then a singular, triumphant shout.

'Vakomana, she is here.'

PART TWO

The Wonders
of the Revolution

29

She awakens to the sight of a gun.

A rifle, the wood burnished, an object that has been loved, cared for, and, in her head, she sees the farmhouse with its ransacked rooms, beds upturned, knocked over, and there, in a hidden place, the bounty of wood and steel.

There have been branches, stones, open hands, fists, words, but now, here in his hands, is the real thing.

He is young and fierce and, on his lips, in his eyes, a burgeoning, vindictive pride: after all the playing around the serious business has begun and he, with the gun in his hands, is chief.

He holds the gun now this way, now that, as if he is testing it out, unable to decide which position it looks good in. On his yellow T-shirt, frayed at the edges, a mouse with big ears and a bow.

He puts the gun on his shoulder, puts his chin against it, brings it down, holds it in his two hands as though he were out in the jungle, stalking some wild animal. Almost there. He moves the gun in an arc, over their heads to the door.

The gun has begun to talk.

At first, the rain falling in a soft drizzle, filtering through the sunny and cloudless sky, feels like a magician's trick, an implausible thing. Gabrielle stands, rocking on the balls of her feet, their nakedness on the earth startling her. What has happened to her shoes? When did she lose them? Have they been taken from her, stolen? When? By whom?

She tries to recall the facts of her shoes, the particular shoes she must have been wearing (When? A day, two, three days ago?). She tries to evoke the memory of them, but this, too, is lost.

She is there, here in this soft drizzle, the sun warm and safe on her face. But the magician packs his bags and leaves. The day spends itself out, the sun never wavering, the sky never blotted by a single cloud. When it is dark, the gun talks again, prodding them back into the barn.

She opens her mouth, inhales the fetid air, coughs, her ribs hurting; Danika there, hovering at her side.

The gun changes hands.

These hands now, clasped tight around the wood and steel as though afraid that the gun might take off, find itself a better suitor. She prays that the gun does this, frees itself, for the hands squeezing it, locked to the metal in nerves, worries the facts of death into her.

'You, name,' she hears.

The gun talks.

The gun points at a man. The man looks at the gun. She watches the man bring up his hand and turn the gun from him as though he means to talk to the boy, the youth, the comrade, without hindrance, but the man says nothing. The boy, the youth, the comrade, looks at the gun, at its new place, at its sudden powerlessness. He squeezes the trigger and the sound shakes the air. On the ground, the discarded metal.

The gun points at a man, at his head, at his chest, at his feet, first one, then the other, and then slowly, slowly up again to the man's private parts, lingers there, draws a circle around them, bulls-eye, and then up until it finds the space between the eyes. The man's eyes wide open, the pupils jumping out.

'My name is Solomon.'

'Solomon, Solomon, Solomon,' the boy, youth, comrade, says, the gun waving through the air. 'Up, two, three, four, up, two, three, four.'

The gun pokes Solomon's cheeks.

'Jump. Jump. Jump.'

Solomon jumps.

The gun prods Solomon's back. Jab, jab, jab. Solomon jumps higher and higher.

'You are here for Enlightenment. Enlightenment is Education.'

The gun has changed hands again.

She tries to look at him. To see him. Who he might be. She tries to take away the gun from him. To diminish the glare in his eyes. To soften his voice. To loosen his limbs. She tries to carry him away from here. To put him in a house. She tries to see him among his own people, people he might love, care about. His mother. His father. Brothers. Sisters. She is, she knows, attempting the impossible, the ridiculous. Trying to strip away at the danger, the menace, to give him a humanity.

She is here. He is here. That is the beginning and end of it.

'Enlightenment is not cheap. In fact, it is expensive. Very EXPENSIVE. You must pay. You must pay.'

He does not say what the currency is but she looks at her body and knows. She watches each comrade survey the goods, make his pick, enjoy the fruits of his labours.

The comrades come in and look about with wild, frantic eyes as if they don't know where they are, what they are doing here, as if they are the captives. They laugh and shriek and fall suddenly quiet. They shout words into the air and grab about with their fingers as if they mean to take their words back, as if they are accusing the air of theft. They rush about and become stranded in the midst of their movement. They are still, their heels digging into the floor of the barn. They are possessed. The spirits driving them now here, now there, demanding now this, now that. She thinks of murderers, so persecuted by the spirits of their victims that they are led to throw themselves off cliffs, to plummet into nothing. Gabrielle wishes this for them.

.   .   .

She turns and sees one of the comrades clutching his stomach, his head bent into his chest. It is probably the drinking but Gabrielle thinks, The spirits are working. The comrade looks up.

He spits on the floor. 'Bitch.'

The comrades seem to have lost their purpose, given up on the slogans, tired of their own fervour and disbelief. Have they forgotten why they are here? They look suddenly like lost boys. The drink wearing off, whatever else that they have been on slipping from them, leaving them marooned. She knows that this too is dangerous. The lost boys will soon become bored boys and then restless, then angry, then vengeful. It is a tide, she knows, that is inevitable, that will sweep through the room, wrecking anything in its path.

She has counted them. Eleven altogether. And how many are we? she asks herself. Fifty. Fifty to eleven. The numbers seem so simple. There is the matter of the gun but that too seems to be a simple matter. One gun, fifty of them, drunk comrades. Surely, they could . . . do something.

Three schoolboys whispering in a corner. Have they absorbed her thoughts, the simplicity of the maths? She should go to them and say something like, 'Look, count me in. I'll be the decoy.' These are film words. The boys would look at her. Dismiss her. If there is any glory, they would want it for themselves.

The boys' hands are shoved into the pockets of their shorts. She sees them there, tight fists of tension. How old can they be? Fifteen? Sixteen? Seventeen? She hears their rising, angry voices full of heat and fear, wants to warn them *quietly, quietly*. She waits tensely for the rush of their gangly limbs, their shouts, but nothing happens. The words dissipate, the schoolboys slink desultorily into their own bodies.

As though suspecting the failed uprising, the comrades regroup.

'You are dogs. Imperialist dogs. Bark! Bark!'

The barn is filled with dogs barking, then yelping, then whimpering.

· · ·

She sees it in the shadow of her fluttering eyelids: the metal stroking the young face, the coldness of it, the terror of it. She hears the laugh breaking over them, spewing dagga, want and drink. Her eyes open. He throws his gun gaily to another, snatches Danika's hand. She lies there, words in her mouth, Danika's hand sliding from her, Danika's eyes, no longer cast down but on her, looking at her, through her. She watches him drag her out, away, the others close behind.

The comrades so drunk and high Danika has left them behind, staggered from them to here, the barn.

Her clothes torn. Her lips swollen, bleeding. Her body huddled, convulsing against the wall.

The figures in the barn recoil from her.

Gabrielle prises her from the wall's embrace, lays Danika's head on her lap, blows gently over her bruised body, caressing her with her breath, seeping it into her skin with her fingers, bathing her with it, washing her clean as though her breath might cleanse the spittle, the sour breath, the hard invading touch.

The comrade punches a piece of paper: the burly pock-marked opposition leader in the hands of the comrade.

'What is this?' the comrade says. 'Is this a man?'

'Is this a man?'

'Is this a dog?'

'Is this a dog?'

'Iwe, is this a dog?'

'Yes. Yes. Yes.'

'Stupid. Stupid.'

'Do you see a dog here?'

'Do you see a man?'

'Iwe, what is this?'

'A ma— a do—'

'Stupid. Stupid.'

'This is a bottom wiper.'

'*You*, show us what this is.'

'Iwe!'

'Trousers, off, off. Off!'

'Wipe. Wipe!'

'Bottom wiper.'

She watches the old man wipe his shrivelled bottom with the face of the leader of the opposition.

The silence around Danika hardens, encasing her, brittle. She looks down and watches Danika, in the depths of her silence, wrap her arms around her body, feels the shiver course through her and wonders if it is the cold or fear or something else.

Shame.

The word strong and heavy in her mouth, bitter too, the taste of it growing and pressing against her tongue so much that she feels she will throw up.

Shame.

The old man gets up and wipes his mouth with the back of his hand.

The comrade laughs.

What does it matter? Any of it.

The comrade takes his gun and dances in the barn, clicking his heels against the butt of the gun, dancing so deep and hard that sweat pours from his face and the music is there around them, pouring out from the heels of the dancing man, storming out of the barrel of his steel instrument, and the music is the sound of The Third Revolution; arise, arise, the comrade twirls to the revolutionary beat and they see, hear, feel in the comrade's rise and fall, to and fro, the farmhouses that must be acquired, the fields that must be set alight, the dogs that must be stamped and stamped upon, the farmer that must be beaten, the worker that must be killed, the women that must be taken and they see, hear, feel the revolution upon them, swoop on them like the mighty eagle, snatch them from the ground, carry them high, high into the air and then let them drop, smashing their useless, flailing limbs onto the rocks of the ancestors.

A voice in her ear, cold lips cracked on her skin.
'Your turn is coming.'

Is she sleeping? Is she awake? All around her in the dark there is the smell of fresh bread, making her giddy. Is she asleep? Is she awake? Her hands are sticky with dough. Her mother's hands are on hers, helping her knead the dough. Is she asleep? Is she awake? The press of her mother's lips on her head—
'Iwe, what are you smiling at?'
The good things vanish.

Danika is ill. There are fits of shaking that assault her weakened limbs, streams of words that burst out sporadically from the parched lips, snatched bits of frantic thought. There are streams of saliva coursing along their chosen path, etching their way down the sides of her mouth. Gabrielle takes her finger and presses on the lines of the young face, traces the arch of the eyebrows, puts her thumbs on the shut lids and, as though working on a miracle, massages the groove there.
She gets up, gently placing Danika's head on the floor. She has to speak. She will draw upon her other life: negotiate.
She walks to the comrade but before she can open her mouth, have her say, he has words of his own.
'Coloured,' he says, the cheap sunglasses fixed on his face.
'Coloured,' he says the word again as though fingering it with his hands, wearing it smooth with his need.
She tries to remember who she is, to hold herself in her mind's eye.
'All the comrades want you. A coloured girl is something else. You have cost me my brand new tennis shoes. Aay, you have cost me too much, too much.'
Cost-Benefit Analysis, she says in her head. She has done this exercise. Weighed one against the other. Hundreds of times.

He waits.

And The Old Man waits in his official residence. Waiting to hear from his minions if they have brought The Third Revolution to the people. Have his people tasted it? Have they had it drummed into their thick skulls, snapped into their limbs? Are his people now duly grateful, singing his praises for their enlightenment?

Stories abound of what can be done, what has been done. Blood drunk from butchered men. She knows that she too will become such a tale. Nothing more. She is but a tiny sweep of a recurring nightmare.

She looks up at the waiting man, the gun in his hand.

It is a slow journey. Her legs, treacherous and true, moving, taking her to a place known and unknown.

An unknown girl walks along this journey for it cannot be Gabrielle, truly her.

There is time to see, to look and behold. A field burnt out, a tractor overturned, the stumps of trees, freshly cut, branches splayed on the dirt, a lone cow shuffling, carcasses on the burnt field, crows inelegantly balanced on them, picking, a black pot, a pan, a tin bucket collapsed on the ground, a red shoe, a hut with a blackened roof, the mangled, charred steel of a vehicle, the entrails of a small animal, a dog cowering at the door of the vehicle, shards of glass on the ground, holes in the window, splinters of wood, a door hanging by its hinges, marks on the floor, on the walls.

'Quick, quick,' he says. 'Time is short.'

She thinks of this.

Of the shortness of his time.

He grabs her arm; pain shoots up it, sears itself into her shoulder, pulsating there. She hears the raspiness of her breath. Sweat gathering on her lips, bristling on her forehead. Her body shaking. Her mind in flight.

She staggers through the doorway into the farmhouse and here, too, the story is in the objects, what has been left behind, dealt with.

There is anger, resentment and spite. It is all there in the TV with its crashed face; the sofas ripped apart, their filling spilling out; the cabinet spread-eagled on the floor; papers strewn everywhere; frames smashed on the floor, glass cutting into family members stranded here in the farmhouse; urine and faeces, the smell of them everywhere.

He stands at the foot of the stairs.

From the banister he picks up a hat.

The farmer's worn suede hat, tattered at its edges. He looks at her and smiles. He puts the hat on his head, pats it down.

'Come,' he says, as if he has watched such a situation unfold before, seen it unfurl on a movie screen, the cowboy at the bottom of the stairs beckoning his gal to the room upstairs, to their future.

'Come,' he says, the gun pointed at her head.

She stands in the ruined room, slowly too becoming part of its contents.

'Come.'

Her feet heavy and slow, her hands sliding on the banister, her body swaying, crumpling.

He knows where he is going; one room and the next. Beds, unmade, an open suitcase on the floor, a comb.

He pushes the door open, steps to one side, prods her in.

It is an improbable sight, grotesque in its beauty now.

In the middle of this room, a bed.

There is: the dark majestic wood, knotted and gnarled, pitted and splintered in parts, sleepers of a dream railway line that would traverse the continent. Teak. A canopy of white over the four poster. Piles and piles of cushions on the bedspread.

The rugged farmer sitting at the edge of the bed, taking off his mud-splattered vellies, wriggling his freed toes; his calloused hands snagging on the white linen; his mind distracted by the work that has to be done – the fence that needs mending, the worker that needs a talking-to, the bull that needs watching, the war vets who must be bargained with. He looks up at his wife who stands there waiting in her white smock.

His hand tight on her neck, he drops the gun on the bed.

'Heh,' he says. 'The others are being afraid. They are thinking that the room is bewitched.'

He picks up the copper urn from the mantelpiece, shakes it in his hand. Ash escapes and falls gently on the ground.

'Heh, they are afraid of this. A murungu in a pot.'

He might toss the urn in the air, let it fall.

But he puts it back on the mantelpiece and turns to face her.

'We will do like in the bioscopes.'

He holds her with one hand while he undoes the zip of his green trousers.

He pulls her closer still, his hand unrelenting on her wrist, his eyes glazed over, his breath ragged.

She is doubled over, looking down at him.

He puts his hand in the black, worn underpants, pulls them down, lets out a sound.

He stumbles on the bed, twisting her arm, his nails digging into her flesh.

'You will put it in your mouth. I will experience.'

There is the urn. She can reach out, take it and hit him. She can run. There is the urn, take it, run.

'Kneel,' he says. 'I will experience today.'

She is there, smelling him.

It is you and him. You can act. You can move. You can wrench yourself free. You can take the urn, hit him. You can run. You will run down the stairs, out, away. He will be behind you. You will run, run.

'Coloured, kneel.'

He lets go of her wrist, clutches at her hair, twists and turns her head.

You will run, run. He will be behind you. Wanting, wanting, wanting. He will take.

She kneels there, between his legs, and he locks her there, pushing her head on him.

'Open your mouth, take.'

.   .   .

He lies there. His body, there.

Run, a far-off voice comes to her. *Run.*

Run into the wilderness, run into the emptiness. *Run.*

Her legs are quivering.

She shifts her body, her arms, her head, piece at a time.

Run, the far-off voice, more urgent now. *Run.*

You are weak.

Run.

The others. They will find you. Take and take.

Her legs, quivering still, hold her.

Run.

'Coloured—'

Run!

'It is not finished.'

Run! Run!

'Now, I must take like a man.'

There is the silence, broken only by his heavy snoring. He lies there on the bed, the hat jauntily perched on one of the bedposts, as though this were his appointed guard. She looks distractedly about the room, her eyes darting from one object to the next . . . the man, his hat, the gun on the bed.

She picks up the gun, stumbles, surprised by its weight and heft. She holds it outstretched from her, knows enough from TV, the movies, what to squeeze if she chooses, what will release the bullet.

She does not know how long she stands, long enough for her body to become familiar with the weight of the gun, so familiar that it is no longer a foreign object but part of her, who she is, who she has become.

She listens to his snores. She smells him on her, in her. She steps closer to the bed.

This is it, she thinks. So be it.

Squeeze and release.

.   .   .

She gathers the clothes about her.

She dresses the body, cloth on flesh.

She sees the urn on the mantelpiece. She takes it in her hands, opens it, dips her fingers there and takes out a fistful of ash. Holding the measure of a man in her hands, she opens her fingers and lets him fall on the bed. Room after room she goes, sprinkling ash on every bed, every bit of furniture she can. There is no thought, no reasoning, just the compulsion to do this thing.

Outside, she looks about her. The scorched field, the dead animals, the burnt-out truck, and beyond these the barn to one side and to the other the open gravel road with its lure of escape, possible freedom. She looks towards the barn and then to the road and it is the thought of Danika huddled against a wall that makes her turn from the road to the barn.

In the burnt-out field stands a solitary tree, its bark charred.

She leans against the ruined tree, heaves and heaves onto the stricken earth.

She steps into the barn.

In the dim light she looks and sees signs of a hurried leave.

There is a single shoe, bits of clothing trailing the floor and, at her feet, a coin which, after a moment's thought, she picks up.

She drags her body around the barn, touching the walls, hearing her lone steps, looking for something Danika might have left behind, a clue.

But there is nothing to be found.

She steps out of the barn, looking, straining for sound, but there is only the faint cry of a bird in the still air.

She stands on the gravel road.

She looks up at the sky. It is so blue. So effortlessly blue.

A bird swoops down from the blue, twirling and whirling in flight, leading the way.

She follows.

.   .   .

Her limbs heavy, her feet treading the ground, hesitantly at first, reluctantly, as though the ground beneath her is not to be trusted, as though fault lines run indiscriminately and, with one step, the ground will open. Her eyes grow sore and so she looks up to the vast sky which causes an ache; its lightness, a torment. She walks through smoke, sometimes just wisps of it, at others great heaves of it so that she has to put her hand over her mouth. She stops at times, paralysed by fear. This is a war zone. She takes in the burnt land, the grass crackling, the crops up in smoke. She walks through the smoke and, for an instant, she is one of the straggling dispossessed, the farm workers who sit on the smouldering earth in the shadow of their burnt huts, waiting. She walks past them, picks her way through what they have managed to salvage, afraid of their loss, of their need, their eyes looking past her, beyond her.

She tries to lift herself from the wasteland, defy it and think resolutely of good times. There he is. He is driving. She is with him. There is his face, turning to her—

But then her eyes fall again on the wasteland.

This is it. The Third Revolution. It is everything she sees, smells, brushes against. It is everything that has touched her. This is what is being done in the name of the Revolution.

She walks; her mind exhausted, emptied, a sheen of white space, until she stumbles out of the wasteland, her feet buckling, her body swaying and rocking then splayed on the burnished land, its heat locked in her limbs, mumbling and moaning, the words entangling in the breath of her burning mouth, in the mesh and web of her spit.

In the film of light and dust, shimmering in the uncertain landscape, something moving, moving towards her, flashes of metal caught in the light, getting closer, closer still, until it stops right at her feet and there he is, getting out, rushing, rushing towards her.

30

'Gabrielle, Gabrielle . . . cosa ti hanno fatto . . . cosa ti hanno fatto?'

She hears him.

What have they done to you? What have they done to you?

He lifts her up from the ground, carries her into the car, all the while whispering her name – *Gabrielle, Gabrielle, Gabrielle*.

She hears him.

The wheels turn and turn – gravel and dirt, asphalt, rough, smooth – round and round they go, moving and moving through space and light and time.

The sky is blue. The sun is shining. The road is a straight, straight arrow.

'Gabrielle, we are almost there.'

She hears him.

'Gabrielle, I am taking you to the clinic.'

She hears him.

'Do you want some water? I have some in the glove—'

She hears him, hears him.

'Gabrielle . . .'

He opens the door, waits.

'Gabrielle, we've arrived. We are at the clinic.'

He moves, puts his arms on her seat, ready to scoop her up again.

'No,' she says. 'No.'

'You need the doctor, Gabrielle.'

She hears him.

'Gabrielle.'

She shifts, moves, pain coursing through her body. She does not want to be here, to be walking in this parking lot, shuffling between cars, through the swishing glass doors opening for her body, past the heads turning and the noses sniffing and the hands flying over mouths, the gasps, whispers, at the state of her. She does not want to be standing at this desk, the girl behind it wrinkling her nose, not trying to hide the disgust she feels at the sight and stink of her.

'Yes, how can I help you?'

The girl does not bother with her. She talks to him.

'We need to see a doctor at once.'

'What's the problem?'

Again, not at her. She does not exist.

'She is— she has been—'

He looks at her, waits for her to jump in – *Gabrielle. Gabrielle. Gabrielle – explain what has been done to you.*

'She needs medical attention,' he says.

Look at her, say his eyes. Just look at her.

'Insurance,' demands the girl.

He looks at her, waits. *Gabrielle. Gabrielle. Gabrielle.*

'Gabrielle, do you . . .?' and then he turns again to the girl. 'Can we do this later, we need a doctor now.'

'Insurance, or cash up front.'

'How much?' he asks.

'Three hundred dollars for the consultation.'

He takes out his wallet, counts the notes, hands them over.

The girl gives him a clipboard in exchange.

'Everything must be filled in.'

She – *Gabrielle. Gabrielle. Gabrielle* – sits down in the front row. No one else now except the two of them. A private clinic, only for the chosen few.

She tries to write, tries to make out the words on the form, but the letters dissolve and her hand starts shaking and he takes the clipboard from her and works through the questions.

He stands up, delivers the clipboard to the girl.

The shaking won't stop. He tries to touch her, hold her, but she lets out a cry and he draws back. He gets back up, goes to talk to the girl again, exchanges words, his voice rising, comes back defeated.

'It's not long now, Gabrielle.'

He sits down, bends his head; she hears his breathing, and then his voice.

'I called you when I landed, Gabrielle. I had to leave early the next morning. When I came back I called again. And then I tried your office. No one answered, and when I went there it was closed. I went to Trinity. She was frantic, Gabrielle. She hadn't heard from you in eight days.'

Eight days. She was there in that place for eight days.

'But she didn't know anything except that an American diplomat was discovered badly injured on the verges of Domboshawa Road. He was dumped there, his car on fire, in the ditch. Trinity said that you were last seen in his company.'

There is something in his voice. A catch in his throat.

'Gabrielle, I—'

There are tears falling from her, gasps of breath coming out from her body. She feels his eyes on her but she keeps her head turned from him.

'I found you, that is what is important. The office got to know about a large group of displaced people on the move and I came in the hope that I would find you.'

He keeps on talking, saying words after words until finally, at last, he is interrupted.

'Miss Langa, you can come with me now.'

She is looking down at the white tennis shoes of the nurse. He makes to get up, holding his hand out to her.

'Sir, you can wait here.'

She follows the nurse to a small room, a cubicle.

'Please undress and put on the gown. Do you need any assistance?'

'No, no,' she says.

She stands in the room alone. An examination table with a sheet of white paper rolled out on it. She will have to lie there. A window, looking out to where, she does not know; the blinds are drawn shut. A stool by the table which swivels. The doctor will sit there. A chair, a small table against a wall. A curtained area where she must undress.

The blouse, once ivory, now shades of brown, rings of dried sweat, blood. Him. The navy-blue, pinstriped Truworths skirt, the hem undone, the dirt mostly absorbed into the blue. Him.

She takes the green paper gown from the wire hanger, puts her shaking hands through the armholes, tries to tie the strings at the back, but her hands won't let her.

She has bruises on her legs and arms, a gash in her head, the blood matted there with her hair. She lifts her hands, smells the blood and gunmetal. She has his semen caked on her legs.

She hears the door open. Breathe.

'Good afternoon, Miss Langa. I'm Doctor Masuka.' A woman.

She steps out from behind the curtain.

The doctor is young and hopeful, untouched. Clean.

She watches as Doctor Masuka puts on a pair of gloves. Doctor Masuka asks her questions. She answers 'yes, no,' closes herself to the touching of her body, the latex gloved fingers inspecting, evaluating.

'You don't appear to have any fractures, Miss Langa, just bruising on your ribs, but we'll take an X-ray to be sure. Your head wound is not too deep. You will not require stitches. The nurse will clean it up and bandage it.'

Doctor Masuka pauses.

'This will be painful, Miss Langa, but I will have to do a vaginal exam.'

'No,' she says.

'It is important, essential for a criminal—'

'No,' she says.

'We must do an HIV test.'

'Yes,' she says.

'We will do another one later, in six weeks, but for now I'll put you on antiretrovirals to cut the risk of transmission.'

'Yes,' she says.

She lets them draw blood from her, do their best to patch her up, fix her.

'Please take me home,' she tells him.

She is at a loss for a moment what her address is, the words and numbers just floating out of her reach.

'We should report this, Gabrielle.'

'No,' she says. 'Take me home.'

'Gabrielle, what they have done is a crime. You must report it.'

The numbers and words for home find her. She gives them to him.

'Gabrielle, I can take you to the hotel until—'

'Home,' she says. 'Please.'

Mawara jumps and leaps up onto the gate, starts licking her face while Giorgio tries to push him away; Mawara growls, flashes his teeth – she has never seen him like this before; the thought flits through her, it's not Giorgio, Mawara smells it on her. Mr Papadopoulos is here now – *Gabrielle*, he says, and then he stops, the look on his face, enough; he claps his hands and calls out to Mawara but Mawara won't be tricked. Good dog, Mawara, she says. Good dog. Mawara wags his tail. Sit, Mawara, sit. Good dog. Her voice is weak but he listens. Good dog. Good dog.

The water falling on her, so much of it, cascading all over her, as if it could drown her, torrents of it pouring down on her, hitting her wounds, opening them up again, stinging, soaking the bandage on her head. She scrubs between her legs, uses the hand towel, lifts the alcohol the doctor wiped there, throws away the towel, grabs the loofah, and then the stone she keeps for her heels, rubs and rubs and still the smell remains underneath. Him. It is in her head. It is everywhere. She retches, throws up. Stands in her sick. The hot water runs out and there is only the cold. She sits down in her sick, in the unclean bits of flesh swirling into the plughole and he finds her there. *Gabrielle. Gabrielle. Gabrielle.* He turns off the taps.

'Gabrielle,' he says softly. 'I have a towel. I am going to put it round you. You must get dry. You will get sick.'

He is speaking to her with great care, afraid of what any abrupt motions might trigger.

He wraps the towel around her as she sits huddled against the wall.

'Gabrielle, please, it's safe here. Please, you need to rest, to sleep.'

She gets up, out of the shower. He has laid out her nightdress on the bed, its arms spread open, and the image of it there panics her. His hands are on her, lifting the towel from her body. No, she screams. No. But he doesn't hear her, keeps rubbing the towel on her body, and then he lifts the nightdress from the bed and pulls it over her.

'I have to change the dressing, Gabrielle.'

He leaves her on the bed, goes into the bathroom. She hears him open the cabinet doors looking for bandages, Betadine, alcohol. She has nothing, just a bottle of nail varnish remover and Dettol.

'I'll go to the pharmacy,' he says. He stands there, looking down at her.

'You're scratching yourself, Gabrielle.'

He leaves the room again, comes back holding two tablets in his hand, a glass of water in the other.

'To help you sleep,' he tells her.

She takes the two tablets he holds out for her, the glass of water. She looks down at them.

'The doctor prescribed them. She gave us these two to start with, Gabrielle.'

She picks one, puts it on her tongue, swallows, and then the other.

She gets in the bed, under the sheets, closes her eyes, but he is there, waiting, wanting, hungry still.

But her eyes grow heavy, closing into the dark, the home-brew and dagga choking her.

She is making noises, cries and whimpers, sniffling and snivelling in the dark; it disgusts her what is coming out of her body. She tries to make it stop, to knock the sounds out of her head, beat and pound them into silence.

'Gabrielle, stop. Stop. You're hurting yourself. Stop.'

Cut and slice herself open. For her to truly bleed. Hurt and kill the pain. Silence it.

'Gabrielle, please.'

She feels a weight on the bed, a mass next to her and she must pull, wrench herself out of the darkness, know that she is no longer there, that the man on the bed, this bed, her bed, breathing next to her, means her no harm.

He will not leave her. He lies next to her. She thinks of telling him to leave but she is afraid to. Afraid to be alone. She has thoughts. She sees blood everywhere, smells it on her.

It feels as if she hasn't slept at all but fallen from a great height and is now coming round. She puts her hand on her throbbing head, stops at the gash, takes her finger away, smudges of blood, some on the pillow, the sheet. When she tries to get up the room dips and slides, and she presses her head back down on the pillow. She has a burning thirst, her tongue heavy and swollen in her mouth. The tablets? She closes her eyes. Hears voices. A man. A woman. They seem so far away. The ache has started again between her legs and that smell rises up again.

'Gabs.'

When she opens her eyes, Trinity sits at her bedside as if this is a hospital visit.

'Did you bring flowers?' she asks.

'Flowers?' Trinity says.

She makes a sound. She thinks she's laughing but Trinity looks at her as if she is looking at a madwoman.

'Gabs,' Trinity says. Trinity is holding out her hand. Trinity wants to help her.

'Flowers,' she says, 'You know, roses, carnations, for the sick or the dead. A wreath, yes, a wreath would be nice.'

She makes that sound again.

'Gabrielle.'

Everyone keeps saying that. *Gabrielle, Gabrielle, Gabrielle.* She should tell them. I'm not her. I am coloured, bitch, mistress of colonizers. *Hure.* These are my names. Who I am.

He says something about getting some food ready, leaves the room; how kind, how tactful, leaving them to divulge secrets, giving her a chance to spill her guts out.

'Ben?' she says. 'Is he alri—?'

'Yes, yes. He has been deported, persona non grata.'

'I'm tired,' she says, turning to the wall.

'You're a lawyer,' says Trinity, 'You can fight this. I'll help you. We can – Gabs, don't let them win.'

She hears. She hears the fighting talk, the outrage, the desperation, all on her behalf.

'Go,' she says. 'Leave me alone.'

She hears. The two of them whispering, out of sight.

'I'll come back.'

'Thank you, Trinity. I have to leave in a couple of days. I've tried to talk to her father.'

'He is useless.'

'I don't know what to— her Colombian visa, for when she was supposed to come, it's still valid, do you think—?'

A door closes.

PART THREE

Flight

31

'Gabrielle, Gabrielle,' she hears in the dark. 'It's time to go.'
He lifts her up and away, again, this shrouded self. He takes her to the New World.

For days and days she lies there, in the spare room of his townhouse in Bogotá. He chose it, once upon a time, with her in mind, ready for her when she came. He had sent her the pictures to entice her to leave her life and join his. That room would be her office, anything she wanted it to be. She would come here and they would play house. They would live happily ever after.

She cannot sleep in his room, that imposing bed, its curlicued wooden headboard from the jungle, forever bearing down on her, wanting.

She eats morsels of the food he makes, dishes he leaves behind in the fridge, on the kitchen counter. She doesn't pick up the maps of the city lying on the dining room table, the routes he's highlighted in yellow, pink and blue, the *Lonely Planet* guide next to them as if she will turn into a backpacker in this new life. There is so much for her to see in this city, he tells her, whole days she can just spend in the barrio of La Candeleria, walking up and down the cobblestone streets.

.   .   .

There are wool carpets on the hardwood floor, beiges and browns woven by the Indios. There are framed rectangles of cloths on the walls, 'molas', inlaid strips of blues, reds, oranges and yellow. There are glossy books on Colombia and pre-Colombian history on the shelves. This is where he imagined she would live. There are African masks along the passageway, masks from his house in Harare. An ethnographic paradise.

Whole days when she doesn't bother with the getting up, the getting washed, the getting dressed, the eating . . . when he finds her, at the end of his day, still on the mattress, a breathing corpse.

One day he comes, a steely determination in his voice.

'You have to try,' he tells her. 'You have to try. I can't take seeing you like this anymore, Gabrielle. Gabrielle, look at me.'

Her back pressing hard against the wall, her arms scraping the brick, her skin shedding onto the stone, her back banging against it as if she means to crack bone, snap it.

Her eyes waver over stone and brick, the wood of the balcony, the vines and the bougainvilleas and below, in the courtyard, the trill of Spanish – ¡hola! ¿qué más? ¿qué cuentas? ¿qué tal? – and the squawking of gaudy-feathered parrots, everything that tells her she is no longer there in the dark, bristling space. The sky, a different blue in the chilly, hilly air.

Breathe, she tells herself, breathe.

Bitterness and fury, raw on her lips, nasty, on her tongue. *You wanted me here, Giorgio. I'm here now, you win.*

He wants to touch her. A hand here, a stroke. A caress. A squeeze. A hug. A rub. All the many ways to touch. The holding of hands. As if his touch will heal her. As if it will erase other hands, other touches, somehow make her whole again.

.   .   .

Noise. The city is full of it, relentless. Busetas screeching and hooting. Gunfire, celebrating goals. Everything done at a fervent, high pitch. Talking, laughing. Dancing.

The breath of people on her, behind her in bus seats. Too much. Too close.

The little tablets thrown away, by him; the bathroom cabinet emptied of pills; the mattress put away. Surrender. Her body on the bed. His. Breathe.

'Gabrielle, we're going out, do you hear me? We're going out.'

Saturday, Sunday. He is there for her, cajoling, spoon-feeding, watchful, hovering. Incessant.

'Gabrielle . . .'

Get up, get washed. Get dressed.

Walking, winding up and down the calles, the carreras, slipping in and out of skaters and cyclists, families. Moving. Always moving.

'Look, Gabrielle.'

She looks. Hacienda Santa Barbara: the market behind the commercial centre.

Home-made jewellery, lapis lazulis in beaten metal, homespun coats – *look look look* – all of it too little, too much. Another life.

'How about something to eat, Gabrielle?'

Baby talk.

'Try this, mmmm, an empanada.'

'You love markets, Gabrielle.'

A buseta to the centre, to the Mercado de las Pulgas.

A man with no hands and one leg. Umberto Eco's *El Péndulo* at his side, a tin cup against the leg stump.

A mother with a child leaning against her – the child, lame and deformed, her face heavily scarred from burns.

A boy beheading chickens, headless chickens splattering blood on passing feet.

She is there, and not there.
Seeing, and not seeing. The grotesque. Her.

Nails scratching her skin, a needle picking at it, a razor gently slashing, and harder now, the solace of her blood, the things that are now her own to do with as she pleases, the sweet thrill of sucking on it, drawing it back to herself. There is comfort to be had in it. The pain she gives to her own body. The control she has over it.

A hat. The dense black colour of it, its wide, ridiculous brim, the red, yellow and blue of its band, nothing like, nothing at all like, and yet . . . when she blinks the hat becomes that other thing, pushed low on a head, spinning atop a bedpost, waiting, wanting.

'Siga, por favor. Señorita, siga por favor.'

He tries to usher her in with a flourish of his chunky arms.

She looks down at his steel-capped cowboy boots, their dandy points. There is a picture of the legendary drug lord wearing boots like these. She saw it on a truck. Registration plates, Envigado, his hometown.

'Siga, siga . . .'

He wants her to come into the shop. He won't hurt her. He wants her custom. Not her.

Tufts of aguardiente from the beseeching mouth, warming her face, bring the other smells, home-brew and want. They are always wanting, always hungry.

'No, no . . . gracias,' she says, taking a step backwards, banging her elbow against the edge of the door.

He has already turned from her, taking the hat off his head, angling it, tossing it on the door handle, just so. He pulls out a black plastic comb, several teeth missing, from the back pocket of his clinging, shiny trousers and runs it through the thick strands of his gleaming jet-black hair, the shop window, a mirror. He takes a step back, pats the hair down, shoves the comb in the pocket, puts the hat back on.

She sees boys in that window, too. Boys who want, who take, whose time is short. Boys who are watching her, waiting, wanting.

She steps away from the doorway, toppling over baskets, clay figurines. Back on the pavement, she stumbles into the path of a military policeman.

The pressure of a gun against her. He can harm her. He has a gun. He can hurt her. He is a boy. Like them.

A gun, a gun waving at her, she sees it there in a flash, come, come with me.

But no, this gun is held tight to his body.

He is wearing a hat too, but it does not make her heart lurch and pound, bring a metallic taste to her mouth. It is just a hat.

'Lo siento,' she says, 'lo siento . . .'

I'm sorry. I'm sorry.

She flags down a buseta, does not even check the number, its route, its destination. Stereo blaring out salsa, merengue, *pegando el pecho, pegando el pecho . . . move those breasts, move those breasts . . .*

Garish hot-red lips on the gearbox, parted to reveal a stretched out tongue, curled just so at the tip.

The Madonna, slung around the mirror, jilting and swinging to the demands of the music.

The buseta squeals and shrieks in and out of traffic. She closes her eyes, her veins pulsing, *give me this, give me that, want want want,* the cacophony of it, flooding her.

A touch on her shoulder, making her jump, her eyes flashing open to the child holding out to her a Madonna. For sale.

She takes the paper Madonna from the child, gives him fifty pesos in exchange.

The Our Lady of Guadalupe in her palm.

Loving protector of life.

An ancient port city. *Cartagena.* Courtyards and cobblestones. A getaway. Music and dancing, poetry in the moonlight. Good food, wine. She smiles and laughs and drinks as much as her body will take. Perhaps more, much more, for she leans against the old city wall and spills herself onto the cobbled street. There is so much of her to let go of.

The sand looks dirty but, when she looks out into the greyish sea, it moves something in her, all that water she cannot see the end of. How small she is against all of that. If something has been taken from her, surely, seeing as she is so small, so little, so insignificant, none of it can add up to much, and perhaps it is only the naming of things that makes them larger than what they are, larger than all this sea; so, if she does not, refuses to give this thing a name, she will be safe. Safe.

Déjame sola! Leave me alone. *Bésame! Kiss me.* The voices, the garish lovers in the telenovelas, her companions, her tutors. Hour after hour. Everything so dramatic, so tragic, so monumental, in Spanish. Déjame sola, she says in her head. Over and over. But they won't leave her alone.

DEA agents in the cafes with local girls who are too young, too beautiful, too smart for them. They have round stomachs, smoke cigars and talk too loudly. They are nothing at all like Ben.

He puts his hand on her cheek, and she makes an effort, keeps herself from flinching.

Mirlande, from Haiti, has stories of voodoo, cholera and poverty.

Carlu, from Corsica, speaks of bombs blowing up the island.

Hannah, from Israel, talks of army training, how handy it was in the Amazonian jungle.

Petite, beautiful Sigrid from Sweden causing commotion everywhere she walks in the city, men drooling and wanting, always wanting, always wanting – her blonde hair, her blue-green eyes, her pale skin – want, want, want – showing them photographs in class when she weighed twenty-three kilograms.

Hans, from Germany, thick beard, bald dome, speaks of the soldier brother of his Colombian wife, kidnapped by guerrillas.

And of her own story she gives them . . . My name is Gabrielle Langa . . . *Mi nombre es Gabrielle Langa* . . . I am twenty-five years old . . . *Tengo veinte-cinco años* . . . I am a lawyer . . . *Yo soy abogado* . . . I am here on holiday . . . *Estoy aquí de vacaciones* . . . That is all.

But they want more.

'Tell us about your country,' Señora Alvez, their teacher, says.

'Yes,' says Carlu, 'it is in the news. Is the president really that bad, killing white people because, well, because they are white?'

'Not as bad as Papa Doc,' says Mirlande. 'He killed everyone he didn't like.'

They wait for her, heads turned towards her, bodies twisted in their chairs.

What words to say, how to say them.

There is a moment when it feels it would be all right to reveal it to them, to put it there among their own tales, for it is just that, after all, a story.

Just a story.

Family.

The textbook open on her desk. There is mother. There is father. Here is daughter, son. Look, there is brother, sister, baby. And there is un perro, dog. She looks at the dog. He is jumping on the white space. He is black, tongue lolling out, tail mid-wag. She puts her hand on his paw. Un perro. He is jumping on her, his tail wagging, wagging, slapping against her leg, his wet, wet tongue, licking, licking. *Mawara, stop. Mawara.* She is looking at the dog, her hand pressed onto his head, his black, glossy head.

'Gabrielle, Gabrielle . . .'

She lifts her eyes from the page, from her other life. Señora Alvez is at her side.

'Tienes un perro?' she asks.

No, Gabrielle says. 'No tengo un perro.'

.   .   .

She goes to the bars on the Zona Rosa with Hans, Sigrid and Carlu and hears more of their lives, their families, their friends, their exploits in this crazy town. They confide in her. Sigrid is in love with a boy from the island of San Andrés; anxiety (does he love her? He is so far away with all those beautiful island girls) is making her have problems with food again. Carlu with his soft face and dreamy, wet eyes tells her he dreads going back to Corsica; his family are nationalists and he is in love with a very French girl from an old noble family.

She listens, she can do that. Standing there sometimes her thoughts float: Trinity there, in wisps of time, space: university Trinity holding court in bars, nightclubs, her laugh, her roll of her eyes, her put-downs, charging onto the dance floor, dragging her along, the pulsing beat of township jive under her feet, travelling up her body. And then there is that other Trinity, the ghost Trinity she opens her eyes to. 'Did you bring flowers?' she asked her.

Hans takes her aside after class one day: in his hand a small velvet pouch. He loosens the drawstring, takes out a crystal, polished smooth, pink; a moonstone.

'It is a healing stone,' he tells her, putting it in her hand. 'It is calming, it has restorative energies. Keep it close to your skin.'

He wraps her fingers around it. A crystal, a moonstone, just for her, because he sees how much she needs it.

'Where have you been? Gabrielle?'

Out out out. Does she say this aloud or just in her head? *Out out out.* He should be happy. She has been out. Drinking, having fun, what the hell is wrong with that?

'Gabrielle, it's two o'clock, how did you get home?'

Two o'clock, is that all? She could have stayed on for much longer. She should have. There were so many bodies, the music so loud it pulsed right through her. Salsa. Merengue. And look, here, now in this room, she is spinning, spinning, the colours smashing, slashing into each other . . . who is that laughing?

'Gabrielle, you're drunk. What is the matter with you?'

Drunk? So what? So what? She has been to a party. She drank, so what? *Aguardiente*. Burning water. Colombian tequila. Shot after shot. She is drunk, she knows that. So what?

'I don't know what to do, Gabrielle,' he says, his voice breaking. Is that her, laughing?

The dark wood looms over her. She feels herself sway, the ground shifting. She looks down at her feet. Her small bare feet on the floor, watches them lift off the ground, her toes first trailing the ground and then up, up and she is floating, looking down on the bed. The door opens and light floods the room but its core is darkness. The darkness swallows her and sinks with her on the bed and she tries and tries to lift herself away, to float again, tries and tries, but the light that is darkness holds her, pins her to the bed and she knows, knows it is coming, it is coming, it will never end.

'Gabrielle, it's time.'

He swoops her up from the bed, away to a faraway land full of the good life. *La Dolce Vita*.

Rome.

The clock hand turns and clicks and the new year begins, the sound of fireworks in the Roman skies ricocheting through her. She thinks of the dogs, whimpering and howling, cowering, she knows their fear, their terror, envies them their voice.

She stands in the square with Marella, Giorgio's sister, watching the dog whose coat seems to be unravelling scamper after pigeons. Mawara could be this dog, dashing this way and that, as ungraceful as any creature can be. She feels if she could only throw her arms around Mawara, something of her life, her self, would be okay. How much she would be happy for him to slosh his wet, heavy tongue all over her. It's ridiculous (petty, stupid, absurd) but she blames Giorgio for Mawara's absence, that he is there, alone, back at the cottage, abandoned by her, under the Papadopouloses' care. But, she does, she blames him. He made all the decisions. He took her away. He brought her here. The other voice tells her, you're being unfair, disingenuous, he had to, you were in no fit state, no one else was there. It was just him. He took care of you, he is taking care of you. You would have died without him.

'Are you cold?' Marella asks her. 'You're shivering. We'd better head back home.'

The dog gives up on the birds and starts rolling about the feet of the old man who bends down to stroke its stomach.

She shakes her head. 'No, I'm fine. It's lovely out here. The temperature's just right.'

She is spending a lot of time with Marella. They share a room. Giorgio has organized that. She isn't to be left alone, unguarded. He is in Geneva at the international headquarters. He phones in the evenings, his voice hushed, which irritates her, as though he is in a hospital. He always ends the same way, 'Are they looking after you?' as though he doesn't trust his own parents, his sister. 'Yes, yes, yes,' she answers. 'They are.'

They are sitting at the little bar in what has become her favourite square in Rome. Piazza Campo dei Fiori, the whiff of fish pungent in the air from the morning market.

The square has a melancholy air to it: rising above the stalls is the grave, dignified presence of Giordano Bruno, in iron, who was burnt on that same spot for heresy many centuries ago. He stands there, his strong, caped body, his hooded head, looking down, one hand clasping the wrist of the other holding a book. It feels to her as though she is looking at someone who has embraced their terrible fate. Someone great and honourable. As usual, there are drunks lolling about the foot of the statue, on the steps. One keeps toppling over, his liquor bottle jangling on the stone. There are carabinieri just at the edge of the square, near the magazine vendor, but they aren't paying any attention. She feels sick. She knows it is the smell of fish, the taste of it in her mouth, but she doesn't want to get up, to leave, so she swallows. Marella sighs. She turns to look at Gabrielle and, while stirring her espresso, says, 'All this running around with my brother. You should settle down here.'

Gabrielle hears shutters banging against a wall. She looks up to find 'the old hag', as Marella calls her, throwing a jug of water out. Then she throws another one, then another, then another. A carabiniere stands under her window gesticulating with both hands in the Roman way and, as he admonishes her, a thud of water falls on his head. Gabrielle laughs.

Marella says, 'What a pain. She is always doing something crazy. The old witch. They're all afraid of her. Peasants.'

She says it in a burst of anger. Marella *is* angry. She lives with her parents and has come to think that this will be the entirety of her life. Gabrielle could tell her that there are worse things, but Marella knows that. She can see it in Gabrielle all the time: Marella has come upon her very late at night, head pressed against the edge of the table, crying. She says that there are times when Gabrielle just disappears. Moments, minutes when she just isn't there. Frightened, she pushes her arm, 'Gabrielle,' she calls out. 'Gabrielle.'

They walk slowly. Marella keeps saying things like watch out, be careful, mind it. She is walking with her eyes on the ground, keeping a rueful eye out for any pieces of skin, an eel, lying about on the stone that Gabrielle might slip on, that this invalid might crack her skull upon. Crossing roads, she grabs Gabrielle's arm and drags her along.

Gabrielle is tired and she is tired of being tired.

There are days when she seems to forget all about it; when she goes on as if it has never happened. Other days when she can barely move, an undercurrent pulling at her.

They watch her. All of them. Sister, mother, father. Giorgio has warned them about knives, razors, but they can't do anything about her teeth; she can bite into her flesh, bite and bite into it until she bleeds, tastes blood in her mouth, until she feels some kind of release, some kind of dulling of whatever it is that has entered her body, this foreign object, monster, that has fused with her cells, that goads and battles her from within. She can bite and chew at herself, draw out blood, traces of the monster she can see, leaking out, trailing against her skin, and when there is enough she can lick this too and spit it out in the bath, sticking her finger, down, down her throat, so that the monster leaves in clumps. But no, *she* is the monster. She wraps herself up in long-sleeved sweaters and jerseys, coats that hide everything.

She wants her mother. Her mother is dead. She dials the Bulawayo number, listens to the phone ringing, and is caught out by the sudden boom of her father's voice in her ears. 'Hello, hello, who is this? Hello.' She listens to him utter an expletive, and then to the *clack* as he angrily puts the phone down.

On the telegiornale, before anyone thinks to switch it off, war vets and youths are kicking open farm doors, beating dogs; bloodied farmers and their workers are standing, dazed, beside burnt fields.

During weekdays, when Marella is busy, she walks on Rome's narrow cobbled streets, starting from the bank of the Tiber where the synagogue lies with its aluminium square dome. She walks, up and down the tunnel-like alleyways. She passes the tailor shops, the kosher bakeries, the restaurants on Via del Portico d'Ottavia, where the day, October 16, 1943 is marked on a plaque, the round-up of the Jews.

She urges her feet up Via della Reginella, into the main square. She stands in the square watching the old men playing draughts, cards or just chatting. Once, like visions, two black nuns walked briskly past them in the direction of Trastevere: a flicker of a memory – Sister Regina, the Ndebele teacher at school, of whom her father had said, *such a beautiful woman, what a waste, how could her people give her up?* She walks on. She looks up at the open shutters and thinks of entire families being taken away by the Nazis, one fateful morning.

She crosses the Ponte Sisto, follows the tourist trail but takes the back streets Giorgio has shown her, wilfully allowing herself to get lost. She walks and walks as if she can outwalk her malaise, pound it into the cobblestones until after hours and hours she collapses into a taxi, her legs trembling, her muscles going into spasms.

Once, in the crush of crowds, tourists, she saw a figure walking towards her and the thought alighted in her head, there he is, *Ben*. A mirage.

Giorgio comes back exhausted, dark circles under his eyes, the clothes seeming to sag off his body. His mother is anxious and keeps tugging at his clothes, touching parts of his body, as if she thinks he is not really a creature of blood and bones; in his place, a ghost, an apparition, that has spirited away her son.

Two days after he arrives, they drive to Assisi.

The village is full of young, earnest people making their way back and forth to the basilica. The Roman Catholic International Youth Convention is taking place. In the church she is entranced by the votive offerings that are attached to one inner wall; she has not seen such a thing before – scraps of paper with names on them, pictures, statuettes, plastic moulds of (healed) limbs, torsos, tufts of wool from a sick sheep – dangling from coloured thread, all in thanks to the Holy Mother for prayers answered. The wall is crammed with them. She wishes that she had some thanks to give, some offering to make. She tries to summon her survival, Giorgio's care; perhaps she is just too mean, ungrateful. Thank you, she wants to say, but she does not feel blessed, beloved. What she wants to do is to leave some part of who she is, what she has become, there, hanging from a coloured thread on the wall, some part that would catch Mother Mary's eye, some bit of the monster.

By night the young, earnest people become lively, raucous youths, their high voices filling up the air, making the village seem both smaller and larger than it is. Her legs hurt. The village is on a slope; there has been a lot of climbing and steep descents into picturesque narrow, cobbled alleyways. She knows that Giorgio is worried, telling her to take it easy, rest, but she senses that there is something else too, something that he is withholding from her, that lies behind his own tiredness. She feels strangely alive. As if she has done something that matters. She doesn't know what it is but for once, since it happened, her body feels truly her own.

Because this is Italy, she drinks. And drinks. Until Giorgio says, that's enough, Gabrielle. His vigilance enrages her. She is not falling over drunk, just unsteady on her feet, what is wrong with that? Can't he just give her a break, stop being so controlling? She wants to escape, drown her sorrows, why won't he let her do that? And so she drinks. He can't keep an eye on her all the time. She says she is going round the corner to the paninoteca, she stops by the bar, takes a nip there. Red wine at first because it is healthy, good for the heart, but this is Italy – white wine and bubbly Prosecco everywhere, so she drinks glasses of that. And then she tries the more exotic drinks, the hard stuff. Limoncello, grappa, things which burn her throat, make her sick.

'They want me back in Zimbabwe,' he tells her, the night before they leave to go back to Bogotá.

The ground cleaves open, and she is no longer there.

'They need someone who knows the place.'

They are lying in the dark and he is talking into it.

'Gabrielle, do you hear me . . . Gabrielle?'

His hand is on her, on her shoulder. 'Gabrielle.'

The ground closes, and she is there, deep under, covered in layers and layers of dirt, his voice, touch, mere echoes on the packed earth.

'I said I would think about it. I can say no.'

She is wrenched up from the ground and she stands there on her grave, dirt in her mouth, bile and blood, tissue leaking from her body.

'There are so many displaced people, Gabrielle. They need some-one who knows the ropes. It is all happening in the rural areas. The towns are quiet.'

He turns towards her in the dark, his breath on her.

'Do you want to go back, Gabrielle? Is it too soon?'

She smells rot and decay coming from her mouth, her body, every bit of herself, dirty and unclean. Where else could she be? Where else could she go? This is Giorgio, who knows. Who has seen it all. And she gives him the words unsaid: worse things have happened, are happening, you too will survive, endure, live, life goes on. She feels him in the dark searching for the right words. 'Perhaps, you need to be ba—'

'When?'

'September.'

Well over a year since she left.

'It's time to go back,' she says in the dark.

His hand finds her again, this body, this corpse, breathing.

She breathes in the garlic on his breath, the white wine, it alights on her skin and she closes her eyes and breathes into the dark.

'Gabrielle,' she hears.

His hand is on her throat, then on her face. She feels a horror as though she were drowning in the water.

Her eyes open and he is breathing, breathing on her – the pasta, the tomato sauce, the meat, the prosciutto, the bread, all there in his mouth, on her body.

'Gabrielle,' he says.

He is pleading, begging, so much want there, so much want.

He is kissing her, on her throat, on her cheek, on her eyelid, but not on her mouth, not there.

'Gabrielle, I love you.'

And his breath, his mouth is on her breast, his tongue moving there, and she closes her eyes, closes them.

And she lets him touch her, enter her, come and take her, Giorgio, Giorgio, who has seen it all, hacked limbs, wombs sliced open, brains spilling from a colleague into his hands, and his hands are on her, on her body, taking, wanting.

There is blood on her hands. The clattering of a gun on a stone floor. A hat jauntily perched on a bedpost, stains of blood on its brim. The last howl of a hyena, bolting her awake.

PART FOUR

Return

32

Through the airplane window Gabrielle sees the long trail of red carpet coming from the foot of a passenger plane. Word has it that The Old Man is inside. A throng of men and women are dancing and ululating in the bright sunshine. Some of them carry placards, jogging up and down: *We Shall Never Be a Colony Again! Down with BBC! Down with Sky! Long Live Our Great Father!*

Gabrielle sits in her seat, her head turned from Giorgio. She pictures The Old Man in election mode – jaunty cap perched on head, fist shaking, a spring in his step, rejuvenated.

She puts her hand on her stomach, then snatches it away. And, because Giorgio is always watching, he puts his hand there where his baby grows.

Six weeks, the doctor said. *Felicidades*.

The captain of their plane, in his thick German accent, asks them to please pull down their blinds. They have received instructions from air traffic control. They are not to witness The Old Man's homecoming.

The runway is eerily quiet as if somehow the scene might have been imagined, but the red carpet still lies there. A rush of nausea, as it ripples and gushes out, spilled blood. But no, it's just the airport workers flapping it, rolling it up.

They separate in the Immigration Hall and, as she watches Giorgio line up in the Diplomatic section, she feels an irrational sense of abandonment, tears gathering in her eyes. She gives the immigration officer her passport. He doesn't even look at her as he flicks through the pages, stamps it. There is no list he has to check, cross-reference. She is nothing. Nobody. One of many.

She meets up with Giorgio at the baggage carousel and, when he sees her, his face betrays his relief.

The office has sent a driver, who looks at her with a puzzled expression. Giorgio opens the door and helps her in.

She feels a kind of numbness. Her neck stiff from trying to avert the driver's looks in her direction. Giorgio takes her hand, gives it a squeeze. She doesn't look at him. She doesn't want to have to deal with his concern. He tried to talk her out of coming now. After the elections, he urged her. You can join me then. After the baby is born. You can wait in Italy. And then, *Gabrielle, I have diplomatic immunity.* He had left that between them. The unspoken, *marry me and I can keep you safe.*

She notices some defaced posters of the opposition leader on a wall. She closes her eyes as they drive past Hatfield.

The receptionist asks for her passport and when she hands it over she gets a little sneer.

'You are sharing one room?' the receptionist asks.

'I asked for a double,' says Giorgio.

'She is your, your—?'

'We want a double room, is that a problem?'

'No, of course not, sir, it's just that we have a problem with prostitutes.'

Gabrielle feels a rush of her former lawyer self, something she could hurl at this undereducated cretin – this is the same kind of thinking that gives the police permission to arrest and bundle into jail any woman they deem not respectable – but the feeling goes as quickly as it comes.

In the room she goes into the bathroom and throws up in the sink and then she takes a long shower.

She finds Giorgio sitting on the bed. Standing by the window, she looks down at the park. She feels a new bout of nausea, a feeling of claustrophobia. She can't stay in this hotel room, feeling bound, useless. What is she going to do here?

'Gabrielle . . .'

His hand on her shoulder. 'We'll start looking for a place soon. They've already given me a list of possible properties. Borrowdale, Highlands, Chisipite.'

She shrugs his hand away. 'Giorgio . . . I . . . I can't do it. I, I can't live with you. I'm sorry.'

'You're tired,' he says. 'It's been a long trip. Have you phoned Trinity?'

'No, I haven't phoned Trinity. I'll phone her when I'm ready. I've already told you.' She is almost shouting.

'She's your friend, Gabrielle. You haven't spoken to her since . . .'

She wants him to stop. To just stop.

'I . . . I can go back to the cottage . . . with Mawara . . . I need to be by myself. I need to . . . I'm sorry I . . . Just for a while, until I know what . . .'

He is standing there, his hand on his forehead, as if what she is saying is giving him a headache.

'I'm going for a walk. I need some air.'

She stands outside the hotel gasping as if she has been out for a run. She has the idea to get into a taxi and go to the cottage, find Mawara, sink into her bed with him at her side and fall asleep. But, as her breath quietens, the logistics of it stop her. The cottage has probably been rented out to a new occupant. There will have to be a talk with Mr Papadopoulos or his wife, and this she cannot do now.

She walks one block, stops at the American Embassy on Herbert Chitepo Avenue. Ever since the bombings in Kenya and Tanzania huge concrete blocks have been placed all along the perimeters of the bunker-like building. She thinks of Ben, his body hidden from her, on the ground. She walks slowly round to the entrance.

She suddenly catches sight of a Peugeot parked at the far side and as she walks she thinks she hears a car engine starting. There is a frantic moment when she is not here but there, her body in that tight ball, muscles and nerves tensed, waiting for the screech of tyres on asphalt she knows now will follow. But there is nothing on this day, just a car idling away in the heat. She looks down at her fingers, trembling. She lifts the skin of her wrists, twists and pinches it. She lifts her hand to her mouth, bites. She walks back towards the hotel, is there now standing at the entrance; she can go in to the calm, air-conditioned room where Giorgio's waiting with his knowing look; it would be a surrender, a defeat. She turns away, heads towards town. First, she is walking briskly, almost running, as if she thinks that the Peugeot might, after all, be following her, but then she slows down, counting each step, pretending she is not really here in this capital; she is in Bogotá, she is in Rome, on one of her walks, but there are smells and sounds that assail her, and she picks up her pace again, trying to leave them behind.

By the time she reaches *The Herald* offices she is panting and she has a pain in her side. She is also surprisingly hungry, light-headed. She looks at the headline on the stand on the pavement: OPPOSITION FUNDED BY BRITAIN: CACHE OF SECRET DOCUMENTS FOUND. No need to read the story, she can imagine the key words: *imperialists, puppets, hijacking the Revolution, traitors* . . . She takes a step towards the door but then changes her mind again, walks past the building. She will get hold of Trinity later. She must find somewhere to sit, something to eat and drink. She walks up to Chicken Inn but, while standing in the queue, she suddenly realizes that she does not have a single cent on her. Someone nudges her on. She is about to make a spectacle of herself by fainting. The floor seems to sweep itself off her feet.

'Ah Gabrielle, Gabrielle, it is you.'

She looks up, sways, feels hands on her.

'Come, come, you must sit.'

Godfrey.

'I will fetch some water.'

He leads her to a chair outside and she sits there trying to stop the circling of legs and buildings.

'Here, drink, I also have a bun. Eat.'

She eats the bun quickly, gulps down the water. 'Thank you. I . . .'

She looks up at Godfrey's face. 'I just came back and I forgot I didn't have any money and I . . . Thank you, Godfrey.'

'No need. No need at all. Trinity would kill me if I let her friend go without water and a piece of bread.'

'How is she?'

'Fine, fine. You don't know? She's been promoted. Deputy Assistant Editor. News Section.'

'Really? I'll have to congratulate her ASAP.'

Giorgio's voice, nagging, flickers in her head.

'And you guys? I read that you had a lucky escape, Godfrey.'

Someone had thrown a home-made bomb at the *Daily News* offices from a moving car. Luckily the aim hadn't been great; the next-door art gallery's windows had been shattered.

'Yes, they are still after us. Every now and then we have to evacuate the offices.'

'You must be very busy with everything that's going on, Godfrey. Zimbabwe is very much in the news.'

Godfrey nods. He drags his chair nearer to hers. He speaks to her in a lowered voice. 'Not as busy as we would like. We try to go to the farms but we are chased away by the police and the war vets. Just yesterday, one of our reporters was badly beaten near Chivhu. There is a farmer there who has been trapped for over a month and the war vets are allegedly threatening to burn down the house. Anyway, the reporter is at the Avenues Clinic now and can you believe the newspaper has hired private security guards to make sure that he is not abducted from his bed? This is not such a good time to be in Zimbabwe.'

A tremor of fear, nerves, passes through her, a bitter taste in her mouth. Her forehead is prickling with sweat and she has a feeling of vertigo, as though she is sitting at a slight angle to the ground.

'But you should read Trinity's pieces, Gabrielle. She is getting into all those hard-to-reach places, interviewing war vets, the so-called new landowners; her descriptions of what's going on in those farms once they have been "liberated" are something else. I don't think her editor really reads those pieces properly.'

A ransacked farmhouse, comrades, youths, passed out. She knows this story. A sudden, overwhelming tiredness descends on her. She puts her hand on her stomach and, conscious of Godfrey once again, takes it away.

'Maybe they're just making a point,' she says, trying to focus, pulling herself back to Godfrey, 'until the elections and then the whole thing will die off. What are they going to do with all those farms?'

'We shall see. But where have you been all this time?'

The question is so vast, it overwhelms her for a moment.

'In, in Bogotá, Colombia.' She rubs her temple. 'Godfrey, please get your lunch. I'm fine now, thanks to you. I'll walk back to the hotel. Thank you once again.'

She can see the confusion on his face. The way she has spoken to him, as if he were a stranger somehow. A gulf has opened up between them. She is not who she was.

She crosses the mall. She looks up at the shop window, up from the plastic legs of the would-be tourist, up from his khaki shorts and all-purpose vest with its multitude of pockets, up, up from its plastic hands holding tight to a pair of binoculars, up over the blank face to the head and, there it is, the suede farmer's hat of another life except it is not battered here, not stained with sweat and grime, not stolen from some farmhouse, not atop a bedpost, witness, and still, even though she knows all of this, her heart quickens, her breath constricts and her eyes close, deep into the other life, self. She smells the hat, its sweat, its blood, its home-brew, and a far-off sound impales itself in her ear . . . *coloured, you are very beautiful* . . . she stands there, paralysed, the evil gathering itself around her until she sees a hand, a hand of flesh and bone, lift the hat from the plastic tourist's head, away.

. . .

She has nowhere else to go, except back to the hotel room, back to Giorgio.

A plane hits a building. For a moment she thinks that she is watching a movie, but no, it's a news programme and what she is seeing is happening in real time to a building in New York. She sits down on the bed. The first building collapses. Then the second. She lies down on the bed, listening to what has happened, the panic and incredulity in the reporters' voices.

She thinks of Ben. Of where he might be. If he is safe. If she will ever see him again.

No, No, she cries. *No!*

But the sound, the earth shattering *boom boom* sound in her dreams, is only the knocking at the door, and then calls of *housekeeping, housekeeping*, and then a key being turned in the lock.

'No, no,' she calls out, scrambling out of bed, 'there's someone in.'

A hesitation at the door, then the sound of the key being removed. 'Sorry, sorry madam.'

Gabrielle listens to the retreating footsteps. She takes the *Do Not Disturb* sign from the handle, opens the door and hooks it outside. She stands against the door looking into the room. She sees Giorgio's discarded shirt, his trousers on the chair, a sock peeking out from under the bed. She notices the sheaf of paper on the bedside table. *At the office. Will be back at 12. Will start house search. Trinity?*

Anger surges again at his ability to deflate, ignore any utterance of hers, to gloss over her wishes, her will. *Of course, you didn't really mean what you said yesterday.* No, it is deeper than that; he doesn't even take her opinions into account, as if she is a child.

She makes to tear the note but something holds her back, so she crumples it instead, throws it on the bed.

. . .

She goes down to the Brasserie where she has a late breakfast. The TV screen is on mute, showing images of the planes, the buildings collapsing, the dust.

From her table she can, through the glass panels, see out into the park. She wants to smash something against the glass, something that will explode into the park where lovers lie entangled in bushes, where women are selling their batiks and baskets, cajoling tourists with their open smiles and lilting voices; she wants to vomit into all that.

Lies. Lies. Lies.

When she looks back at the TV, cartoon mice are chasing each other.

Giorgio finds her sitting by the poolside going over *The Herald*. The whole paper is full of the attacks in New York, but she has the page open on the classifieds. She turned there to get away from the planes, the rising panic she has over Ben, but, looking through the sparse jobs column, despair and disorientation set in. She is a tourist in her own country.

Sitting up high in the Land Cruiser, Giorgio at the wheel, on the Borrowdale Road, a picture from another time when she was just a student, and here she is now, as if time has done a loop, found her and deposited her in this same place. They pass the racetrack and the 'new' developments on the roadside, some of the houses still not completed, money run out. Just before Sam Levy's Village they turn. She is breathing softly, gently into herself, watching the car move, until finally it goes through an open gate and stops, the engine ticking to a rest, and while the car is still and Giorgio has stepped out, she sits there, breathing. The estate agent is talking to Giorgio and their voices come to her as though she were under water, bubbles of indistinct sound. She is thinking of Ben, the red car, their drive on the Borrowdale Road to the flea market. She is thinking of the rain falling on them and their bin liner raincoats. She does not know how long she sits there, lost, how long it takes for Giorgio to realize that she is not with him, but suddenly she brings herself back, hears her name and she looks up to find him standing by the open door of the driver's side, his head ducked inside.

'Gabrielle,' he says. 'Come on, let's go and take a look.'

She opens the door and puts her foot on the step, takes in a breath, exhales.

They have spent the day looking at houses with their sparkling swimming pools. Gardeners and maids who pause in their work to look her up and down. Houses where the estate agents look past her and talk only to Giorgio. Houses for a diplomat, a head of mission. Houses in which she will be expected to entertain.

This last house she likes. Not the modern main house with its unstructured open spaces and French windows, but the cottage behind a low hedge in the back garden. It looks and feels exactly like the advertisement in *The Herald*: . . . *old English country-style cottage with thatched roof, exposed wooden beams, stone walls and authentic fireplace, offset by a stream and lovely big trees in the golden triangle* . . . I can live here, she says to herself. This, I can manage. The absurd thought streaks through her head, I can pay rent to Giorgio; I can be independent.

Giorgio is impressed by the main house.

'Look,' he says, 'the baby's room.'

There is sunlight streaming through the window, splashing out onto the marble floors, everything bathed in a golden glow. She sees what Giorgio sees, what he wants for his child.

'We'll get it,' says Giorgio to the estate agent.

'Very good, sir, I'll draw up the rental agreement.'

'No,' says Giorgio, 'we want to buy it. It is the perfect place for our family.'

Giorgio looks at her, takes her hand, squeezes it. The estate agent turns to her, parts his lips in a sickening smile, the first time he has taken any notice of her.

'It is, sir,' he says, 'perfect.'

As they discuss the details she hurries away from them, to the back of the house, looks out over the stream to the cottage, her body shaking with rage.

She sits on the edge of the bath in the hotel room, listening out for Giorgio. Quietly, she takes out the razor from its packet. She holds her breath in and then she flicks the razor on her skin. A pearl of blood sits on her brown skin. She bends her head to it, sucks, draws it back to her body. She pushes the sleeve of her T-shirt higher: here they are, her tiny flickers of light.

33

'You weren't here, were you, George,' she hears from somewhere in the depths of the circle – it takes her a moment to realize that George is Giorgio – 'when that young American chap, driving around in a red car, got beaten up, a year or so ago?'

She is a guest at a 'soiree', hobnobbing with consuls and vice-consuls, a diplomatic spouse, in every which way but the law. She is at the edges of the circle, a drink in her hand, water she has dribbled some white wine into, stranded in the ebb and flow of the chatter. Until a moment ago the room was full of talk of the planes in New York and the bombings in Afghanistan. And then it shifted to local affairs, the latest gossip: hyperinflation, South Africa turning off the power supply, and now this.

'I remember that,' another voice pipes in. 'He was out in the bush with a local, a girl. Apparently he was in a right state when they found him.'

'Heard as much; they really worked him over.'

Giorgio stops the car on their way back to the house, switches off the engine. It is dark all around, only the distant whir of generators coming through.

'Cazzo!' he shouts, banging his hand on the steering wheel. 'I'm sorry, Gabrielle. I didn't know.'

She looks out into the night. The baby moves but she doesn't tell him.

'Gabrielle . . .' he says.

'I'm fine. I think I'll get in touch with Trinity, like you said.'

Their conversation falters and wavers over their drinks, and their university anecdotes sound stale and forced. Even their greeting was awkward, a half-hug, Trinity saying something about the baby bump she didn't quite catch.

They are silences where they concentrate on their food, look at the things in the room. They have met up in their regular student haunt, Makadors, which looks more dingy and tired-looking than she remembered it – she and Trinity used to go to the disco downstairs until paunchy, greasy men turned up with worn-out Eastern European girls. Pole-dancing and stripping took over, the place soon overrun with fat cats looking for a good time.

There are moments where Gabrielle feels that Trinity is waiting for her to 'open up', but every time Gabrielle feels herself being pushed there, she pulls back, *no, no*.

Trinity insists on paying the bill, pushing aside Gabrielle's hand.

'Please, Gabs, I get a super discount here, I can manage. Can you believe it, it's now almost one thousand dollars to the US, we're going the way of Zambia, fast track. Come, take me for a drive in your four-by-four. We can talk there with no fear.'

In the car, Trinity opens her bag, takes out a folder.

Gabrielle feels prickles of sweat on her forehead. She is about to be taken to a place she does not want to go. She thinks, before it goes any further, I can tell her to stop, *just stop*. She feels a resentment towards this friend of hers.

Trinity hands her the newspaper articles. Gabrielle silently reads the first one.

The Ambassador of the United States has filed a formal complaint with the Ministry of Foreign Affairs concerning the alleged mistreatment by unknown assailants of an American embassy employee. The male employee was alleged to have been attacked and beaten in a location out of Harare and has since left the country. The Ambassador alleges that these assailants are known to the government. The Ministry of Foreign Affairs spokesperson vehemently denies this accusation, calling it salacious and thoroughly unfounded. He took the opportunity to say that diplomats should not abuse their privileges in Zimbabwe and that the matter was being investigated by the police.

'Gabs?'

'I saw them beat him up, Trinity.'

She lifts the other page, reads:

'The observer from the South African Parliamentary Mission is an opposition white MP. In her press conference she claimed that she and a group of observers had found a torture camp run by Party Youth militia in Marondera. The Ministry of Foreign Affairs categorically denies this claim and says that the lady in question must be suffering from hallucinatory issues and is working to subvert the democratic process in Zimbabwe. The Minister says why have these so-called victims of the alleged torture camps not been identified, and further, why have there been no complaints to the police by the so-called victims. Zimbabwe is a country of Law and Order and will not be derailed in its democratic right to hold free and fair elections.'

'If you need to talk Gabrielle I'm . . .'

Gabrielle looks out at the people walking up and down the pavement, going about their lives.

Trinity sighs. She fishes in her bag, takes out a pack of Madisons, taps a cigarette out, dives back in her bag again for matches, stops, looks at Gabrielle's stomach.

'You don't mind me smoking, do you? I mean, the baby, all that stuff about passive smoking that's coming out.'

Gabrielle thinks she could do that, sit here in the car, a cigarette in her mouth, sucking poison into her body, into the growing lungs.

'It's all right, Trinity, just keep the window open.'

But Trinity stashes the cigarette, the matches, back in the bag.

'They go door to door in the townships. People just disappear. Zimbabwe is not the same country – the food riots really shocked them – but anyway, you're Ndebele, you've known the dark side of this place much longer than us, up here.'

'Yes.'

The Gukurahundi massacres in the 1980s when The Old Man had unleashed his feared Red Brigade to quell the 'dissident' uprising in Matabeleland. Thousands of ordinary people killed, bodies dumped in mineshafts.

'Now, you have soldiers back from the DRC. Ten thousand of them deployed in the rural areas to make sure that the vote goes only one way. What is happening there – Gabs, I have people who've seen things. This is not Zimbabwe. They're burning women alive in huts. A member of the opposition's wife, she had her hands hacked off and she was locked in her hut and they set it alight. Bodies are being found in ditches. Ha, we were so naive as students. Remember, even when we were calling him Vasco da Gama – we all thought he was essentially a decent man, it was those around him that were the bad apples. No more.'

Driving out of the city centre towards Westgate, Gabrielle listens to everything pouring out of Trinity.

'There're some units stationed in the high densities, beating up people, checking ID cards. The other day they stopped a commuter bus that had opposition posters on it and made the driver torch it. Also, with the farmers, their twenty-five-day grace period is up so the war vets have been busy that side, truckloads of so-called black settlers are, quote unquote, 'reclaiming the land'. And you must have heard about the white High Court Judge who's been arrested because he ruled against the justice minister. Things are falling apart, or more to the point, power is being consolidated.'

Gabrielle feels herself in that dangerous place of memory. At one level she continues to listen to Trinity and, on another, she turns away from her friend's words and delivers herself into the stretch of road, into the tread of the tyres on the patchwork of tar and the hum of the engine; she fills her head with these things, dulling out the past.

'Being a *Herald* reporter gets me into some off-limits places. I was in Hatfield Police Station three days ago and they brought in three opposition youth leaders. What the police were doing to them, Gabs,

I saw one go into a room with pliers – *pliers*. So, I'm writing some articles, eyewitness accounts. I'm getting them out through someone.'

Gabrielle looks at her friend.

'In between all the fairy stories I'm being made to write I'm getting some serious things done.'

'You are taking a huge risk, Trinity.'

'But this is what I want to show you.'

Gabrielle parks the car on the verge.

She looks at the booklet in Trinity's palm. She is afraid to reach out, take it.

'This is what they have been learning in the DRC. This is what they're implementing. There's also tribute paid to Sierra Leone, Rwanda. The Old Man is going to win these elections. The African Way. The Youth Brigade has already been busy in Ruwa and Mabvuku.'

Gabrielle feels a surge of revulsion and a sense of encroaching evil.

'I can't validate the booklet. I got it from a former CIO who has gone over the border. I want to find some way to bring this out in the open but I have to find someone high-ranking who is willing to turn.'

'Trinity, no. This is way too big for you. You don't know these people. You don't know what they are capable of.'

And, suddenly, she's crying.

'Gabrielle, I'm sorry, I shouldn't have just forgotten everything, I . . .'

Gabrielle clutches hold of Trinity's arm.

'That's the problem, Trinity. That's the problem with us. We are always forgetting. Look at me,' she says, 'I . . .'

But she can't go on.

Trinity puts the booklet back in her bag.

'What about Godfrey?'

'I haven't told him anything.'

An army truck rolls past them. The soldiers wave at them and Trinity waves back.

'We all have to stand up and be counted, Gabrielle,' her friend says, looking on at the truck as it disappears round a bend. 'You have to go back to your work.'

. . .

The Centre has become the offices of a driving school. She sits in the car watching people go up and down the concrete stairs, copies of *The Highway Code* in their hands. Where is Constantina? Is she still in the country or has she fled, a refugee in South Africa? She closes her eyes and sees herself in her office, getting ready to leave for court. Waiting for Danika. *Danika*. She gets out of the car, stands there, her back against the metal, breathes, breathes. She led Danika from this place to the courtroom to the barn, as if it had all been foretold, all so clear, inevitable. She did this. She has spent so long not thinking, and now here she is. Her responsibility, a girl she told could get justice, a girl she saw brutalized.

I – I – have missed my period, Miss Langa.

Miss Langa, Miss Langa, I am here.

I am very sorry.

They will come back.

There is something undone, incomplete, a reckoning she must make, but there is the fear, the terror, the hyena's breath. She breathes, here, now, all this air, and yet it is not enough, her mouth opening, closing, frantic, gulping, panting. She slides down onto the ground, the hardscrabble earth, claws at it, digs it up with her fingers, brings it into her mouth, takes it in, again and again, until she throws up there, empties her body out, but there is still the baby, its heart, growing, beating, beating, alive.

34

'Gabrielle, if you don't feel well we can drive you home.'
'I'm fine. Just resting.'

She's not 'fine', but she is going on this trip.

'It's an eighty-kilometre drive, the last ten on dust roads.'

'I'm pregnant, not sick. I want to go. You should be happy I want to do something, become engaged with the world. This is a positive step.'

On the road to recovery.

'I don't understand, why . . . it's out in the bush, Gabrielle.'

She waits. Waits for him to say the unsayable.

'I can take you on a mission nearer town.'

Of course he won't go there. She's delicate goods. She'll *make* him go there.

'I can't avoid the bush, Giorgio. Most of the country is the bush.'

'The baby, Gabrielle—'

'Will be fine.'

The car slips off the tarmac, rattles onto the dirt road, her heart drops into the bottomless past, the car rattling and shaking on the gravel, her body in the tight, hot, unyielding space. She opens her eyes into the red dust coating the car. Look, she tells herself, look. They might have taken you there, here. The drive seems endless, this choking dust, clogging her breath, her lungs, thick on her tongue. She could tell Nelson, the driver, to stop the car, she could get out, collapse on her hands and knees, lick the ground, take it into her. She was here, she thinks. I was here. A body in the boot of a car. A body thrown off the road. A car bursting into flames.

She sits quietly, stiffly in the car. She is fine.

The Hope High Primary School, partner school of Tongogara Refugee Camp School, sits atop a mound of earth that once was a grand colonial farmhouse and which now appears to be a series of outhouses in a state of breathtaking decrepitude. These 'outhouses' are the school classrooms. They are welcomed by much singing and ululation. Some part of her wants to scream, 'What's the matter with you people? Why are you so happy to see us? Look! Look!' As she gets out of the car the children start singing the national anthem. The headmaster is moving forward. She feels a moment of disbelief here. Is this really her, standing on this spot, school children singing, the gangly headmaster about to start fawning over . . .?

'Your Excellency, it is such an erstwhile pleasure to welcome you to . . .'

Yes, it *is* her.

Giorgio inspects first the new toilet block, where the law that each government building contain a picture of The Old Man has been strictly, scrupulously obeyed – there he is in the toilet, supervising the washing of hands. Then it's over to the three new classrooms and the renovated teachers' accommodation. Off he goes, down to the newly sunk well, watches as clean water is pulled forth. One of the children is called out. He recites a poem, his own, about the dangers of drinking water from rivers without treatment. *Bilharzia.* A small, timid-looking girl recites *The Life Cycle of the Bilharzia Parasite* in a sing-song voice. They are taken round to the vegetable garden. There are rows of cabbage, carrots, spinach, tomatoes and choumoellier. She can't turn her eyes away from the choumoellier while the headmaster goes on and on about 'Education with Production', the slogan from the 1980s. A high-pitched soliloquy on the wonders of germination, natural resources and crop rotation snaps her back to the present; a boy, a stub of a figure, stands between the cabbage and choumoellier, shouting his heart out. Two girls put on a little play about the joys of electrification and its dangers.

All the children erupt into 'Thank you, Mr Development Aid, thank you. We are so grateful to YOU!' And clap and clap and clap.

Giorgio gets up from his seat and stands before the expectant gathering.

'. . . And so I must express my utmost gratitude to you for allowing me to share in all the different areas of development that you have spearheaded and carried out so well. I can see that you have worked hard to create a wonderful place of growth and learning. Congratulations!'

They clap and clap and clap.

The car is on the road when, several minutes into the drive, they pass a convoy of Party supporters in three pickup trucks going towards the school. The sides of the trucks are plastered with The Old Man and youths are crammed in the back wearing red kerchiefs and white T-shirts with The Old Man's face emblazoned on them. *We should go back to the school.* The thought is there in her head. It is there as the wheels turn swiftly, effortlessly, on the tarmac towards away. It is there as she rests her head on the plush head-rest. It is there when she presses her hand on her heart, closes her eyes, willing sleep. *We should go back to the school. That is where they are heading. We should go back there to chase them away, use Development Aid bravado. We should go back to protect the voluble headmaster, the timid girl, the stub of a boy, schoolboys, schoolgirls* . . . but the car moves away, away.

35

This is what her childhood home has become: youths slung over the gate, hissing out at them; youths in groups on the property, the smell of home-brew, so strong it floods the open windows, settles into the car.

'Let's go back,' she says to Giorgio. 'I'll phone my father. I don't know what's going on here.'

She wants to lean back on the seat and sleep through all the hours on the road that will take her back to Harare.

She doesn't want to be here, with these boys. She came to bring her father news of her pregnancy, a fool's errand, she realizes now. She might be his only legitimate child but he must already have a whole busload of grandchildren to his name. What does one more matter? Time to face reality.

Giorgio is about to start the car when her father lumbers out from a group of youths, towards them.

'We can still leave,' Giorgio says.

She watches her father instruct the youths at the gate to open it. 'No, let's go in.'

When she steps out of the car the air seems to form a vice around her. She looks up at Giorgio and then away from him to her father, who is standing between two youths looking at her.

'I was expecting you earlier,' he says.

'There were roadblocks, Mr Langa.'

Her father winces. 'Comrade Red Danger,' he says.

She feels a burst of laughter in her throat.

'We are at war here,' her father says.

She looks beyond her father up to the house, at the verandah. She is going to be sick. She used to do her homework there in between her mother's elephant-ear plants. Now, there are big black drums, the smell of home-brew coming from them, youths with pots, cups, plastic tubs, scooping it out. She doesn't want to know what is happening inside, who is in those rooms of her childhood, what is being done.

There are rooms throughout the country, in Comrade Hitler's medical surgery in Budiriro, for instance, torture chambers. Youths, war vets have moved themselves in, kidnappings, beatings . . .

'Why have you come?' her father asks.

She feels her hand moving to her stomach, instinctively ready to cup the new growth, and then she stops herself, stands there before him, her hands behind her. If he has eyes he will see, he will know.

'Mr Langa, Gabrielle—'

'I am not talking to you,' her father says.

Her father knows what happened to her. While she slept in the cottage, he came and saw, heard from Giorgio what had been done to her. And still he went away, left her to fend for herself. He warned her, didn't he, that she was playing with fire? His allegiance is to The Old Man, isn't it? Why has she come? She knows now. Not for him. Looking at the house, seeing into the rooms where her mother once sat, glancing out back into the garden which her mother loved and where she once tended a wounded bird, no longer there, nothing but dirt and rubbish now, she knows that she came to seek out her mother. But her mother is not here. There is no refuge to be found in this place.

'Why are you just standing there? What is wrong with you? Khuluma!'

But she won't give him the pleasure of her words. She turns and walks away.

That night she dreams: snatches of that day. Ben and her in the cave, the sound of rushing feet, the voice calling out. She sits up in the

196 · IRENE SABATINI

dark, Giorgio on his back breathing noisily into the quiet. She has all this time tried not to think, worked hard not to get there. But she has come back. Ben lying on the ground, the men gathered around him. She closes her eyes, goes back to that place when she first set eyes on him, the type of person she thought he was, how he charmed her. And then there is his body on the ground again, stilled. He is back in America now. He has to be safe. She tries to imagine him there. In Connecticut. Tries to see him on a boat, sitting there fishing. She knows so little about him, but enough. They have between them that moment when terror came to them both. She pulls herself out of bed, clumsy with her weight. She walks slowly to the little room next to the baby's nursery and she types his name on the computer, searching.

Ben.

How strange it is, in that time together, she never once asked him for his surname.

Ben. Just Ben.

She looks at it for the longest time, touches it with her fingertips. And then she bangs the laptop shut.

PART FIVE

Breath

36

Here he comes, Mawara, dashing out from whatever he was digging up, slapping his paws on the front gate, barking and barking.

'Good dog, good dog,' she says, cuddling his head. 'I've come to take you home. Good dog.'

She rings the bell on the wall and waits; she is a guest now.

Before she can say anything, Mr Papadopoulos gives her a gentle hug, and then two kisses, one on each cheek. 'Come in, come in,' he cries.

She follows him into the house, down a passage into a large sun-filled room, and from there, out of the windows, she sees the cottage, her cottage.

'Sit, sit,' he tells her, and so she does. 'Do you want something to drink, to eat, my dear?'

The cottage calls out to her, and she takes another furtive glance at it.

I am here. I am unlocking the door, Mawara all over me.

'It is such a pity Sofia is not here, such a pity, she is in Cyprus,' he says. 'She would be so happy to see you.'

She smiles politely at the mention of Mrs Papadopoulos.

'You want to go and see the cottage, my dear? We have not rented it out since—'

She shakes her head. 'Mr Papadopoulos, thank you so much for—'

'It's nothing, nothing, my dear,' he says, waving her thanks away. He gets up suddenly. 'Wait here, I have something for you,' he says. 'I will go and fetch them.'

She sits there alone, her eyes cast down. She hears his heavy steps on the wood, the opening and closing of drawers. And here he is now, his hand, stretched out to her.

There are three brown A4 manila envelopes. She reaches out her hand, takes them. She is surprised by their weight. One, two, three – the envelopes are marked. Her name on top of the numbers.

'They are letters,' he says. 'I did not have a forwarding address.'

She sits at The Italian Bakery, the envelopes on the table. She lifts the flap open of 1, takes out the letters, twelve of them, unopened. She reads her address, looks at his handwriting, sees the stamps are from America, and then she lifts the last one, Tel Aviv, Israel. She looks out, as if she were expecting to see him come bounding up the steps.

She takes her bill to the cashier.

'Is Charles at the back?' she asks him. 'I would like to say hello to him.'

The cashier looks at her and shakes his head. 'No. Unfortunately he is no more with us. He has passed away.'

'Oh,' she says.

She is at the door when one of the waiters comes to her and whispers, 'He was badly beaten by the youths on his way home – he did not have a Party card to show them.'

She sits on the bench, under the oak tree. She is ready now to hear him.

New Haven, March 28, 2000

You're alive, Gabrielle.

I phoned the cottage and spoke to Giorgio. He said you were resting, sleeping. I woke up on a hospital bed. They wouldn't tell me anything about you. And then they shipped me out. I'm here, back home. You're alive. That's all I can think about.

Ben

She reads his words, over and over, until she knows them by heart. March 28, twenty-eighth March. Days and days after, he sat down, on this day in Connecticut, writing to her. He thought she might be dead. She could tell that the writing took effort and perhaps pain, how the pen pressed into the paper and then seemed to jerk off it, leaving the words jagged. She tries to think of him, to remember him, the details of him, the length and breadth of him, his voice, and she tries to see him, far away now, in his mother's house, the cuts and bruises on his face, his body slowly settling down on some chair, his head bent down, the pen in his hand, the discomfort, pain, and him writing down her name, *Gabrielle*. He called. She was resting, sleeping. That is what Giorgio told him. And, what more? Don't call again. It's not a good idea. She could imagine Giorgio saying those words. I know what's best for her. Yes, I'll tell her you called. He was doing what was best for her, taking care of her. None of that matters now. She has Ben's words in her hands, his voice clear to her.

In the next envelope there are pictures, five of them, and he's written on a white sheet:
   Gabrielle, one day, you and me, here.

A cabin in a forest.
   The Amistad Memorial.
   Van Gogh's *Night Café*.
   A boat in a harbour.
   A bench by a river.
   A man sitting on that bench.
   Ben.

A hat, pushed just behind his hairline, reveals that his hair has been left to grow. Dark glasses over his eyes. A muffler over his nose, mouth, so that all she sees are slivers of skin. She touches the bits of cheek, the bit of ear sticking out. She thinks, what terrible truths lie under the hat, the dark glasses, the muffler, what is hidden there. Is his flesh

cut open, wounds still to heal then, stitches. She tries to peer through
the glasses, cloths, to decipher who Ben is there.

Washington, May 15, 2001

Gabrielle,

*Mr Papadopoulos says that you've gone. Giorgio has whisked
you away.*

I'm here to get my next posting. Where are you?

Ben

She reads his words again, slowly this time because she wants to hear him.

On a single white sheet:

Tel Aviv, June 26, 2001

Gabrielle,

So, I've made it to the Middle East.

Ben

There are seven postcards.

The Western Wall.

The Bet Alfa Synagogue.

The Dead Sea.

The Church of the Holy Sepulchre.

The Shrine of the Friend in Hebron.

The Church of the Annunciation in Nazareth.

A cafe in The Jewish Quarter: on the back of this he's written: *I sat
here (x marks the spot) and thought of you eating apple strudel at Mimi's
in Sam Levy's Village.*

Haifa, August 3, 2001

Gabrielle,

*I phoned again, in case you were back. The more it rang the more
I had this idea that you were there, somewhere, in the bathroom, under*

*the shower, just coming in, and if I just hung in there you'd pick up so
I kept at it, just holding the damn phone . . . I've talked to the embassy
in Harare and they say that things are not looking good, so I hope
that you're not there; I know, I want you to pick up and for you to
be anywhere but in Zimbabwe. I want you safe. Are you in Rome?*

*There is so much going on here, I run around doing the assistant
cultural attaché thing, but it's the craziest thing that I find so many
places of quiet and they scare the hell out of me. I think of slipping
back into Zimbabwe, but you're not there, are you?*

Ben

She can hear the children next door splashing about in their swimming pool. She presses her back against the wood, puts the envelope to one side. She is in Zimbabwe. It is not where she should be, where Ben would have her be.

They have shared something terrible. But, there was also something beautiful that came before. Whatever it was was just beginning. It might have meant nothing. It might have ended as fast as it began. It might have been a mistake. Or there might have been what they called 'chemistry' between them; it had all seemed somehow so effortless with him.

She reads all the letters, twenty-four altogether, some of them pages long, some of them just singular thoughts, observations, as if she was with him and he had to share that moment, that experience, with her just then.

A single sheet of paper with a phone number. There is no date. When she turns to the envelope she cannot make out the date of the postmark. She does not know if this was written, sent, before the planes, if he was in Israel when terror struck in New York, or home.

A dog whimpering, scratching at a door, a car twisting and turning on a dirt road, a sharp cry in a moonless night, lights moving in the dark, grass rustling at the passage of feet, a white horse leaping out of the night, dust particles swirling, the slam of a door, her eyelids struggling, struggling to open in her dream, sleep, in her awakening, terror pulling them closed, until will, the sheer force of panic that she will forever be in this state, tears them apart and her eyes flash open into the bright dancing sunlight, a moment of unbearable loss and confusion, *where is she, where*, and then the sky, the ground, the air settling, the sprinklers *tsk tsk tsking* away, droplets of water falling on her, Ben's words dissolving in the rain.

She picks up the phone, begins to punch in the numbers, stops. She looks at the numbers on the screen, and then she puts the phone down. She drops the piece of paper on the table. For a while she sits there, slowly drinking a glass of water and then she picks up the phone again, punches in the numbers, all of them, and waits.

'Yes?' the voice says, A voice she thought was lost to her, forever.

'Yes?' As though they were simply picking off from a conversation, and perhaps they are.

'Hello, hello . . .'

She puts the phone gently down.

She is just coming out of the shower when it rings again. She looks down at it, lets it ring and ring until it wears itself out, stops. And then it starts again.

'Gabrielle,' she hears. 'Gabrielle.'

She sits on the bed, drawing the facts around her. Ben, who is in New Haven, about to leave in a couple of days for Israel; he had come home to bury his father. His voice had come to her, etched in tiredness and grief so that she saw him as she had never seen him before, imagined his face drawn with sorrow.

'I'm so sorry, Ben,' she said.

She knew so little of him and yet, here they were.

'Thank you,' he said. 'I can't believe it's you. You, Gabrielle.'

What did he look like as he said those words?

'I'm, I'm pregnant,' she said when the silence grew too much and she was afraid that soon there would be only the hum of his absence.

'I'm not married, I—' she said. She wanted to tell him so much but her voice caught in her throat.

'Ben, I, I can't believe . . .'

'I know,' he said.

He sounded exactly the same, and yet . . .

'Are *you* married?'

'No,' he said.

They hung onto the silence until finally she breathed into it.

'Okay, Ben, I just wanted to . . .'

'Gabrielle,' he said, 'how are you?'

'I'm fine,' she started, then stopped.

'I'm managing,' she said. 'There are good days, bad days. And you, Ben? I mean—'

'I wake up thinking of you, of—' he said. And they breathed into the silence again.

'I want to see you,' he said.

37

Ben's phone call – hearing his voice, knowing him to be well, alive and that he has not forgotten about her, that he has a need to see her – has put her, in these past few weeks, in a different space. Her day-to-day detachment from what is happening to her body, her life with Giorgio, what she will do after the baby is born, has given way to a kind of restless anticipation, of looking away from what is here to what might suggest itself. So, more than ever, she has not been seeing Giorgio. But now, she sees him, and he makes her fearful.

He shakes his head, tries to smile but it turns out more like a grimace.

'Nothing, nothing. We just had a visit. Let's enjoy our lunch. Any major movements today?'

He puts his hand on her stomach and a hump suddenly protrudes.

'Looks like she's got a big head,' he says, smiling up at her, the shadows under his eyes lifting for a moment.

'Who visited?'

He picks up a grissini, snaps it in two, gives one half to her.

'CIO. They wanted to have a chat.'

She puts the grissini down. Her mouth is dry.

'About what?'

'They wanted a list of all the NGOs we're funding. And they also expressed their disapproval about my visits to rural areas. They seemed to know a lot about what's going on at the office.'

'You have to get rid of Judith.'

Judith, Giorgio's flighty secretary with expensive tastes, who always looks at Gabrielle when she comes to the office with an exasperating mix of scorn and pity – *why haven't you been married by my white boss, obviously you are just being taken for a ride and now, look at you, pregnant, used goods*. The office gossip was that Judith was intimate with someone in the Cabinet and, hence, it would be dangerous for the organization to fire her.

'No, at least we know who it is. Besides, I don't think it's just her. I suspect a couple of the local officers. I hear one of them got allocated a farm in Ruwa.'

'How can you even bear to be around them?'

He shrugs.

She looks out of the window. An army truck has just pulled into the parking lot. She watches the soldiers leap out and head for the bank, thinks of the soldiers in the Congo, wreaking devastation on women, children, plundering diamonds.

'The woman from Save the Children, Sara, was she with you when they came, didn't you say you had a meeting?'

'Yes, she was.'

'She must have been frightened.'

'She was much more calm, cooler-headed than me. If she hadn't been there I might have said some regrettable things.'

'Good for Sara.'

'You can't stay here, Gabrielle,' Giorgio says.

She does not move her eyes from the images on the screen: clandestinely shot footage on CNN of a funeral which took place a day ago at the Presbyterian Church in Highlands, a farmer bludgeoned to death by war veterans. Pictures of the farmer fill up the screen as he once looked, vital and alive, descriptions of his brutal murder in front of his wife and two daughters, his body so savaged that he had to have a closed casket. Pans of war vets packed in tractors wielding machetes, the invasions in full force now, and then over to the church again where a crowd of youths and war vets are chanting at the mourners making their solemn way into the church.

'Gabrielle . . .'

She turns the TV off. Giorgio stands by the doorway, the satellite phone in his hand. Yesterday he came home with it, and, watching him testing it out, call out the code names, roger this, roger that, she had had an image of Ben in his flat talking into the phone as the Youth Brigade were marching up Tongogara Street.

He waits for her to say something, but she is transfixed by that phone in his hand.

'The war vets are dragging people out of beds at Avenues Clinic, Gabrielle, even the maternity ward. The office is already on code yellow, two more steps and we will have mandatory evacuation of non-essential staff, family members. I don't want to take the risk.'

You knew all this before, Giorgio. When they asked you to come, you knew what it would be like. She can't say this out loud to him. She just wants to sleep. Sleep. That's what she's become good at, the baby growing, growing.

'Gabrielle . . . I've made plans.'

'What plans?'

'Cape Town. You can go there. There are beautiful guest houses. I can stay for a week and then I can come during weekends. You will be near a clinic if . . . Gabrielle, it's for—'

'Yes, yes I know, it's for my own good.'

'Don't be like this. I'm only—'

'Okay, Giorgio, you're right, it's the best thing.'

38

'Welcome, Mr Fiori,' the white manager of the guest house beams at Giorgio, cricking his neck back into the 'at rest' position, having satisfied himself that no, there is no one behind the gentleman who might really be his wife, companion, other than the very pregnant, coloured, black, *it's hard to tell sometimes*, girl next to him.

He will register even more disappointment when she opens her mouth and he finds out that the female is not even the right kind of African, African *American*. So much for Cape Town being the sophisticated, cosmopolitan, racial-tension-free zone that Giorgio had promised her it would be, free from all that bad stuff down there in Jo'burg.

The guest house is in an exclusive enclave in Clifton Bay, inside a gated community. It's lovely and peaceful-looking with its whitewashed walls and flower gardens and it's only a five-minute walk to the beach. She can smell the sea and, when she is standing at the edge of the raised verandah, she has an incredible view of Table Mountain.

The fridge is well stocked and, on the glass dining room table, there is an extravagant silver dish of implausible looking fruit; she picks an apple up just to check that it is real.

'Do you like it?' asks Giorgio, who is standing in the archway that leads into the bedroom. 'There's an old-fashioned bath tub. Come and see. You'll love it.'

She follows him. She looks down at the claws of the bath and she is suddenly overcome by exhaustion and dizziness. The claws seem to her ominous.

'I think I need to lie down for a bit,' she tells him.

'I'll make something to eat. There are fresh prawns in the fridge. Do you think you can manage that? With some rice.'

'Maybe later. I'll have an apple now.'

She would like to take a walk to the beach on her own, sit down on the sand and just watch the sea.

There are sleek, gleaming vessels in the water. She imagines that they are full of playboys and oligarchs, beautiful women. She looks around her and comes to the realization that she is the only non-white person on the beach. This, she knows, should cause her discomfort and upset; she should say something to Giorgio about it, get up in protest and go back to the cottage, even insist that they go back to Harare and that she face the elections just like any other pregnant Zimbabwean woman. But she has no energy, no desire to pick a fight. Not now.

'Again, again.'

Turning, she watches a young blonde couple swing a squealing child, a girl maybe five or so, up and away into the surf, her feet wriggling in the air.

'Again, again,' she cries when her feet scrape the sand. 'One more time, pleeeeeeeeeeeease.'

Further down on the beach there are some boys playing cricket.

'Zimbabwe seems so far away,' she says, watching two men spreading a blanket out and then begin to unpack a picnic basket, a bottle of wine and two glasses.

'That's the point. Relaxation.'

She feels flooded with a sense of well-being, the cool sea air making her giddy.

'I love you,' she hears, Giorgio's lips against her ear, his finger moving strands of her hair over her ears.

She moves her head, shaking him off, shivers, draws her jersey tighter.

The little girl is now carrying a bucket of water with utmost con-
centration, the tip of her tongue sticking out. She pours the water into
the hole her father is digging and then she collapses onto the sand
giggling. Her mother turns, sees them and waves, calls out, 'Hello . . .
beautiful day.' Giorgio waves back.

'And look, Leah's happy too,' Giorgio says, putting his hand on
her stomach. 'Yes, she is doing a dance. The cha cha cha.'

There are tears gathering in her eyes and a tremor on her lips.

'What's wrong?' he asks.

'I, I don't deserve you. You're a good person.'

For a moment the thought sears itself into her that she might tell
him everything.

'Leah,' he says, his hand on her bump.

She picked it from a book of children's names. She thought
if she named the child she would love it. Giorgio was so excited
and encouraged by her initiative; he didn't seem to mind that
the name wasn't Italian.

'It looks like she will be quite a handful, non-stop energy. You will
be a great mother, Gabrielle.'

And something in the way he says that, the reassurance in his voice
that she will cope, the need he feels to give it to her, the presumption
he has of her fears, snatches her back into herself again.

She struggles up from the sand.

'Let's go,' she says, ignoring his hand.

She can't believe that in two days he'll be gone. The thought both
frightens and excites her. Since she's been here she hasn't woken up
once from a nightmare. She hasn't felt the presentiment of evil on
her bedside. It's as if she's been given a period of grace and she wants
it to go on forever. They haven't seen much of the area. She's been
content to either sit in the garden of the guest house or on the beach,
reading silly fashion and gossip magazines, dozing off. They've been a
couple of times to the Waterfront, both visits leaving her exhausted
and bad-tempered. Another time Giorgio rented a car and they

took a drive through the garden district and had a sumptuous meal in a hotel in Stellenbosch, overlooking some vineyards. She keeps telling Giorgio to go ahead and explore on his own, to go up Table Mountain, go over to Robben Island. But he feels he has to be here with her.

He reaches out his hand, touches her belly, smooths his hand over it.

And something inside her flares up, recoils; she swallows the anger, the bitterness, the disgust, swallows them back into her body, into the child growing, becoming.

'You will be okay?'

'Yes, Giorgio, don't worry.'

'I've stuck the manager's, caretaker's numbers on the fridge.'

'Yes, I saw them.'

'And the doctor . . .'

'Giorgio, I'll be fine.'

'Maybe we should arrange for someone to live in . . .'

'Giorgio, I'll be fine. Lots of pregnant women live on their own, plus I am in the most developed country in Africa. I'll be fine.'

'I'll be back during weekends. If I can, I'll try and leave late on Thursday.'

She stands by the edge of the water watching a child's beachball get picked up by the wind and spun into the sea. A man in red trunks jumps into the water and gives chase, his head bobbing in and out of the water, his hand reaching out for the round of inflated air, only for it to be whirled and twisted away by waves in their own game of chase. Further and further he swims, the ball seeming always just within his reach. And once, she thinks his fingers graze it before wind and waves laugh it away. She sees the man's wife and child waving their arms in the air, hears them screaming, their voices lost in the wind, *leave it, come back*, it's just plastic and air that he's risking his life for. The water laps at her swollen feet, her hands cradling her underbelly; Leah, warm and safe.

The man gives up, swims all the way back, comes out of the water, shivering, an air of embarrassment about him, his hands empty, dripping the sea.

When she looks down, she finds a fish lying, dying, on the wet sand. The tide deposited it at her feet. She watches its tail beat the wet sand, weakly. Its mouth gulps for air. She lets out a low, slow, strangulated cry, and then the tide carries it away.

39

He has come straight from the airport to the guest house. She struggles to her feet and is at once supremely conscious of what she looks like to him. A duck. A waddling duck. She stands looking at him as he lifts the latch of the gate. He is dressed simply, jeans and a white T-shirt, deck shoes; he might have just stepped off a sailing boat in Connecticut.

'Gabrielle,' he says, when he is still too far to reach out to her, touch her; he stands there as though he can't move, as though he is taking a measure of her.

'Ben,' she says. 'Ben.'

It is awkward, and yet . . . he walks slowly towards her, one, two, three steps, that's all the distance it takes and he raises his hand to her face, her cheek, and then he kisses her lightly there.

'Ben,' she says again, taking his hand in hers, and they stand for moment like this, listening it seems to the water crashing on the rocks below, the sound of seagulls wheeling and keeling above them, and then he bends over and kisses her gently again, on her lips, a chaste kiss.

They touch each other, their hands working on each other's faces, arms as though they are searching for broken bones, kneading, setting them back into place.

She finds scars; along his right ear, a thin scraggly line, as though someone has taken a jagged piece of glass to his skin.

He draws back the sleeves of her dress, finds the story etched there on her skin, and she lets him look, massage his fingers over them as though he can rub them away.

You're alive, he'd written, and she is, here with him.

She looks down at his feet and as though he understands, he takes off his shoe, sock, and shows her the scar on his left foot. She wants to reach down, cradle it but she is clumsy with her weight. And she starts to cry, softly, quietly at first, and then the sobbing racks though her, her shoulders heaving until she grows afraid that she is damaging the child somehow, and she hates that he sees her like this; she takes gulps of air, tries to calm herself. When she looks up at him she sees that his face is in his hands and when she takes them away they are wet with tears.

She cannot tell him what she feared. The car in flames. The two planes crashing into the buildings.

The sun sets and it grows dark. They sit there in the moonlight, listening to the water.

They go inside and they eat; there is fruit, cheese and bread, milk, water.

'Where are you staying?' she asks him, and he tells her of a hotel.

'I should be going,' he says, because he's misunderstood her question, the intention of it.

'Stay,' she tells him.

And so he sleeps there with her, the two of them on the bed, his hand resting on her belly, as if it is the most natural thing in the world, and she breathes him in, every particle of him, this man, and she closes her eyes, opens them, closes them again. He is here.

She wakes up, and he is no longer there. She finds him on the terrace, a cup of coffee in his hand. She has spent months and months of not knowing, the minutes, and hours, the days and months, ticking, falling away. And now he is here.

He turns.

'Good morning,' he says.

'Good morning.' She stands with him, looking out into the water. 'It's beautiful, isn't it?' she says.

'Yes. Gabrielle—'

He wants to talk, she can see that. It is too much, too much. She wants to be here, here.

'Ben, let's just, let's just . . . you're all right, aren't you, that's all I need to know.'

He looks at her and says, 'Yes, I am,' and before he can ask her she says, 'And so am I. You're here.'

It is the second day. Tomorrow he will leave. He will go back to Israel.

They walk down to the beach, he in front of her, his hand raised to hers, leading the way. The sea has calmed down, and the sun is shining, a chill in the air; the seagulls looping and diving into the water. They are alone.

They talk about their walks with the dogs in the gardens – Rum, she finds out, is still in Harare, a beloved embassy dog – their first meeting, his red car . . . and then they fall silent and listen to the things that are in the air between them, unsaid.

The baby moves and her hand flutters over her stomach onto the fist or leg or elbow there; and her body, what remains of it that is hers, shudders. He's watching her, and she him. She watches him to see if he's judging her, or if he has already condemned her, and when she doesn't see any of this she says it anyway. 'This,' she says looking down at her stomach, 'it just happened.' And the tears are there again. 'God, I'm pathetic,' she says. 'What's wrong with me?' The question takes up the air and he holds it and turns it back to her.

'Gabrielle, we should talk about what—'

'No,' she says. 'No.' She is trembling, shaking. She is here in this place, now. She does not want to go back, there. 'Just hold me,' she says. 'Hold me, Ben.' And he does.

It's evening: she lies there, her head on his lap, her belly a mountain she rests her hands on, his hands on her hair. And she knows that they have come to this point, and she breathes and says, 'Tell me, Ben.'

The hands lift for a moment, brush against her forehead, his finger on her cheek.

'I wanted to get back in,' he says. 'Through South Africa, Botswana, Zambia.'

She feels his hands in her hair again, his fingers on her scalp.

'The embassy said they were doing everything they could.'

She listens to him, her eyes closed.

'Gabrielle . . .'

'Gabrielle,' he says again. She knows that he has come to the place he has tracked, back and forth, since that moment they stepped out from the dark into the light and now he is here.

'Gabrielle, I'll never forgive myself, I . . .'

'Don't,' she tells him. 'Don't.'

'The very worst thing was,' he says. 'Waking up, and not knowing about you. No one would tell me anything. I thought that they were keeping some news from me, that they were in a hurry to ship me out before I found out that . . .'

She struggles up from his lap, sits there, looking at him.

'I felt, I feel responsible, Gabrielle. Completely responsible. Those first words, Gabrielle, those first words we heard, they ran loops and loops in my head, the sound of that voice. But just before that voice I felt something, the atmosphere had changed. It was . . .'

And now, she is telling their story too.

'Evil. I couldn't see you properly after they were around you, Ben. I heard all those terrible noises, and then silence. I kept thinking, come on, Ben, say something, say something. I wanted, needed you to be okay. As long as you were okay I would feel safe, that whatever was going to happen wasn't going to be too bad, that's crazy but it just felt so unreal, I . . .'

She weeps with him there, in the small room by the sea.

He leaves her, on the third day.

She lies in bed, watching the elections on the big TV screen, her hand on the remote, switching from channel to channel. Giorgio has been instructed to stay in place, in case a humanitarian disaster unfolds, something that might require his particular expertise, if enough people are beaten, killed, displaced, starved, if enough youths are unleashed to do The Old Man's bidding. He calls every hour, as if she's the one in danger; she must keep him abreast of her movements so that, at any moment, he can leap on a plane. But, of course, it's the baby he's worried about. The manager of the guest house checks in on her too (Giorgio's instructions); she knows he's seen Ben but is too tired to worry about him telling Giorgio, or about the looks he gives her. She has broken some code, she knows; she has done Giorgio a wrong, but there is Ben in her life again.

It looks like all of Zimbabwe is voting. She phones Trinity, but can't get hold of her. She worries about her friend, what stunts she is willing to pull to follow her story, how ignorant she is of what can happen. Brave, reckless Trinity.

She falls asleep and when she wakes up, the voting has ended. The waiting game begins.

The drama and brutality of the presidential elections has yielded The Old Man his victory – so onwards with land confiscations, indigenizations, beatings; what does he care if the international community condemns him, if the Commonwealth suspends his country's membership, it just shows what a revolutionary he is.

Giorgio waits in place for another week, and then he is on a plane to come and take her home. They will have to drive back because the airlines won't let her on the plane, but she insisted to Giorgio that Leah, her daughter, was going to be born in Zimbabwe.

PART SIX

Captive

40

A n emergency caesarean because the baby is breech: the terror of the general anaesthetic, the doctor filling her veins with sleep; a primeval fear, unconscious, unresponsive, helpless, unknown hands touching her; she had woken up feeling that something terrible had happened, that the baby was damaged somehow, certain that the voices hovering over her, whispering, knew the awful truth. Those first months spent in a perpetual state of fear, of what could be done to Leah by anything, of what damage she could do to her. There were visions in her head, grainy images that haunted her, a child lying still and unmoving in the water because she had forgotten, lost herself elsewhere. There were times when she got up over and over and over again, to check, to make sure, that she hadn't done something, hadn't forgotten, hadn't harmed. She imagined herself as one of those mothers who forgot their children in a locked car in the heat of October or who drove off with the car seat on the roof. Or she was the other type: the type that deliberately harmed, who drove their children, fastened into their car seats, into a body of water; called them into the bathroom, one by one, and slit their throats; muffled their breath with a pillow. She felt herself capable of such horrors. She was terrified, so she distanced herself from the growing creature, from its care, its wants, its cries. She left her to Giorgio, who had fallen hard in love. He cradled the baby in the crook of his arm, swayed it gently to sleep. She would come upon them both, asleep on the armchair that Giorgio bought for her when he imagined her nursing Leah; Leah and her, mother and daughter, for those moments when Leah would lie snuggled against her breast, suckling away. But that hadn't happened. She couldn't bear the *tug, tug, tug* of the child against her breast. She felt repelled by it, by how much of an animal it turned out she was, her tits hanging out like any cow, dog, monkey, feeding its young. She hated the sight of the baby's milk (*her* milk) drooling out of the tiny mouth, the smell of it, curdled. The nurse suggested she express, which seemed to her even more disgusting, milking herself into a plastic bottle or getting it pumped out of her. She lasted five weeks, and then it was over to the bottles. Her breasts punished her for her pettiness; they ached and heaved with the wasted milk, they heated up, the cold cabbage leaves she put in her bra wilting within seconds. But in a week they had shrunk and, for the first time, she felt she could look at the baby as an object apart. She could watch it grow.

'Pa pa, pa pa,' demands Leah. 'Pa pa, pa pa.'

Gabrielle feels something inside her shake loose, plummet. No, no, not now, not now, when everything was going so well. They have got through the day. She packed it with events at Greenwood Park, aided by Trinity and Patrick. Train rides and baby trampolines and merry-go-rounds and boat rides. They have had dinner. But, as soon as she mentioned bath time, Leah flipped. Because bath time was all about pa pa, pa pa.

'Pa pa, pa pa,' cries her daughter, pointing to the door. 'Pa pa, pa pa, come, *now*.'

Leah flexes her plump fingers and toddles to the door.

'Pa pa, come, *now*.'

Something shifts and turns, flutters in Gabrielle. Don't panic, she tells herself. Don't panic.

'Pa pa, come.'

Gabrielle hears the rise in her daughter's voice, the tremor there. *Don't panic. Be calm.*

Leah stands by the door, looking up, up at it, waiting. The door will open and her wonderful pa, pa will be standing there, ready to sweep her off her plump feet.

Gabrielle breathes.

Gabrielle counts, one, two—

'Pa pa, pa pa, come!'

'Leah,' Gabrielle says, 'Papa's at work. He's coming later.'

Oh God, how false she sounds. How can she expect Leah to believe in her as this mother being when she sounds so fucking false.

'Pa pa!'

Leah is standing there, talking to the magic door.

'Pa pa come.'

Gabrielle walks, she walks to the door, to where her daughter waits for magic to happen.

'Leah,' Gabrielle says, 'Papa's working. He's coming on Tuesday. Sunday, Monday . . . Tuesday!'

Leah's fingers splayed on the bad door, *slap slap slap* on the big bad door.

'Pa pa, come!'

'Leah—'

Slap slap slap.

She grabs her daughter's wrists, too hard, too hard. Leah screams and she lets go. Leah's legs, arms, jerk up and down, thrashing on the carpet of the room, letting out blood-curdling screams . . . *pa pa! Pa pa!* . . . and Gabrielle can do nothing but watch over her until she is tired out, exhausted, asleep on the floor.

She looks at Leah, asleep there. Same thick, curly dark hair and pouty face, same sparkling eyes as Giorgio, two years old.

Giorgio had been nervous about leaving her alone with Leah. If she'd said that to him he would have denied it angrily; it wasn't part of his script, to have doubts about her. But they were there. He wanted her to be a normal Madam, to fill the house with a live-in housekeeper, house-girl, cook, and perhaps, who knows, even wet nurse, masking his fears as attentiveness, wanting to make life easier for her, par for the course of his, their station, the accumulation of servants. She had refused. She had had a lifetime of house-girls at her childhood home.

She had seen their handiwork but, what was more, what she felt deep inside, was that she didn't want any witnesses to her culpability, her ineptness with Leah. She didn't want any spies, any report backs to 'Sir'.

In the morning she had watched him pick up Leah, kiss her forehead. 'Bene,' he said, standing by the door with his bag, and then he was gone, off to his meeting in Pretoria. She had stood there alone in the room in a state of shock. There were the two things to take hold of. Giorgio did not say goodbye to her, and she was alone. Alone, with Leah. The whole of Sunday loomed. What would they do? What would she do? What would Leah do? What would they do to each other? There was no escaping: the crèche was of course closed and even if she ran off to the agency, just to sit alone there in the office, what would she do with Leah?

Giorgio was furious with her when she got the job at the employment agency. Her job was to be de facto wife and full-time mother. Leah was too young, he said. Wait until she starts at the international school, he said.

Twice, they have been called by the crèche, once for hair pulling and the other time, the more serious case, for biting. The supervisor showed them the bite marks on the little boy's arm. Giorgio's immediate reaction was that Leah must have been provoked somehow. He only ever saw the angel child, while she got the brat. Tantrums were left for her and others to deal with. Giorgio brought out the cherub; she, the devil child, Chucky One, Two and Three. Leah pulling her hair, her earrings, biting her ankles, thrashing about the floor like some rabid dog – Giorgio dismissed all of it as the terrible twos.

'She's energetic, easily bored.' Meaning he thought he had sired a genius.

And then, 'She shouldn't be in the crèche in the first place, Gabrielle.'

'I have a job, Giorgio.'

'At an employment agency.'

She was, apparently, too good for an employment agency. If she was going to do anything it should be something in the legal field; he had, after all, dragged her law books all the way from here to Colombia and then back again; they were now gathering dust in the garage. He held out the carrot of consultancy work with aid agencies; he had the contacts.

There *is* something wrong with her. How can she feel so detached from Leah, as if she is someone else's child? She named her but, in her innermost thoughts, she knows there is a hole where that thing called love is meant to be.

A teaspoon of cough mixture. Mother's Little Helper, was what one of those ladies at the mother and baby group called it, her secret remedy. *It has a sedative, works wonders, especially on long air trips; my paediatrician recommended it. And it's just the thing to quieten an over-excited child. No harm done. A bit of peace and quiet all round.* Gabrielle pretended shock like some of the other mothers but, in her head, there was the pulse beat of recognition, excitement, and the knowing of it; the lure of that secret remedy made her deadly afraid. Because, she, *she* would not stop at a teaspoon, she knew it in her heart, she would give the child more, just a little bit more, for peace and quiet.

Giorgio is right. She is not to be trusted.

Leah does not come running into the bedroom as she usually does when Giorgio is around, as if she knows that there will be no fun and games today. No scooping up from the floor and twirling up high, round and round, and kisses kisses until she is squirming, hysterical with them.

Gabrielle gets out of bed, walks over to Leah's room, sees her still asleep, arms and legs spread open like a starfish, the sheets, blankets kicked away, still dressed in yesterday's clothes because she, Gabrielle, mother person, didn't have the guts to take them off, change her into pyjamas, in case she woke up and the drama of the missing father started all over again. She had picked her daughter up from the floor, but first she had considered just letting her sleep where she was, covering her body in blankets.

She will have to wake her up. She will have to bathe her, brush her teeth. She will have to get her dressed. She will have to get her breakfast. She will have to make sure that she eats it. She will have to coax her into the car for the trip to the crèche, get her buckled into the car seat. She can't think beyond that. She just can't. After six months at the crèche, Giorgio tells her she still wails for him when he leaves.

She sits on the edge of the bed, contemplating action. She looks at her watch. Forty-five minutes to get her act together. Too little time. She puts a tentative hand on her daughter.

'Leah,' she says, 'Leah.'

Her daughter blinks her eyes awake, and Gabrielle tells herself she is being truly pathetic when she thinks that it's disappointment that she sees in Leah's eyes.

Leah allows herself to be dressed (Gabrielle forgoes the bathing and the brushing of teeth), to be sat at the breakfast table, allows herself to eat and to be coaxed into the car. Gabrielle is grateful for her acquiescence, but strangely appalled. It's as if her daughter expects nothing from her, has already given up on her, knows truly where love and nourishment are and knows they are not present today.

There is no wailing at the crèche. Not for her.

She unlocks the door of Fisher Employment Agency and walks straight into her office. She has been doing this for six months now. Each morning there is the thrill of knowing that her day will soon be owned by the jobseekers who will come through the doors of the agency, either with a spring in their steps or a resigned shuffle.

It was funny how she secured the job, having sent in her CV with a bold line on top – *Any work except in the legal field*, which pretty much nullified the value of her CV. Isobel Fisher had called her in to the office, asked her gamely, so why *not* law? and she had replied, I just want to spread my wings.

The thought of practising law again had filled her with a rage that frightened her. She could not trust herself in a court of law, what might come out of her mouth once she swallowed away the fear, what truths she might spit out. She could become a lecturer at the university and feed those innocents lies upon lies? No. She would become something new, even if it meant starting from the lowest rung. She would work anywhere, be anyone. Maybe she would retrain as a teacher. Yes, teach English in secondary schools. Or go and work in an advertising firm. Administrative work . . . she would do something where she didn't have to think: sell clothes, shoes, coffee . . . it did not matter. She would start all over again.

Isobel had given her a querying, searching look, and then laughed and said, Well, what about spreading them around here then?

Isobel was a white Zimbabwean in her thirties with sharp, angular features, married to a Swiss archaeologist, Tomas, who was a lecturer at the university.

They had become friends, having lunches together, watching each other's backs in the cut-throat world of the business which was, according to Isobel, teeming with poachers and sharks, 'Oh, and of course, racists, that goes without saying.' Gabrielle was still reeling from last week's meeting of the Annual General Meeting of the Union of Employment Agencies, which had taken place in one of the townhouses opposite Ben's complex. Isobel had warned her that it was going to be dire, packed with bitter white hold-outs who did not have a good thing to say about working under the black government even though, in the early, post-independence years, business had thrived, what with the inflow of aid capital and donor-sponsored projects which required labour.

'The dears will be careful about what they say with me around, and you, Gabrielle, you're coming with me, that will really throw them off.'

Isobel was prepping her over gin and tonics for the horrors to come.

'I know that the trick is for me to keep cool, dismantle their rants calmly but Gabrielle, honestly, I never manage it. The cunning bastards have probably already had the real meeting. This one's just for show, keeping up appearances. They'll probably bring in some black face, call him a manager, public relations. You'll see them in action.'

And she had. The trouble started with Mrs Dickson of Dickson and Dickson (Isobel had warned her that was where it would most likely arise from), which was the oldest agency in the country.

Mrs Dickson apparently did all the talking at these meetings. She was the voice of experience, reason, vitriol, the good old days.

'I want to share a recent experience with you all to keep you on guard. One of my placements, a sales rep, actually had the nerve to come into the office, all threatening and what, shouting that I was stealing money from him. Can you believe it? He doesn't want to pay the commission. I told him that that was the contract. Two salaries, fifteen per cent each salary.'

She stood there in all her puffed-up indignation, heads nodding vigorously. Yes, theirs was a tiresome calling.

Gabrielle felt Isobel's pent-up fury, the deep breath she took before she opened her mouth, saw that her friend's hands were trembling.

'Two salaries, fifteen per cent each salary, that's a bit much, isn't it?'

Bodies and faces turned to look at her, and then slipped over to Gabrielle, pursed lips.

'That's thirty per cent.'

Mrs Dickson took a breath of her own. 'Time and labour, girl. It took us forever to get this young man a placement and you can no doubt see why. I wouldn't be surprised, now I think of it, if he isn't related to a former terr— I mean, fighter; they're getting clever these days, wiping that out of their applications. Can you believe, we used to have application letters signed by the likes of Spillblood, Comrade Stalin? Delightful. I'm sure people will be falling over themselves to employ that.'

There was a heavy, protracted silence. No one could quite bring themselves to look at Gabrielle. Mrs Dickson had been in full flow, everything but her own outrage shut out. Isobel stepped valiantly into the breach.

'That's just bullshit.'

'Isobel!' This was from Mrs Smith, the evening's hostess. 'Language, my dear.'

'Well, I'm sorry, but it's bullshit. You can't just arbitrarily take thirty per cent from someone's salary. We should have guidelines as an organization, on fair practices.'

There was a lot of huffing and puffing, tut-tutting.

Gabrielle opened her mouth. 'As a lawyer, I must warn you that you could be liable for severe damages should a case be brought before the courts.'

A thousand eyes bored into her.

Afterwards, she and Isobel had celebrated their triumph over a bottle of wine.

'You see, I'm the one with "the Ideas",' Isobel said. 'And they blame it all on my mother, "the Artist". One day I'll tell you all about her, Gabrielle, how she scandalized these small-minded gits.'

Isobel comes into the office wearing one of her long Indian skirts, beaded sandals and a dreamcatcher earring. She looks every inch the rebel, hippy, foreign, exotic specimen that the agency ladies can't get their heads around.

'Gabrielle, I need your lawyer brain,' she says, plonking herself down on the chair where the jobseekers usually sit in front of Gabrielle.

'It's about Tomas. He's been contacted by some group calling themselves the Relatives of the Slaughtered. It's about that report that's going around, about the massacres in Matabeleland in the eighties.'

Gabrielle feels something swoop onto her, heavy on her shoulder.

'They want him to help with pressuring the government to dig up the mass graves.'

Gabrielle had received the Catholic Commission for Justice and Peace report in her inbox, forwarded to her by someone she didn't know. Giorgio had a hard copy of it. She had scrolled down the document, reading snatches of it and then she'd deleted it. Days after, she was tense with the thought that the government, with their new Chinese technology, could track down every single person who had received the document, those who had opened it. Giorgio, together with other Heads of Missions, had been summoned into a meeting by the Foreign Ministry where they were lambasted about the ownership or dissemination 'by any means' of the document which was 'full of untruths and exaggerations, a treasonous fabrication of the opposition and its sponsors'.

'They think because he's European he'll give their cause publicity—'

'He'll get expelled.'

'Exactly! That's what I told him. His work permit is coming up for renewal and – Gabrielle, what's wrong? You look a bit woozy.'

'Nothing, nothing, probably low sugar; I didn't have breakfast.'

'Here, I've got a doughnut.'

While Isobel rummages around in her straw bag, Gabrielle seeks refuge in last night's phone call with Ben, the relief of his voice after Leah. She talks to him every week on the phone: in the beginning she made the calls in public phone booths, but she has become careless, reckless, calling him from home, even though the numbers show up in the itemized phone bills, and Giorgio can see how often she calls, how long she stays on.

'What's wrong?' Ben asked her.

'I'm just tired,' she said.

He was on home leave, in New Haven, getting ready for his next posting. He wouldn't tell her where it was.

It has been more than two years since those three days in Cape Town. Two years. They have talked about seeing each other again, talked about where and how, and there's always something that keeps her from taking that leap.

Then, there was the long period of silence from him when she thought he was with someone.

I want to see you. The thought had jumped into her head that he wanted to see her again to say goodbye. To put an end to their story, as he began his new life with someone else. So that he could have a clean slate. *How you are.* It was as if he was reaching from the furthest place right deep into her, as if he understood how lost she was, and that he was offering her a respite from all the pretence, where she wouldn't have to try so hard to snap out of it and get on with being a mother, a 'wife'. Four years was enough, wasn't it, to get over it?

'Here,' Isobel hands her the doughnut. Gabrielle brings it to her mouth but the smell makes her nauseated.

'Where was I? Oh right, so Tomas thinks he should do the right thing, you know, join the cause, so I need some kind of iron proof argument about why he can't. Suggestions of deportation won't cut it.'

'It's dangerous, Isobel.' She sees in her words Ben beaten on the ground. The thud of feet on him. His silence. They could have killed him. Easily. They could have put him in the red car, set fire to it with him inside, simulated a car accident, like they have done before.

'I know. That's what I keep telling him but he just won't let the thing go. To be honest, I'm scared, Gabrielle, and trust me, I don't scare easily.'

Gabrielle is distracted by Isobel's dreamcatcher, the feathers and beads hanging from the 'spiderweb' hoop that will catch all the bad dreams and evil. Isobel gave her a proper one to hang over Leah's cot. Her daughter needed protecting, that was for sure.

Isobel is looking at her expectantly.

She can only reiterate what she has said before. Don't get involved. But then she thinks of Trinity and what she is doing, how she is involved, and how Trinity expects her to be involved, to get back to her lawyer, activist self. It is exhausting what this country demands; after everything it does to you, it still wants more of you to beat up.

'Isobel,' she says at last. 'He'll do what he thinks is right.'

'Bugger it,' says Isobel. 'I know.'

There have been no incidents at crèche today. In fact, Leah was unusually quiet. She receives the words as accusation, admonishment. What did she do to Leah to make her so *not Leah*? But as soon as they reach the house, and the gate slides open for the car, something seems to click in her daughter because she starts up again.

'Pa pa, pa pa . . .' her fists banging on the car door window.

Gabrielle drives in, tries to get Leah out of the car seat but there's kicking and scratching and biting.

'Leah, stop,' she screams. 'Stop.'

But there is no stopping her. No stopping her unless she can magically produce Giorgio, magically teleport him here, now. And so she does as yesterday, stands there, useless, grateful for no witnesses, except for Mawara, allowing her daughter to scream herself out, except this time she's strapped in, she can't harm herself. Gabrielle knows that this is not right, *this is not right*. So she tries again, manages to snap off the seat belt, manages to lift her daughter's rigid, arching body, tries to get her out of the car, gives up (fearing that she will bang Leah's head on the edge of the door), tries to put her back on the seat, to strap her in but Leah won't have it; she slides down to the floor, her body now wedged between the passenger seat and her own booster seat.

'Pa pa, pa pa . . .'

On and on and on.

Until at last it is over, and Gabrielle lifts her and carries her into the house.

Dinner. Bath. Bedtime.

Giorgio will be back tomorrow. The clock will be reset.

The phone rings and she thinks of not answering it because she knows it's Giorgio, then does because it would be criminal to make him worry, and all that ringing might wake Leah.

'How is it going?' he asks her.

'Fine, fine. She's asleep.'

'Already? I was hoping to—'

'She had a very active day at crèche.' The lie slips out of her so easily. What is wrong with her?

'Ah good, I was worried that—'

'She's fine.'

'Good, good, okay, I have to go to a dinner. See you tomorrow.'

There was a time when he would never have ended a conversation without saying he loved her.

'Why?' he asks again.

They are sitting outside on the verandah. He is holding a glass of wine; she watches him put it down on the wrought iron table between them. For once she has not drunk anything, as if she knew that she would need a clear head; funny how Giorgio tonight was intent on making her drink, as if he wanted to forestall her.

She looks up at him, at his wounded eyes.

'I have to,' she says. 'He was there.'

He flinches as if she's hit him.

'He knows,' she says.

And that's what it is. The everything of it. He knows. He was there.

'Then talk to me, Gabrielle, talk to me.' His words, so weary, a plea, a cry. Tell me what it was like to be there. Let me in.

'I can't, Giorgio. I can't. I'm sorry.'

'So, you want to go to be with him. And I'm supposed to say, *yes, that's fine, you have my blessing.* Is that what you want, Gabrielle?'

She latches onto the one thing, and she knows she's doing it, validating her position, invalidating his. *His blessing.* It is always about him.

'I have to go.'

She sees the twitch of his lips, knows that he is holding back things that could so easily come out of them.

'We have a family, Gabrielle. What about Leah?'

He has not said, what about us?

He takes her hand, squeezes it. 'Listen to me, Gabrielle. If you go to America, I'm sorry, but if you go there, our life here will be—' He drops her hand and for a moment they are the two of them together, the unsaid word bristling between them, and then he gets up and goes back inside.

PART SEVEN

Shelter

41

She is going to this far-off place to meet a man she knows, and does not; a man she has shared very little with, a whole life. She is coming back to him. But, what is there to come back to? An image, images. A first meeting at the vet's surgery. A few walks in the gardens with their dogs. Cappuccino and pie at Mimi's. A gallery visit. The drives in his red, shiny car. A lunch, pasta, in his flat; a barbecue. A kiss. Kisses. Their bodies curled up against each other in the dark of a cave. The harsh light of their awakening, the words slicing through them. Three days in a guest house by the sea.

Letters. Phone calls. Emails. Pictures.

She sits in the plane, his words on her lap. There are tears and smiles, up there among strangers, her heart beating, slow, fast. There is no sleep. She is there in the clouds; should the plane explode, her body might float out there for an instant before it begins its tumble. The image is there: her arms outstretched, her eyes closed; there is grace and beauty, eloquence in the still, moving body, her body returned to her. Or, she could disintegrate, just like that, bits of her hurled into space. She is nothing, and everything.

A story was beginning with him. It might have ended, or endured . . . become something ugly, distorted with truths, untruths, the unsaid, or grown into a thing of beauty, a love story, a romance, a life; there might have been heartbreak.

She woke up this morning, kissed Leah goodbye, Giorgio standing in the doorway, watching her take the taxi, away from him. *How can you do this?* were the only words he spoke to her. How can you be so cruel, so unkind, how can you spit on everything I've done for you? How can you do this to us? To Leah? It was all there in his eyes. This was something he would never forgive, she knew that and still she left.

After hours and hours of flying she has arrived. JFK International Airport. She follows the signs to Immigration, her head throbbing with a growing conviction that she has made a terrible mistake. What madness is this that she has come across the world to see him. What stupidity. Walking to Immigration she looks out for signs for the toilet, *restrooms*. She wants to splash water on her face, try to fix her hair, take out her travel toothbrush and, when there is no one by the sinks, quickly brush her teeth. She wants to straighten her T-shirt, rub water under her armpits. She should have packed a change of clothes in her carry-on. She wants to spray herself with the tiny perfume spritzer that she got at the perfume counter at Oliver Tambo Airport. But there are no restrooms.

The more she walks the more she is certain that the immigration officials will single her out, take her to a back room where they will ask her probing questions about the nature of her visit. And when she gives her ridiculous answers they will send her packing on the next plane back. They will look at that green passport of hers with the Zimbabwe bird on the cover and already have their suspicions: ah, one of those who will overstay their welcome. They will look at her visa with scepticism, despite the embassy contacts Ben gave her to expedite the process. But the immigration official turns out to be friendly and when he hands her passport back he booms a cheery, 'You're all good to go.'

She collects her suitcase, hands in her customs form and then makes her way to the Arrivals Hall. It has been so easy, so far. Too easy, she thinks. The hard part is coming.

She scans the waiting crowd, can't see him, feels a flutter of panic, takes a step back, bumps into a trolley and then she hears,

'Gabrielle.'

And there he is.

There he is.

He kisses her. He puts his arms around her and kisses her, literally sweeps her off her feet. It must look like the thousands of greetings that take place at airports all the time. How would anyone know that they have not seen each other for so long, how strange and complicated their situation is.

He is wearing, it seems, the exact same clothes as the ones she last saw him in, in Cape Town, as if he has just stepped off a boat. His hair is short again, not as short as in Zimbabwe, but shorter than when she saw him in Cape Town.

'You're here,' he says, when he finally lets go of her.

They are silent for a time as he manoeuvres the car in and out of the gridlock, the road surging with those iconic yellow taxis she has seen so many times in movies. THE EMPIRE STATE, she reads on number plates. She sits there taking it all in. She is here. In this car, weaving in and out of traffic, somewhere now in THE BRONX, she reads on the road signs. She is here with Ben. But this time he is driving just a normal, modern, black four-wheel-drive, an SUV, one of several that she sees on the road, nothing that stands out, that draws attention to itself.

Halfway across the bridge, over the vast expanse of water, she feels herself close to tears.

'I, I didn't know bridges could be so . . . so awesome,' she says, smiling, remembering how that word sounded when he said it.

'Oh, wow,' she says, as she catches sight of the skyscrapers of Manhattan, the famous skyline, and in the next instance she can't help but think of those two planes flying into those towers.

There it is. The Big Apple.

'I can't believe I'm here, Ben. I feel like I have to pinch myself. It's so strange.'

He puts his hand on her thigh, and she puts hers on his.

He turns into a road that says Exit 6. They are on Interstate 95, going straight out of New York to New England. Connecticut.

A police car, lights flashing red, white and blue and siren sounding shoots up alongside them and then past, tails the car in front of them until it comes to a stop on the verge of the road, the police car behind.

'Have you ever been stopped?' she asks him.

'Not by a state trooper; a few times by regular cops. Not as much as in Zimba . . .'

His voice trails off, and she wonders how careful they will have to be with their words, their memories.

'You good, Gabrielle?'

'Yes, yes, just a bit tired.'

Her eyes fluttering, opening into the moving car, a pulse of confusion as she looks out into the road.

'Hey,' he says.

She is here with him.

'How, how long have I been asleep?'

'Oh, about an hour.'

Somewhere in the state of Connecticut, the nervous tension had completely left her body.

'We're almost there. How you feeling?'

'Fine, fine.'

How small and imprecise that word is. How can it describe the jumble of emotions that she is experiencing at this very moment? The shock? The bewilderment? The relief? The conflicted joy?

They drive past little towns and, looking at the smart, double, three-storey houses made of wood along the road, neatly laid out side by side with small, well-tended lawns, she is incredulous: they are completely unfenced, no walls, no burglar bars, expensive-looking cars parked casually in their driveways, as if thieves and murderers don't exist here. She says so to Ben. Some of them don't even have *picket* fences. We have guns, he says. There are flags on just about every house, *the stars and stripes, the star-spangled banner*. She tries to imagine this back home, a flag proudly displayed; everyone would think that you were a rabid Party supporter.

The car glides along – past rustic farmhouses, swathes of greenery on either side, heading up, up to that famous cabin by the mountains.

She can't get over the abundance of everything: water, trees, mountains, sky, air.

Him.

There it is. Here it is. The cabin. His cabin, nestled among the tall pine trees.

'There used to be many more trees,' he says as she stands there, taking it all in. 'They were destroyed in a tornado.'

She breathes it in. All of it.

There is the smell of something sweet: crêpes, waffles, pancakes. She finds him in the tiny kitchen, a stack of pancakes piled high on a dish. She spies on him until he must feel her there, breathing quietly, for he turns round and she knows that this is not a faraway dream. She is here, with him.

'Hey,' he says.

'Hey,' she says back. She walks the few steps of the room, past the wood stove and the basket next to it with wood chips, past the two chairs with leather seats which bring to mind the handmade furniture at Doon Estate in Msasa, just outside Harare, her bare feet stepping on the three rugs and then she is there, standing in the little nook, the pine seating forming a booth around a square table, the pancakes on it. Above the kitchen sink, she can see a path meandering through the towering white pines, perhaps all the way up to the mountain.

He has watched her short walk, said nothing as she came to him. And now that she is here, she is aware that she is wearing the first thing she found in her bag, one of those Nelson Mandela shirts which she bought for him as a kind of joke.

He kisses her.

'You look really hot in that.'

'It's actually yours.'

'Okay, not too sure I can pull it off. How you feeling?'

'Good,' she says.

She *is* feeling good, tired but good. She woke up several times in the night, disorientated, but then she felt him there in the dark, breathing, and she had drifted back to sleep.

'What time is it?'

'Eleven o'clock.'

She tries to do the maths.

'Five o'clock in Zimbabwe,' he says.

A shadow passes over her, the thought of what she's left behind, what she might come back to.

'You must be starving,' he says. 'Come on, let's eat.'

They stay in the cabin for the whole day. A few words pass between them and then silence, touch. That's enough.

He takes her for a walk, a fishing rod in his hand, a bucket of bait, worms, until they reach a stream. She's never seen so many trees. Never. Not even in Nyanga. The air's so fresh, clean and pure, she feels it almost a travesty to breathe into it. She watches him leap over some rocks and then cast out his rod. *Fly fishing.*

Evening, and he grills the trout he's caught in the stream. They sit outside on the verandah, *porch* he calls it, eating.

She listens to the night sounds. The call of animals she knows nothing about. Could one of them be the leaping moose she has seen on road signs throughout the drive?

She thinks of Leah and Giorgio, but they seem in another world now.

She closes her eyes, breathes in this night. She has so much to say. She tells him everything but the one thing. She will not say it, name it. She will let its memory, its telling, float and sink and be lost for now. She is with Ben, here.

42

The house, a mansion really, is white and spread out over three, four floors, one of the grandest of what Ben calls *New England colonials* which line this street with its plentiful trees and pristine, manicured lawns, a street she imagines a paper boy cycling up along in the mornings with his basket of newspapers, tossing each paper onto the porch.

He rings the doorbell twice and then he puts his key in.

Gabrielle stands in the hallway, light streaming through the windows. The light catches her by surprise.

'Mom!'

'I'm in the kitchen.'

A light, musical voice.

He leads her through a winding passageway until they must be somewhere in the back of the house.

A woman, shorter than Gabrielle, her face, seemingly without make-up, gently lined as though someone has delicately traced lines over paper, her hair, an undyed white, cut into a wispy bob, is standing by the kitchen sink, wiping her hands on a towel.

'Ben,' she says. 'And you've brought along your guest.'

There is an elegant girlishness to her. She could be any age, from fifty to seventy. She is, in every conceivable way, the very opposite of what Gabrielle supposed a maths professor, a maths professor at Yale, would look and sound like. There is nothing at all severe about her.

She moves towards Gabrielle, her arms open.

'Hello, I'm Eva. Ben forgot to say that you are quite lovely.'

Ben holds his hand splayed on his chest.

'Shame on me.'

'Well, it's true. Come on, now, let's get out of here. Let's go to the living room,' Ben's mother says, reaching out for Gabrielle's hand; Gabrielle has the eerie feeling of a small bird, a robin, a woodpecker, brushing against her hand.

The sliding doors of the living room are wide open and, outside, there is a deck which leads out into a wooded area; beyond that, there is a glimpse of water.

'That's the Quinnipiac,' says Ben, following her gaze.

'It's so beautiful here,' she says, a catch in her throat.

'You should really see it in the fall, Gabrielle,' his mother says.

'That's autumn,' says Ben.

'I know,' says Gabrielle, smiling up at him.

He is standing there between them, one hand in his pocket, the other in his hair, looking on, watchful.

'Well, fall in New England is quite something to behold, Gabrielle. Ben must have told you.'

'No, no, he hasn't,' she says and her mind is swept back to one of their very first conversations when he told her about fishing and skiing and sailing and she had wondered if these were the normal things an African American man in New England did.

'The leaves turn gold, vermilion, orange and that's just the maple trees. It's quite a sight. I'm originally from the Midwest, prairie country and, after all these years, fall in New England still takes me by surprise.'

'Heads up, Gabrielle,' Ben chimes in, 'there are six gigantic leatherbound volumes of pressed leaves somewhere in this house. Don't let her talk you into looking at them, you'll be stuck for hours, they date back from nineteen fifty—'

'Hush now,' his mother says, waving her hand at him. 'Don't listen to him. Come, come sit down, Gabrielle.'

She turns to sit but her eyes fall on the half-moon table of hard-wood across the room – on it, the curves and shallows of a sculpture set against the white wall, caught in the shaft of light.

She can't look away from the sculpture, and suddenly she is walking across the room, putting her hands on the stone, the coldness warm and familiar. In the stillness that has enveloped her she traces the lines of the stone, chiselled there she knows, but they are so smooth that they seem organic to it and she sees now what Ben meant by the face of Modigliani's women there in the stone, coming out of it, which is the face of the masks of the ancient kingdoms of Benin.

'An Ant Eating a Woman,' she says.

'Yes.'

She hears in his voice his concern, his worry, that perhaps the sculpture should not be here, in this room, that she should not have seen it.

'It's perfect.'

'Gabrielle, would you like something to drink? Lemonade and something to eat, sandwiches, I'll . . .' Ben's mother makes to get up.

'No, no, I'm fine, thank you.'

Gabrielle sits down on a sofa, one of three in the room, although there is no possibility of lounging on it – *settee*, seems somehow more appropriate; it is where the Victorian ladies of the Brontë novels she read for school might sit, doing needlework and gossiping. There must be other rooms for lounging in. Don't Americans have 'dens'? Is that where the TV and comfortable chairs are? The house is big enough for two, three living rooms. They must now be in just one wing of it.

His hands rest on the sofa back, just above her head, a finger grazes her forehead, hair. She feels herself stiffen, conscious of how they must look to his mother, her son, this foreign woman.

'Thank you, thank you for having me here. You have an incredible home.'

'Ben's father's grandparents built it, and it's a great pleasure to have you here, Gabrielle.'

Suddenly she has this feeling of being overwhelmed. What is it? Ben's mother's kindness? Tiredness? Ben must see it for he picks up her bag and puts his hand on her shoulder.

'Mom, I'll just show Gabrielle up to her room.'

'Come here,' he tells her. He is sitting on the bed.

She sits down on his lap and he starts undoing the buttons of her blouse.

'No, Ben.'

'*No?* Why?' His head cocked to one side, his fingers slipping between the buttons to her skin.

'Ben, your mother, not in her house. It's, it's disrespectful.'

His hands are cold on her neck. He bends down, nibbles on her ear.

'No, Ben,' she says, trying to wriggle out of his hands.

'We'll have to check into an inn then. I'm not staying here without being able to touch you, that's just crazy.'

'Don't be silly.'

The word, unexpected, out of her own mouth, takes the breath from her.

'Gabrielle, what's wrong?'

'Nothing, I, nothing, that's the word Leah uses all the time, *silly*, I . . .'

'Tell me about her, what is she like? Show me a picture.'

'No, Ben.'

'Why – why not?'

'Because I'm here. And they, she doesn't belong here.'

Her words shatter something between them. For a moment she sits there stiffly, and then she gets up.

'Ben, I'm sorry . . . I came here. I left them in Zimbabwe. I . . .'

'I'm not asking you to choose, Gabrielle. I just wanted to see a picture of your daughter, that's it.'

'I don't have one,' she tells him. 'Strange, isn't it, a mother who doesn't carry around her daughter's picture.'

She looks out of the window, at the silver of water beyond the foliage.

'You grew up here,' she says. 'I thought I'd never see you again, Ben.'

The shared memory is there between them, so thick and potent she feels that she could touch it, give it words.

43

He wakes her early and, after a quick breakfast of coffee and a doughnut, he takes her for a walk, up and down the streets of his neighbourhood – Quinnipiac Avenue (Quinnipiac, Ben tells her, means *long-water-land* in the language of the Native American tribe that lived here) and Lenox Street; the historic river district with its colonials, its sweeping Greek- and Italian-style villas, and fantastical gothic manors which look like something the Addams Family would live in. They stop often so she can take pictures of the magnificent homes, all the while Ben peppering her with the history of the place: a fishing and oystering village founded in the eighteenth century, called Dragon by the settlers, which later became part of New Haven.

'When oystermen got richer they moved away from the shoreline to here. It's a real mix of people in this area.'

'Yale professors and—?'

'Other professionals,' and, as if he has understood her other, underlying question, 'African Americans, Italian Americans, Puerto Ricans; I hate to be a walking tourist board ad but you don't get this kind of diversity just anywhere in New England, ma'am.'

'As long as you have money,' she says, and regrets it instantly. It sounded like she was accusing him of something, the audacity of that given where she lives in Harare.

'You're right. Although quite a few of the homes are rentals. Further up, on top of the hill, there's public housing.'

'The projects,' she says, without thinking, and then is momentarily confused as to whether this word from the movies isn't somehow derogatory. Would it be better if she had said 'the hood' or 'the ghetto'?

'Yes.'

She wants to ask him about crime, but doesn't know how to without being offensive.

'New Haven gets a bad rap.'

'How so?'

'I don't mean to put you off but, as we speak, it's currently slated as the Number One Most Dangerous City in New England.'

'Oh,' she says. It's hard for her to believe this statistic in this quiet street.

'But I'm safe with you,' she says, playfully nudging him.

They stop at the church where his family worships. St James Episcopal, its granite or sandstone masonry making her think of the cathedral building near the school, back in Bulawayo. She tries to see him here at his father's funeral, going up those stairs with his mother, and she wonders if that's why his mood has shifted; he seems to have retreated into his own thoughts, as though something has started to bother him, weigh on him.

She would like to go inside, but he takes her hand and they walk down towards the water.

He says it without any fanfare as they stand there on the bridge, as if it is the most natural thing in the world for him to say.

'I love you, Gabrielle.'

There is a silence; she follows the arc of a bird sweeping from the bank, over the bridge, along the water until it disappears out of view.

When she turns to look at him, he is not looking at her but out at the water.

'Ben . . .'

His eyes, looking intently at her now, carry his words, hold them.

She is, all at once, overcome by a feeling of annoyance; no, it is stronger, sharper than that, irritation and anger at his words. What does he love? Exactly what? What can he love? Is this part of his guilt trip, loving her? It strikes her then how many times Giorgio has said those words to her. She has never said them to him.

The bridge is starting to get busy with pedestrian traffic so they too move, to the other bank. They watch some fishing boats going out. Further down, by the boat house, there's a man putting a canoe in the water.

She leans into him, breathes in the morning air. She could now say those three magic words back to him. She only has to open her mouth and let the words out.

This river is calm and gently meandering, nothing like the rivers in Zimbabwe, unpredictable and full of hazards: bilharzia, crocodiles and hippos. There is no walking on a muddy track, at least not along this part of it; there is a concrete pedestrian path following the turns and bends of the water. They pass a man casting his fishing rod over the green rails. Ben tells her how polluted the river was – he points out the old brewery, one of the polluting culprits – that and overfishing killed off the oyster industry; it's only recently that they've started to clean it up. To her it is all idyllic: the trees, oaks, beeches and willows, the ducks, and the timber houses in whites and pastel blues, greens, the church spires, all of it full of a quiet charm and beauty.

They walk up along Front Street, Ben calling out a *hello* or a *what's up* now here, now there, stopping to introduce her to some folk, marina types who ask him about his boat, who seem genuine in their warm greeting to her. She is highly conscious of herself in this place, aware of walking with a native son; startled passers-by giving her the once-over, checking to see who one of their own has brought home.

Ben points out the old oystermen cottages. They walk past the luxury townhouses and flats, *condominiums*, and then up along East Pearl Street, Grand Avenue, where there is a brick church which Ben says used to have a really tall spire called the first skyscraper of New

England; it was so tall it swayed in strong winds so it was removed, and, behind the church, the cemetery, many sea captains buried there. His father, he tells her, was cremated. He doesn't say about the ashes and she doesn't ask him.

They double back, have lunch at a restaurant that overlooks the river; its walls are full of pictures of the neighbourhood in the eighteen and nineteen hundreds, oystermen working, milling about. She has clam chowder with fresh bread rolls, which she likes a lot, and there's the thought of him, the apron tucked into his waist, bringing the plate piled high with pasta alle vongole, the first time she had ever had clams. She has so many questions to ask him, and she gets in as many as she can, interrogating him again. Does he still paint? *Yes, occasionally.* What happened to his pictures, the ones in Harare? *No idea.* The thought of them still being on those walls in that flat stuns her.

She wants to know him. How he seems so different to everyone around him and yet is so himself. Comfortable in his own skin, she supposes is what the books call it. The pictures she's seen of him on the landing in that grand house, a hippy-looking student – she was right about that haircut back then. There are no photographs of his mother or his father and she wonders about that. Is it a kind of modesty or his mother's sense of privacy and decorum? Are those pictures in another wing of the house or in his mother's room, in albums deemed too personal, too intimate, too revealing? She wants, for instance, to hear more about the legal fight to build that incredible house on that street, did it go all the way to the Supreme Court? She wants to know more about his great-grandfather, who owned a grocery store and a quarry, who built wharfs and worked as an oysterman at some point. A black man in the eighteen hundreds in America, an entrepreneur, like her father it could be said, about all the battles that were fought so that he, Ben, would get to live this life.

In the afternoon, he drives her downtown. He shows her around the Yale campus with its faux medieval buildings, what he tells her are neo-gothic arches and turrets, but impressive to her because she does not know what the real thing (in Oxford, he says) would look like, or if it would look any different. Sitting on a bench they watch a group of students, male and female, play a game of *pickup* football, the American kind which is like rugby. Some of them are wearing T-shirts with a 'Y' and the face of a bulldog in it, Yale's logo for its teams. They are running, shouting, wrestling each other, calling 'touchdown!' There are some couples further away on the lawn, some studying, others just hanging about. A male student stops by a statue, puts his hand on the tip of the shoe of the man sitting on a chair and rubs it, burnishing the tip even more. Ben has already told her that it's a tradition or 'superstition', rubbing the shoe for luck. She thinks of the UZ campus, tries to think of a piece of such well-manicured lawn, open to students at any time, but there's nothing to compare. UZ has shabby tennis courts and a neglected swimming pool, all of it surrounded by untamed bushes and grass.

She hears another shout of 'touchdown', and watches the victorious players give each other high fives and slump down on the grass. What could these students possibly have to complain and protest about?

'Lobster rolls.' She says this out aloud and Ben looks at her, puzzled.

'Remember,' she says. 'That's what you told me you Yale guys protested about.'

'I was exaggerating,' he says laughing. He gets up from the bench. 'Come, the gallery will close soon.'

They pass students walking, riding bicycles, jogging. There are some lingering by a noticeboard.

'Let's see what interests Yale students, Ben,' she says, tugging him over to the board.

'Probably some Yale–Harvard match up, brinkmanship is the name of the ga—'

There are flyers tacked on.

STOP THE SILENCE – FIGHT RAPE ON CAMPUS

A joke was already on her lips – *oh, not lobster rolls, Ben, but . . .*

She reads a flyer silently, feels that she is nodding her head. She knows that Ben is still with her, standing just behind her. That he is reading what she is reading. Thinking what she is thinking. Or maybe he thinks she is thinking of Danika's court case and soon he will make a comment.

'Let's go,' she says.

They cross the park – *The Green* – where he points out the tall elm trees which gives New Haven its nickname, 'Elm City'. There are homeless men on the benches under the trees, nursing drinks hidden in brown paper bags. Supermarket trolleys piled high with clothes, mattresses and blankets, and whatever else has taken the men's fancy, are scattered along the path – *vagrants* is what *The Herald* would call them. They pass a woman having a spirited conversation on her cellphone, shouting sporadically into it, 'Where he at? Where he at?' They cross the street and he shows her the Amistad Memorial in front of City Hall, in the exact same place where the prison used to be which held the slaves. She takes in the bronze monument, its three panels, the reliefs of body parts of the slaves who jumped or were thrown into the sea. This happened in the eighteen hundreds, not that long ago in the history of mankind – what does it mean to live and be part of a country that has done that to your ancestors? She thinks of that conversation they had in his car when she was ashamed of her ignorance. He takes her hand.

'I'm going to Iraq,' he says.

When she turns to look at him he is not looking at her but at the memorial.

'Iraq?'

'Iraq.'

'Why?'

He looks at her now. 'They're short of volunteers for the embassy. I volunteered.'

'No, Ben, no, it's dangerous, you could—'

The absurd thought flares: he is punishing me. As if all she needs to do is to say the magic words – *I love you* – and he would take back this madness.

'It's the right thing to do, Gabrielle. The embassy's highly fortified. It's probably the safest place in Baghdad.'

On the plane here she saw the pictures from Abu Ghraib in one of the newspapers, the Iraqi prisoners being abused by American soldiers. She read of the anti-American protests erupting in the Middle East.

'I, I don't understand, Ben, why can't you wait till after your elections, everything could change—'

He squeezes her hand.

'It's done, Gabrielle.'

At the university art gallery he shows her Van Gogh's *Night Café*. He waits for her to say something, to call back the quaint memory in Harare when he told her about it, but she is silent, unmoved. Her feet echoing on the wooden floor as she follows him around the maze of white walls, trying to focus on the works of art hanging on them, the colours and the brush strokes, catching fragments of his words – *Hopper, Pollock, Basquiat, O'Keeffe* – her eyes glancing over a group of primary school children seated on the floor at Picasso's *First Steps*. She tries to bring, fix, herself to the moment, to be moved, enchanted like Ben wants her to be. But she can think of only one thing. He is going to Iraq.

They are supposed to meet up with some friends of his who are in town. Dinner at a place called Pepe's for 'the best pizza in America', and drinks. She tells him that she's tired but he should go, she'll have an early night. She's relieved to find that his mother's not home, so she can go upstairs to bed with no need for polite chatter. In her room – she is even more grateful now that she has her own room – she thinks of going downstairs to ask Ben if she could use the phone. She wants to hear Leah's voice. But then she remembers the time difference. Zimbabwe is six hours ahead, isn't it? So, it must be way past midnight. She lies on the bed, closes her eyes.

'Gabrielle.'

'Yes,' she says, her eyes still closed. And then, 'Come in, Ben.' The words sound so formal and stilted, as if they are strangers and he is a guest in his own home.

'I want to show you something,' he says. 'It won't take long.'

44

In the morning, when she awakens in his room, he is not there.

Standing on the stairs she hears sounds coming from the kitchen and she is just about to go down there when, turning round, she spies Ben's mother sitting out on the deck, reading. It would be rude to tiptoe past her. Gabrielle steps out of the room and, for a moment, thinks of turning right round again because Ben's mother seems deeply engrossed in work. But then she looks up and smiles.

'Hello,' says Gabrielle softly, feeling awkward to be here without Ben, to be presenting herself alone to Ben's mother so late in the morning.

'Good morning, Gabrielle.' She puts a finger to her lips, says, 'shuuu' and points towards the kitchen.

'Ben's putting together a picnic basket, let's leave him, shall we? Come, sit down.' She pats the wicker chair next to her. 'Have you had something to eat?'

Gabrielle sits down on the wicker chair.

'Yes, thank you.'

She is too shy to say that when she opened her eyes she found a breakfast tray with a wildflower in a glass on the dresser.

'He's taking you to Lighthouse Point. There's a beach and park and probably the oldest carousel in America. When he was a boy he just loved to ride the one horse, Man Man, he called him, he's white with a red saddle, and it had to be just that one.'

There is a moment of silence between them, Ben's mother lost, it seems, in some memory, perhaps of a day when they went up to this

Lighthouse Point and she watched Ben going round and round on the horse, hugging it tight, squealing his delight.

'He was heartbroken when they closed it, the wear and tear from the sea air and hurricanes. But they've fixed it up now and reopened it.'

She has the feeling that Ben's mother has been patiently waiting for her to come downstairs. She is struck with unease at the direction that any serious conversation between the two of them might take, although there has been nothing from his mother's gestures that has conveyed disapproval, dislike.

'Ben says your country's quite beautiful, particularly in the east, I think.'

'Yes, Nyanga and Vumba. The pine trees in Nyanga must have reminded him of this place.'

Ben's mother smiles. 'So he took you up to his little cabin.'

'Yes.'

'Not the most accommodating of places.'

'It was how I imagined it might be like up in the mountains here, how an American cabin would look like – that sounds so inane . . .'

'No, when I first came here I was also taken by it. It is a charming place.'

There is something in how she says charming, something sad, regretful, memories.

'Gabrielle . . .' Her hand is on hers, pressing faintly down. 'He was so excited about going to Africa. He even got that ridiculous car of his sent over. He'd been tinkering and tinkering on it since high school. You should have seen it when he got it – junk, pure junk. He had to have it towed here, that's how awful it was. And he fixed it up. He did that.'

His words resound in Gabrielle's head – *Nineteen fifty-nine, El Camino, a coupe utility vehicle, good for town and country. A classic.*

'I don't know the extent of what happened in your country, Gabrielle, but when he came back it wasn't just his broken bones that troubled me. There was so much grief and a rage in him. I had never seen him so off-kilter.'

Gabrielle looks down at their hands. His father was alive when he came home in that state, perhaps just diagnosed with cancer.

'And then one morning he was standing just there by the door and I was sitting here and he said, "I've found her."'

Gabrielle remembers that moment when she found him.

'I knew immediately it was you and when I looked at him I knew then that he would be fine. He would be fine. He started to paint again, soon after.'

Gabrielle breathes in. He came back home to bury his father. Ben's mother is telling her that, in that time of grief, finding her, Gabrielle, again was a type of salvation for her son. How much has Ben told her? What does she know of this Gabrielle who has come to be with her son in her house? Does she know that she lives with someone, that she has a child? Upset and anger would be reasonable reactions for her to have if she were to know this about her son's lover. But from the very first moment Gabrielle set eyes on her, Ben's mother has only given her kindness and warmth. She realizes, as the tension slowly leaves her body, that she has been bracing herself for some kind of scene, an explosion of anger and accusation. A confrontation where Gabrielle and her dysfunctional country would be made to account for the harm they brought to her son.

'He won't let me see or hang any of his new work. They're all down in the shed, his studio. Perhaps when he's done with all this wandering about he'll . . .'

She shakes her head free of the image of her son in a war zone, in danger again, Gabrielle thinks.

Ben took her to the shed last night. When he had switched on the lights she had gasped, like so many years ago in Harare. The canvases were everywhere. Once again there were the colours, but more muted now except for the one painting which stood on the easel where its burst of yellows fixed her gaze and brought the tears to her eyes: it was her as he imagined, remembered her. She stood there, dazed.

'I started sketching them in Zimbabwe,' he told her, 'as soon as I got back from the open day at the vet's surgery.' And there she was, sitting under that flamboyant tree, her head turned, looking at something out of the canvas.

'I knew it then,' he said, as she took in what it meant that he had held who she was for so long. 'I knew it.'

'He came late in my life. I was in my forties, an unexpected gift.'

Gabrielle thinks of Leah. The weight of her in her arms, newborn.

'He loves you, my dear. You do know that, don't you?'

She tries to understand what it is his mother is telling her. Don't hurt him. Don't play with him. Be honest with him. Lie?

'I—' she begins, but then Ben's voice suddenly blows into the room.

'Okay, Gabrielle, let's go!'

Looking about her she is once again caught up in the spell of this trip, that she is here in this place, that she is standing against the backdrop of a lighthouse and an antique carousel and beyond, the beach, the promenade, the sea, the view of New Haven, all of it as if it were a dreamscape. And Ben standing beside her with the picnic basket, smiling at her, at her wonderment.

'Seriously, how can you *not* be happy here, Ben? Just look at all this, the boats . . . Ben, where is your boat?'

She feels shy, as if she has spoken out of turn, said something too personal, indiscreet. He puts the picnic basket down and wraps himself around her again. He slides his hand under her arm, lifts it so that it travels over the water, and is pointing out to the eastern shore.

'Over there. We actually drove past it, she's moored at the New Haven Yacht Club. I was thinking we could take her out tomorrow.'

'You mean . . . go sailing?'

'Yep, I figured I'd let you get past the jet lag before taking you out to sea.'

'That sounds . . .'

She can't find the word to say, to give this thing that is being given to her, the breadth and depth of her emotion.

She thinks of suddenly doing something crazy like taking off, running across the sand, barefoot, into the water. She spins round instead, points over to the carousel.

'You have to take me to see Man Man, Ben!'

For a moment he is startled and then he throws his head back, 'Ha! So, Mom's been talking. Manny, I think is well and healthy. Later, you can hop a ride, become acquainted.'

'I hear you were quite heartbroken when they put him—'

'Yep, I won't be leaving the two of you alone again.'

She helps him lay down the blanket and then she sinks her body on it, her eyes closed, happy to have the feel of him around her.

The music from the carousel mingles with birdsong and the high cries of excited children. A sudden pang when an image of Leah arises: her daughter rushing into the pavilion for a ride on the antique horses, the pleasure of her squeals. The dreamscape suddenly shatters and she is standing on shards. She sits up abruptly.

'What do you want, Ben?'

He is busy unpacking the picnic basket and now he stops, a bottle of wine in his hand. Something snaps in her head. She is caught and fixed on this image of him. She is blown away by the past that comes barrelling into the present: a picnic basket swinging from one hand, her hand in his other. What's in there, Ben? she'd asked him. She had never found out, the basket left unopened on the ground.

'What do you mean, Gabrielle?'

The picture dissolves, but she still wavers between now and then, is upset that he does not see what she sees, does not feel the past's pull.

'You must have had . . . you must have . . .'

He won't make it easy. He won't give her words.

'Come on, Ben. It's been so long. You can't tell me you haven't had someone, other girls.'

'You're here, that's all that matters.'

'Ben, I, I just can't. I—'

And then the words thrust themselves out of her.

'I was raped, Ben.'

She covers her face with her hands, breathes into them.

'I'm sorry, Gabrielle. I'm sorry.'

She takes her hands from her face, shows herself to him. He is there. The same Ben from moments ago, before she spoke.

'I've never said that out loud to anyone. Not Giorgio. Not Trinity. It's always there in my head.'

She closes her eyes, breathes into the quiet.

'I, I was lucky. It was just the one.'

Danika is there in front of her.

'I was raped.' She says it again to him, to herself.

His eyes are ever steady on her, not wavering, still.

She is not alone.

45

She does not know anything about boats but the beauty of this boat, which Ben has just stepped on, speaks for itself, the polished wooden parts setting off the white. *Eva.*

She is standing on the jetty – a new vocabulary that he gives her, *jetty.*

'So your dad's company built this?'

'Actually, he built this one almost single-handedly. Mom was terrified of going out on a boat, so dad said that he would build a boat and the boat would be hers.'

'That's so romantic, Ben.'

He looks up from the rope he's untying. 'Yes, I guess it is. It's the first boat my mom ever stepped on.'

'And sailed on.'

He shakes his head, smiling. 'No, she stepped on it and then right off it.'

'It's still romantic.'

There is a faint breeze and the air is filled with the tinkle of wind chimes or bells. She marvels at the boats, pristine and inviting – Ben has shown her a *schooner* – the wonder of its many sails – like he promised he would back in Harare. She looks out at the sea. She breathes it all in, deeply, and when she turns back to him, he is there on the boat, watching her.

'The bells,' she says, as she too gets into the boat, his hand out-stretched for her.

They both stand there, listening.

'It's the lines vibrating on the mast,' he says, and he points them out to her.

'It's magical,' she says.

He bends down, kisses her.

'We'll make a New Englander out of you,' he says.

The words seem to her both an invitation and a promise.

'But first,' she says, 'I'll probably throw up all over this lovely boat.'

She sits down, watches him work on the boat, opening and closing boxes, taking out rope, sails from their canvas bags, attaching them to the mast. He unhooks the boat from the buoy. She watches him working on the *winch* which hoists the sail, and then they're moving out of the harbour, his hand now on the wooden lever, the *tiller*, steering; the boat gliding in the water, effortless, the silence of it so profound, like an ache.

'I thought I'd be afraid,' she tells him when they are in the middle of nowhere, just water for as far as she can see. 'I can swim, but I like to feel the ground beneath my feet.'

She sits on the deck, her jeans rolled up, the sun warm on her bare shoulders. She tries to think of Harare, Bulawayo, Giorgio, Leah; but when she opens her eyes they are lost in the blue water, the blue sky, the seagulls overheard and this boat out at sea.

She has been to Cape Town and now she is here, sitting on this beach, just the two of them, the boat anchored. He points to the island, dense with greenery; they could walk to it on the long strip of pebbles that stretches out, over the water, if she dared to go so far out. It's a bird sanctuary, he tells her, and treasure is rumoured to be buried there. He points out the dunes behind them and tells her of the salt marshes, the woods further back and then he just stops and kisses her.

They go back to the cabin. They spend the days, a week, walking bits of the Mohawk and Appalachian Trails, sometimes they sleep in the cabin, sometimes in inns. She has never thought of herself as a nature lover, someone who would enjoy the effort of walking up trails, sitting still on a rock, a bench, and just looking out at trees and mountains, at bodies of water, waterfalls, at birds and squirrels, and, yes, once, an actual moose. After their walks, Ben is scrupulous in checking her for ticks because he says they are not just nuisances, the deer ticks carry a disease called lyme which attacks the neurological system, and there is no known cure. Later, so as not to freak her out beforehand, he tells her about the skunks, raccoons, the (shy) black bears and the rattlesnakes. She loves the hiking boots her feet have broken in, bit by bit, and the satisfaction she feels the more her muscles get used to the work. Each night, whatever bed they sleep on, they make love, and whatever happens after, whether she cries or withdraws into herself, he is there, and she never wants him not to be there.

46

She sleeps for a large chunk of the flight, exhaustion catching up with her. The Air Zimbabwe connecting flight from Jo'burg to Harare is delayed for three hours for 'technical' reasons, so she finds herself at Oliver Tambo Airport writing a long letter to Ben. She posts it, and she thinks of him reading it, perhaps up in the cabin or, more likely, in his room in that big house while he makes his preparations for Iraq. Or maybe he will already be in Iraq by the time the letter arrives and it will lie on his desk, bed, unread for months. I love you, she wrote. *I love you.*

After an hour stranded in the Arrivals Hall, after calling the house repeatedly and his cellphone with no answer, she takes the taxi home. Mawara comes ambling along, tail wagging. She pats him, and this older Mawara does not have the energy to jump and fuss for her attention. He slumps down, contentedly, by the gate. The garage door is open, empty. A moment of disorientation and then, in a kind of dazed panic, she leaves her bags in the driveway, rushes up the front steps, fumbles with the house keys, drops them, finally unlocks the door, her heart in her throat. She runs into the bedrooms, checking cupboards, flinging open wardrobe doors – *his clothes are still there, Leah's too.* They have not left her. There is nothing to do but wait, so she sits at the kitchen table and waits for them.

She hears the car pulling into the driveway. She is lost: should she get up, rush to them, put on a show or . . .? She stays where she is. She listens out for Leah's pitter patter, waits to hear her call out, 'Mummy!' She hears Giorgio's steps and she stands up to go to them.

Giorgio stands in the doorway, Leah asleep in his arms. Gabrielle's hands are shaking. Say something, she tells him silently, say something. But he turns and walks away.

Later, she finds him standing on the verandah.

'Giorgio—'

'Did you sleep with him?' he asks, not turning to look at her.

'No,' she says in a heartbeat.

He turns to face her, looks at her.

'I'll sleep in the spare room,' he says, when he has taken the full measure of her.

PART EIGHT

The Breathing of Spirits

47

'So, what's going on, Gabs?' says Trinity, pushing away her empty plate and looking intently at her. 'You're a mess.'

Straight-talking Trinity; this, after they've finished eating the only dish available on the menu, pasta with cheese.

'I'm just tired.'

'Tired? You look like a zombie, *sha*,' her friend retorts, clicking her fingers in front of Gabrielle's face.

It's true, she hasn't been sleeping well. There have been the anxious waits for the phone calls from Ben, then the relief on hearing his voice again, that he is okay out there in Baghdad despite everything she hears in the news, but as soon as she puts the phone down, a flood of sadness and panic hits her.

And there has been the new life with Giorgio.

'Did you see the breakaway opposition?' she asks, trying to divert Trinity's attention away from her.

They had the show on the news last night. The opposition leader, acquitted of the latest treason charge, standing outside the High Court, a shadow of himself; he had obviously been beaten while in prison. Then, it was over to a clip of the spokesperson for one of the breakaway groups. It was none other than their former Student Union President, Jeremiah. In his usual bombastic style, he slammed the dictatorial tendencies of the opposition leader, declared that now, his new wing of the opposition, the *true* opposition, would work for real democratic changes. *Aluta!*

272 • IRENE SABATINI

'Yes, I saw the fool.'

They talk for a bit about the possibility that Jeremiah has been co-opted by The Old Man to sow division ahead of the 2008 presidential elections. Divide and rule. And that perhaps those rumours were true all along at university, the CIO turned him.

The waiter brings their bill in a chipped saucer. Trinity picks it up and starts opening her bag.

'Come on, Trinity, I'll pay.'

They both look at the pile of notes that Gabrielle fishes out and puts on top of the bill. She insists on paying because she has access to foreign currency (Giorgio) which she can change in the black market; Trinity has to survive on her local dollar salary which is being daily reduced to nothing.

'Can you believe it?' says Trinity. 'This is what Zimbabwe has come to. I can hardly lift my handbag with all this paper stuffed in it, those printing presses at the Reserve Bank are working overtime. Man, I can't even afford Madisons these days, and don't say anything about smoking kills, blah blah blah.' She starts biting at her nails, a habit she's picked up since the restricted smoking.

'Monopoly money,' Gabrielle says. 'One of the nuns at school was always talking about the hyper-hyperinflation Germany had before the war and I remember us kids laughing at her because we didn't believe that you would need a whole suitcase of bills to buy a loaf of bread.'

'Well, we're getting there,' says Trinity.

Gabrielle nods. Every day at the agency she sees how desperate things are, the lines of young men winding from the small reception area all the way down the three flights of stairs, the scuffling that sometimes breaks out, how Isobel has had to hire a guard. Some of them must sleep outside on the pavement. It's not even full-time employment that they are demanding – anything, by the hour, the day, anything at all.

'My work is almost done,' says Trinity.

'Work', Gabrielle knows, is a code word for her project, the eyewitness accounts she's putting together.

'And then what, Trinity?'

Trinity looks at her. 'Well, maybe the zombie will wake up and use it, maybe even tell her story.'

'Trinity—'

'Stop feeling sorry for yourself, Gabrielle, okay, and I'm saying this as a friend, as your best friend.'

Gabrielle looks at her watch and then at her bag and then around at the empty tables, anything to keep from meeting Trinity's eyes.

'Gabs, I'm going to tell you this because maybe you need a jolt, something to wake you up.'

She is already up, snatching her bag from the seat. She is not going to sit here and listen to Trinity lecture her about how others suffer more than her, how strong they are, what they have been through, but Trinity's hand is firm on her arm, halting her escape.

'Hold on, Gabs, listen, remember that girl you were representing before? Danika?'

The name sweeps the ground from under her feet so that, if Trinity was not holding her arm down, fixing her hand on the table, she would collapse, fall. There is an eternity of time and space where she waits for Trinity's next words.

'Well, I was doing a story on prostitution at Matapi flats, you know those male dormitories in Mbare, and I saw her coming out of there. I'm sure it was her.'

Trinity has seen Danika. Danika Dube. Her thoughts, as she sits on the bench in Africa Unity Square, continually swirl around these new facts. *Outside a block of flats. In Mbare.* She looks about her at the jobseekers sprawled on the grass going through the classifieds in *The Herald.* Some of them she might see later, desperately clutching the CVs that the typists in Rotten Row have typed out on their ancient machines. But they offer no real distraction, her thoughts pulling her back to the new knowledge. *Trinity has seen Danika Dube.*

She furtively pops a spearmint in her mouth, contraband. She has been coming here during her lunch break for three days now. She eats the cheese sandwiches she makes at home by her desk, away from the many hungry eyes and mouths here. It's as if she is on a pilgrimage, as if a sign will come to her at this very spot, tell her what she has to do.

She gets up from the bench, says *no* to a street photographer leaning against the wall of the dry fountain, even though he tells her how beautiful she is, how much that camera will magnify her beautifulness; she says *no* to a flower vendor who says that he will throw in a love request for her so that she will be married soon with many many young ones; she says *no* to the children who've started to tail her, some of their stomachs distended, a sight she thought she would never see in Harare, asking for, demanding money or offering to procure her some dagga, and when she keeps saying *no* they scatter to find someone else to harass. In happier times those children would have been frolicking in their underpants in the pool of the fountain. She starts walking back to the office. She is vaguely aware of the shadow of things, a queue outside OK supermarket, snaking down the block. A consignment of sugar (Cooking oil? Bread?) has arrived – matches? Or perhaps nothing at all, just the rumour of something; strangely enough what the shops seem to always have enough of are salt and condoms. In her head, the same words keep going. *Trinity has seen Danika. Danika Dube. Outside a block of flats. In Mbare.* She walks, repeating these new facts. She comes to an abrupt stop on the pavement, allowing herself to be jostled about, and then she finds herself walking to the lot, where her car is parked.

She sits in the car looking out at the flower and curio vendors opposite the Meikles Hotel. She is going to drive to Mbare. She is going to do it. She starts the car, is about to reverse, when two police trucks screech past her and stop in the middle of the road. One, two, a dozen riot police leap out of them. For a moment they seem confused as to where to go. Left to the Meikles, or right to the vendors? Gabrielle hears a yell and then the riot police snap into action, right, to the vendors. The flower vendors, some of them holding out their roses, their carnations, caught in mid-smiles, mid-sales talk, watch the riot police as though they believe that this is a ZBC TV movie, and then the soundtrack gets into motion, the crack of batons on the buckets and zinc tins filled with flowers that line the pavement, the swiping away of stone Zimbabwe birds, wooden giraffes, the crash of wooden crates containing paper wreaths and crosses. A furious flurry of feet as the vendors flee, some towards the city centre, some into the square. The riot police kick anything in their path until, in what must be only minutes, the pavement is eerily quiet, strewn with flowers, birds, giraffes, crosses, wreaths. The riot police stand amid it all. One, two of them bend down, pick something from the floor and stuff it in their pockets. One of them looks up in her direction and flashes a smile. They walk slowly towards the trucks and pull themselves in, drive away.

She gets out of the car, surveys the devastation. She hears someone behind her, 'This is just nonsense,' and, when she turns round, she sees a young man, his face contorted in a futile rage. Office workers and the unemployed who were busy reading the classifieds in the square are wandering around, or standing still, in shock. Some vendors begin picking up the pitiful remains of their livelihood: broken stones, wood, flowers. Then someone shouts, 'They are coming again,' and everyone starts running. But something keeps her still in the scene so that she witnesses the ordinary police force take charge of the pavement, forming a cordon around the goods, and then the municipal workers, coming to sweep it all away.

She drives slowly out of town, down onto Simon Mazorodze Road into Mbare. There are so many potholes on the road, some of them so deep the car could easily disappear in them, that it would be quicker and safer if she abandoned the car and just walked on the patches of tarmac.

She hears the bulldozers before she sees them, shaking the ground. They are surrounding Mbare Musika, clattering their way through the market stalls and cabins, their wheels trampling over masks and herbs, the love potions and home-grown Viagra, spare parts and clothes and mbiras, tomatoes and pumpkin leaves, all the million different things that the warren of stalls has to offer.

The air is also full of wailing, market women tearing at their hair, beating at their chests. *Why? Why? Why?* Some of them even daring to tug at a policeman's sleeve. A baton comes down. Surely there will be trouble from the township boys. Surely they will come out on the streets, come out from the alleys where they drink, play cards. When Gabrielle looks up towards where the buses are parked she sees a swarm of men and as they move closer she sees that they are dressed in those old, green, army-like uniforms, worn and torn with use. She steps back into the car and, for a moment, she cannot think of how to start it, and then the passenger doors are flung open and she hears a shout, 'Reverse, reverse, drive!'

What is happening?

'Drive, drive!'

In her paralysis, something gets through, the voice is in panic and fear, not anger. It is a plea for help.

Her hand shaking, she turns the key in the ignition and spins the car away from the market.

'Turn here,' one of the men says.

'Yes, yes, left. Don't worry, we are the opposition.'

'Those Bombers were after us, we are community organizers.'

'They are causing maximum destruction, so much burning, people are crying.'

'They are punishing the urban dweller for supporting the opposition.'

'Here, here is fine, thank you. You must get out of here. Those thugs, I'm sure will be coming to the flats. They know that this is the ghetto. Thank you, thank you. You know the way forward? Just straight.'

The men, three of them, rush into the flats. The notorious Matapi flats, overcrowded, dilapidated, hotbeds of discontent. The smell of open sewage is already permeating the car. She puts the car into reverse and flees.

She returns to the flats the following week during her lunch breaks, a foolish, dangerous thing, what with soldiers patrolling the streets to make sure that the decimated market stays so, but she can't let go of Trinity's words. The flats are still standing, but there are charred marks on the walls. She sits in the car, waiting, each time for only thirty minutes or so, before her agitation gets the better of her and she leaves. On her fifth visit, just as she is about to give up, the main door of the flats opens and a figure comes out, stands at the foot of the stairs as if she is expecting someone.

Gabrielle switches off the engine. She keeps her hands on the steering wheel, looks out at the figure by the stairs standing there wearing a denim miniskirt, a tight pink T-shirt, white scuffed shoes, her uncombed hair in tufts on her head.

She gets out of the car, walks up to the girl, the woman. 'Danika?' Gabrielle says.

After all these years, is it possible that she is standing before Danika Dube, her client, the girl in the barn? Is this how time works, that all things will come to pass? Can this really be her?

'What do you want?' The dull, clouded eyes are sliding away from Gabrielle when something flickers in them and they steady, and hold their gaze.

'What do you want?' the girl, woman, asks again.

Gabrielle feels the question as accusation and demand.

'I'm Gabrielle Langa,' she says. 'I, I was your—'

'What do you want?' the question again, a third time.

'I, I don't know,' Gabrielle says.

Gabrielle looks at the cracked heels of Danika's feet, how small she is, how thin, a chalky white crust lining her mouth.

'You have a big house,' Danika says.

Gabrielle looks at Danika's hands, folded in her lap, the arms that were once plump, protecting her breasts from the youths' wants, now so slender they might snap. She has brought Danika here, begged her to get in the car, to come with her. What has she done?

'I can be your house-girl,' Danika says. 'I can clean.'

Danika looks around the room, her eyes moving slowly until they find Gabrielle again.

The youths are in the room, breathing, wanting. Danika stands up, moves towards the closed French windows, and looks outside.

'You have a nice place,' Danika says. 'You have done well.'

Gabrielle closes her eyes. Danika is in her arms.

'You know what they did when you were in the house with that one. You were lucky you were with that one. The other boys, they took us deep into the bush.'

There is home-brew and want, the youths breathing, breathing, wanting, taking.

Danika reaches out her hand, pushes the handle down, opens the door. She walks onto the verandah, stands there, looking out. Mawara, lying by the gate by the stairs, lets out a bark.

'Quiet, Mawara. Good boy.'

'Yes, you have done well.'

Gabrielle looks out at her bounty, all that is hers.

'Danika, you, you can stay here for a while. There is room in the house. There is a spare—'

Danika opens the gate, pushing Mawara out of the way, walks down the stairs.

'Does anyone live in that place?'

Danika is looking out at the cottage.

'No.'

'I will stay there,' she says.

It is a statement, the decision out of Gabrielle's hands.

'Yes, of course . . . I, I will get the keys.'

Gabrielle goes back into the house. She finds the keys in the jar on the kitchen counter. For a moment, she stands there, lost, unsure, and then she looks out through the window, sees that Danika is already by the stream, then up on the bridge, walking on until she reaches the cottage.

The cottage has a bedroom, with a single pine bed, a pine wardrobe, a small lounge and dining space with two cane chairs and a table, a kitchenette with a two-plate stove, shower and toilet. A mortifying mix of shame and embarrassment descends on Gabrielle; after the main house, what must Danika think? Cobwebs and dead spiders on the ceiling, dust balls nestled in corners, and droppings of lizards, mice, rats.

'I will bring you some plates, dishes. No one has been living here.'

Danika sits down on the bed.

'Do you want to go back to get your things?'

Danika lies down on the bed, looks up at the cracks in the ceiling, unmoving.

She picks up Leah from the international school. Grade One Leah, all five years of her, who seems to consider any of her mother's queries about her life: how was school, what did you do today, did you have fun, who did you play with . . . as so much small talk, things to be batted away with a 'nothing'. She knows it's different with Giorgio. They have conversations. They have shared jokes. Laughter. Squeals and squeals of it. They have a coded language, private. Italian. Today, she does not even try to engage Leah. She is grateful for the silence on the drive home and for Leah's retreat to her room, door closed until dinner time. Giorgio phones to say goodnight to Leah. He has another late-night meeting.

She sits at the kitchen table, looking through the glass outside into the vast darkness, and then a pulse of fear, the sense of eyes watching her from outside; they will see her, she will not see them. Or is it Danika she fears? She jumps up, draws the curtains shut. She is surrounded by the flickering light of candles – another ZESA, unannounced blackout; she was too tired to go out and switch on the generator. She tells herself to relax. She meant to go back to the cottage after putting Leah to bed but she ended up here, just sitting in the semi-dark, waiting for Giorgio. She goes to the kitchen sink, opens the cold water tap, but no, the water's out too. She opens the cabinet, finds the bottle, uncorks it. Pours herself a glass. And then another.

.   .   .

The rattle of keys startles her awake.

She hears his footfall in the dark, and before he can disappear into the spare room, she speaks.

'Giorgio, wait, there's something I have to tell you.'

He stands in the doorway, a spectral figure in the candlelight.

'I found her, Danika, the girl who was with me. She's in the cottage.'

'She's in the cottage?'

'Yes.'

'Why are you are doing this, Gabrielle?'

A flash of anger makes her want to pick up the wine glass and smash it on the wall.

'You do not bring a stranger—'

'She needs help, Giorgio. You help people.'

'Gabrielle. This is our home.'

'She is my guest.'

She comes with her basket of supplies and a plastic bag of clothes. She knocks on the door, waits awhile and then she opens it. She puts down the basket on the table and she goes into the bedroom where Danika still lies. She puts the plastic bag on the ledge of the window. When she turns, Danika is sitting on the bed, watching her.

'I want to help you,' she says to Danika. 'I can help you go back to school.'

Danika scratches her arms.

'I can pay the school fees. I can pay for the school uniform.'

Danika drops her hands, lifts her face.

'There is no need for school,' she says. 'I am a woman. They made me a woman. All of them.'

48

Gabrielle, her head throbbing, has dragged herself out of bed to find Giorgio and Leah gone on their Saturday jaunts, a party or the park, or horse riding, as Leah has fallen head over heels in love with Black Beauty.

The ringing of the bell is like the clash of cymbals in her head.

'Yes?' she says into the intercom.

It's Trinity. Through the fogginess, she remembers the frantic phone call she made last night.

'Trinity, she hasn't come out of there for two days. I leave food outside. She doesn't eat. I don't know what to do.'

And here is her friend now, coming to sort out this mess with her brisk, no-nonsense attitude.

'Gabs.'

A flicker of distaste in Trinity's face. Gabrielle is still in her dressing gown even though it is already three o'clock. Her hair is all over the place, her face still crusty with sleep, her breath, no doubt, giving off stale tufts of alcohol.

'I'll go and talk to her,' says Trinity without any pleasantries, as if she is desperate to get away.

'Talk, but not interview.'

'Gabs, from what you've told me it sounds like she wants to have her say.'

Gabrielle feels the impatience in Trinity's voice. Trinity has the voices of victims in her tape-recorder, their words in her notebooks.

They have been brave, these victims. And they are out there with no one to protect them. No white man to shield them. No diplomatic sanctuary to put their feet up on. No big, lavish house. These are the things she senses in her friend. You have it easy. You have options. And you choose self-pity.

'I'll, I'll come with you.'

'No,' says Trinity. 'We'll be talking in Shona. Some things you can only say in your own language, with your own people.'

Trinity's words hit her with such force, as if she has been physically punched.

'I just mean, Gabs, she will be more comfortable.'

'She is traumatized, very traumatized,' says Trinity when she comes back from the cottage.

There are stories you read about, these are not your life. She thought this once. Mere jottings in a reporter's notepad.

Trinity stands there, looking at her, forever pouring judgements.

'I don't know what to do.'

'You're a lawyer,' says Trinity. 'You know what you have to do. And your Giorgio, isn't he in the business of saving lives?'

Mawara's frantic barking jolts her awake. When she reaches the lounge Giorgio is already there, opening the French windows.

'What is it?' she asks him.

'He just started.'

Mawara lets out another staccato of barks. He is standing by the stream, barking towards the cottage.

She follows Giorgio down the steps. Mawara comes running towards them. This is the most active he has been in a long time.

She gives him a pat and then he is agitated again; he starts barking, his face turned to the cottage.

'He's not used to her yet,' she says.

'He shouldn't be getting used to strangers in the property. He won't know who is an intruder and who isn't.'

'And since when has Mawara ever been a guard dog?'

Giorgio starts to say something and stops. Mawara is frantic, barking and jumping, rushing in the direction of the cottage and then rushing back again as though some kind of force field is keeping him at bay. They watch as Danika walks towards the stream, up onto the little bridge and stands there looking in their direction. They are in a tableau: Danika, Giorgio, her and Mawara.

'This is not normal,' says Giorgio. 'I don't like it.'

The uncharitable thought enters Gabrielle's head that if Danika was some girl, some woman, in a refugee camp, Giorgio would have a completely different demeanour; Trinity's scornful words in her head.

Danika takes a step on the bridge and, for a moment, Gabrielle thinks that she will walk over it, towards them; she will come and greet Giorgio, thank him for allowing her to stay here, and Giorgio will *see* her, that she is someone in need of care, that she is harmless. But Danika turns round and walks back towards the cottage.

'I don't like it,' says Giorgio again.

Gabrielle says nothing. The truth is that she too is spooked by Danika.

'Papà! Papà!'

Giorgio walks past her, back into the house, back to Leah. She is left alone looking at the cottage, wondering what is going on with this girl, this woman, Danika Dube, why she came out of the cottage just then, whether she was disturbed by Mawara's barking or if she really intended to come to them and then changed her mind, or if she was taking it all in, if she was making an accounting of things.

49

The note is propped up against the stove-top espresso maker. *Emergency meeting. Police Commissioner/Permanent Secretary in the Ministry of Foreign Affairs. All Aid Organizations.*

It's just past eight. She takes the note and puts it in her dressing gown pocket. She lifts the espresso maker. It's cold. He didn't have time to make himself a coffee. She busies herself with the maker, feels a headache in the background. She didn't sleep much, her head going over the question of Danika. And now she feels she has come to a resolution. She places the espresso maker on the stove, stands there until the coffee comes out, pours herself a cup and then she sits by the table sipping it. Absent-mindedly, she takes out the note from her pocket, smooths it out on the table. How many notes over the years has Giorgio left her in that calligraphic handwriting of his, so precise and beautiful at the same time? She turns it over as if she is expecting other words. But it's blank.

She will go and talk to Danika with clarity and understanding. She will be that person she was back then at The Centre. They will decide, the two of them, on a course of action, a plan. She works at an employment agency, after all. They will work on a way to get Danika back on her feet. Yes, that's the way forward. She stands up, puts the cup in the sink; maybe she should get dressed first before she goes and talks to her. No, she has momentum on her side now. She will do this without any more delay.

The phone rings as she is walking down the stairs of the verandah.

She hurries back into the house, worried that the ringing will wake up Leah. She thinks it's Giorgio, filling her in on the meeting. But it's Trinity. For a few moments she can't understand what she's saying. And then something about Party Youths in *The Herald* office, rampaging through it, looking for sell-outs, and Trinity not being able to produce her Party card.

'They slapped me for a bit, Gabrielle. They accused me of giving the opposition a platform.'

'I'll come and pick you up, hold on,' says Gabrielle.

And then, suddenly, Trinity seems annoyed with herself for having called. 'No, no. I'm fine, fine.'

'Are you sure? I can—'

'Yes. I have to go now. I've been suspended by the paper until further investigation. Bye, Gabrielle. I—'

Trinity's laboured breathing fills the air.

'What, Trinity? Anything, I'll—'

'If, if you can pick up Patrick. I was just here to finish something. Godfrey is out of town, Patrick's in the neighbour's flat. I'm a mess right now and I can't—'

'Okay, Trinity. I'm on my way.'

'Thank you. Thank you.'

Gabrielle goes to check on Leah, finds her still asleep. She could wake her, bundle her up in the car and hurry to Trinity's place, but she can't deal with a cranky Leah right now. The thought rushes through her that she could just leave her there sleeping – how long would she take? Thirty, forty minutes . . . and come back to find, what? Leah, awake, screaming blue murder? She will have to wake her up.

'She is beautiful.'

Gabrielle gasps, jolts in surprise. She turns round to find Danika in the doorway. With the simple cotton dress she is wearing, one of hers, and barefoot, Gabrielle can see glimpses of that long-ago schoolgirl in her.

'She is beautiful,' Danika says again. And then, 'The kitchen door was open.'

'Yes, yes,' says Gabrielle. Her mind is rushing from one thought to another. She must get to Trinity's. She must pick up Patrick. There is Leah. Should she call Giorgio? No, that's impossible. She looks up at Danika and the words rush and fly out of her, as if she is in the grip of a fever, without thought.

'Listen, Danika, would you mind— can you stay here, for a bit, I have to go and do something. I will be back in thirty minutes.'

Danika looks at Leah, and then back at her. 'Yes, I will do it.'

She is driving way past the speed limit, all the way down Borrowdale Road. She turns into Josiah Tongogara Street, drives down to Trinity's government-built, brick flat complex, nothing like Ben's swanky one on the other end in the Avenues. She doesn't lock the car, simply gets out, only just remembering to take the key out of the ignition, runs to Trinity's, rings the doorbell like a madwoman, then remembers that Trinity said Patrick was next door. She rings the doorbell there, impatiently makes small talk with the neighbour until at last she is able to get Patrick, and can speed back home. All the way she berates herself. What kind of a mother is she to leave her child with a stranger? A stranger, that's what Danika is. What if Danika has kidnapped her, harmed her in some way? What if Leah is now – she shakes her head, looks over at Patrick, who's playing with a Spider-Man figurine. For a moment her mind goes back to Trinity. Should she swing by *The Herald*, check . . . no. What if Giorgio has come back? What if there is an empty bed—?

She runs back into the house, Patrick behind her, her head about to explode, some untold catastrophe has happened in her absence—

But, there she is, still asleep, Danika watching over her, standing by the doorway as if she hasn't moved a muscle.

'Thank you, Danika,' she says, ashamed of her panting.

Danika simply nods, brushes past her and walks away.

.   .   .

'So what was it?' she asks him, getting up from the couch.

She's been waiting in the dark for him. The electricity went off at six and she kept the generator on till nine. A candle flickers in a saucer on the table. He draws up a chair, sits down. It's tragic how romantic this scene could be. A man, a woman, at a dinner table, in candlelight, a scene that's become an almost-daily affair, romance orchestrated by a broken-down government unable to pay its bills.

She sits down opposite him, has an urge to pick up the saucer, bring it close to his face, truly see him. He sits there looking, not at her, but at whatever images the meeting has left behind.

'What, what did the Commissioner say?'

He sighs, the candle almost snuffing out with his breath.

'International organizations are to stay away from several designated areas in the coming days because the government is going to be undertaking a *clean-up operation*.'

So, what she saw in Mbare, that was a foretaste, a practice run perhaps, getting the logistics right.

'What designated areas?'

'Mbare, Glen Norah, the whole of the high-density areas. Oh yes, he muttered something about an urban beautification exercise and that, if anything, we aid organizations should be highly supportive, because we're always complaining about overcrowding and unsanitary living conditions in the townships.'

She thinks of Giorgio sitting there, the humiliation of it, having to stay there and take it, the police commissioner relishing his power over these international people, his fingers tapping his belly.

'Just in Harare?'

'Nationwide. They're getting ready for the presidential elections, destabilizing the urban population, clearing it of registered voters, that's my guess.'

She thinks of a conversation, long, long ago with Giorgio, one of their first ones, and what had she so smugly told him – *there are no displaced people in Zimbabwe*. Well, there are plenty now.

'And the Permanent Secretary?'

288 • IRENE SABATINI

'A friendly reminder that we are guests in the country and any attempts to interfere with the activities of the forces of law and order will lead to immediate expulsion.'

He gets up. 'I'm going to have a shower. They kept us waiting for three hours in a small room. You should go to bed.'

'There's no water.'

'Of course.'

He stands there, exhausted.

'Leah?'

'She's fine, we just hung out here.'

She doesn't tell him that Patrick was here, doesn't want to risk the possibility of an inquisition, it slipping out that she left Leah alone with Danika.

'That's good.'

In the flickering light she sees that the broken vessel in his eye has returned. A doctor friend told him that it was stress and he has to be careful.

'Was, was Sara there?' she asks him.

The question so odd, something lying behind it, unsettling her. *Why are you so late?*

'Yes, she's mad as hell.'

'I thought she always kept her head in these situations.'

'Gabrielle, she's just come back from Chipinge. She saw children digging into dry earth for roots, anything to eat, a rat is a feast.'

'I'm sorry, I didn't mean—'

'Goodnight,' he says.

She sits for a while in the dark, listening to him in the house, until his footsteps disappear down the passageway, away from the bedroom they once shared, into the spare room.

The cottage door is wide open. Gabrielle steps inside. The room looks as though it's been ransacked, the bed turned over, the two chairs knocked onto their side, the mirror that was hanging on the wall now face down on the floor, bits of glass poking out from the pine frame, and the smell . . . Gabrielle walks into the chaos, into the narrow passageway and follows the smell into the bathroom. She stands by the doorway, her hand over her mouth. In the sink and on the floor there are buckets and jars full of rotting organic matter: pieces of meat, teeth, claws, roots, perhaps even faecal matter and, hanging from the shower curtain rail, a snake's shed skin. Looking down, she gasps at what she sees on the stool. There are locks of curly brown hair on a jagged piece of mirror.

Leah.

She steps back and finds her passage blocked.

'Now, you have seen,' she hears. 'I will destroy them. I have paid for strong medicine.'

Gabrielle turns, looks up at Danika.

'I will find them. I will have my revenge, one by one. Already that first one, the one we came to you about, do you remember that one?'

Gabrielle remembers. The fifteen-year-old schoolgirl, Danika Dube, who came to the office with her father and found her. Danika Dube with those big brown eyes, looking at her to see if she was going to be judged.

'Yes, that one, he has become a madman. A madman.'

Gabrielle knows nothing about what became of him, the defendant in their case. Here today, gone tomorrow. It happens all the time in the Party.

'And you, you do not want to find them, those other ones? You are a lawyer. What about your justice? I am not afraid. They will pay.'

Gabrielle feels herself swaying and she reaches out, touches the stone walls.

'I am calling upon the spirits. They will come. They will come.'

There is blood pouring out from the bed, a river, a flood of blood sweeping her out of the farmhouse away, away.

'Danika, you have to leave. I'm sorry.'

'You are afraid.'

'Yes, I'm afraid,' she says.

'We are damaged,' she hears. 'Now it is our turn to do the damaging. One of those boys, he is at those flats, Matapi.'

She is aware of the one thing: Danika standing there patiently, watching, waiting.

'I will clean up, go,' she hears. 'Go!'

'Danika, it's not worth, it's not—'

'Do you want to see what they did? Do you? Then look! Look!'

Danika clutches and snatches at her clothes, tears them away from her body.

'Look!'

Cigarette burns branded on the skin, the acronym of the opposition carved into it.

'I have seen him,' she says.

Gabrielle hears the words, hears them and knows.

'The one who laughed like a hyena. I have seen him.'

This is the beginning of all things, the end. This is life, death. This is a girl, a woman, Danika, whose words fill up the acrid room, who has lived and died and lived.

'I used to believe in God. I prayed to him for revenge but he was just laughing at my suffering, making those boys run free, unpunished. So now I am using traditional medicines. They will work. They have power.'

'They can't, you can't, Danika—'

Danika draws close to her, her breath blowing rage on her. 'And what are *you* doing? Nothing. Nothing! Go!'

Gabrielle stumbles out of the cottage into the cold sunshine. She feels the failure beating, soaking up her palms, her scalp. Danika will act. She, Gabrielle Langa, will be in this suburban house, with her suburban child, her de facto suburban husband, her dog. She will be one among them, living her calm, faked life.

From the verandah, she sees Danika walk up to the side gate, leave. And she sits, sipping, drinking the imported white wine, watching the sun set. She will sit here and drink because she found Danika and did nothing, is nothing, because, she will tell herself as the white liquid courses through her veins, you are a mother, de facto wife, homeowner too, you live a charmed life, you do this and it is good, and the white liquid will satiate her veins, until her eyelids flutter, flutter, flutter . . . the hyena lies on the bed. He snores. Suddenly his eyes dart awake. The feel of metal on his skin. Squeeze and release. Squeeze and release. Squeeze and release.

Opening her mouth, she breathes into the dark, the smells in the air thickening around her, home-brew. It is there, caked on her mouth, skin. She sees a dark figure, framed in the doorway, looking down at her. She is suddenly bathed in light, she blinks and the figure moves, bends towards her, picks up the wine bottle, her, and she thinks, that is strange, first the wine bottle, then me, and in the house as he puts her to bed, she hears the child's high-pitched singing, the splash of water, until her eyes close again, into the dark.

Her mouth burning, parched. She tries to get up but is pushed back on the bed by the pressure on her head. She throws her hand out, fumbles for a light switch. The light seems to slice through her. She keeps her eyes closed, counts to five, and then opens them. She lies there as though paralysed. She listens for sounds of Giorgio, Leah, but there is only this alcoholic sludge of silence around her. Her mouth feels as though she has thrown up and when she puts a hand to her lips there is a crust. She closes her eyes and then slowly lifts herself off the bed, fighting the shifts of pain beneath her eyes, through her head. She shuffles to the windows, draws the curtain to one side and is astounded by the glare of sunlight. She turns, picks up her watch from the table and sees that it is four o'clock. She feels a wave of nausea and self-loathing. She slumps down on the bed, sees herself knocked out, Giorgio, Leah, finding her. She goes into the bathroom, into the shower, runs the water over her and scrubs herself clean. She puts on her clothes, makes herself a mug of coffee using the espresso maker for six. She does everything deliberately as though these may be her last acts. She swings the door wide open and a breeze flutters the curtain back in. She ties it to the hook on the wall. She sits down on the step of the verandah. The coffee is too bitter, much too strong. She puts the cup down on the step. She feels a wave of sickness building and she leans her head against the gate, prickles of cold sweat on her forehead.

'You need help, Gabrielle.'

She hears him, through the fog of wine in her veins, her arteries, pumping out of her heart, making her sick. He is standing behind her.

She needs help.

He comes, sits down next to her. 'Here,' he says. 'She is very experienced.'

He puts the card in her hand and when she looks down at it and reads what it says, what it offers, what he wants her to succumb to, a surge of anger and revulsion overcomes her.

'I'm not one of your projects. Don't—'

She makes to get up, stumbles forward, Giorgio's hand stopping her from toppling down the stairs.

'Gabrielle,' he says, 'Please. You can talk to her. Give it a chance. Yes, you're not one of my projects. You're Gabrielle, the mother of my child.'

He sits beside her, waiting for her to succumb, waiting for her to say yes, she will go and see the good doctor, go and tell her what's going on in that head of hers. And then, when she gives him nothing, he sighs, gets up and leaves.

She sits on that step long after he is gone. She sits there thinking, I am the mother of his child, his words. Not, *Gabrielle, you are my love, that's why, my companion.* She sits there thinking of everything that has come and gone, and what she might want from her life. She thinks of Ben holed up in the Green Zone, doing whatever it is he is doing. In his emails he has let slip that he ventures out of the security zone. She thinks of Trinity. How far apart they have grown. Trinity, putting herself in danger with her continual investigations, the dossier she is compiling with a passion that frightens Gabrielle, the zeal of the newly converted.

'What are you going to do with it?' she asked her.

'You're a lawyer, Gabrielle, tell me. I have the names of hundreds of victims, tortured, dead – what should I do with them?'

She had no answer for her friend.

'How are they going to seek justice if no one wants to take up their cases? *No one*. So, maybe I'll go international.'

How many times has she felt Trinity looking at her, questioning: when are you going to act, when are you going to join the struggle again? She has never told her what happened in that camp, so that all Trinity understands of it are the generalities. Even as she is busy collecting all the testimonials of what happens in those places, she doesn't really know, doesn't understand, have it deep in her bones, the smells, the fear. Trinity thinks it is something that you can put away, and then you get on with life, that the lawyer Gabrielle Langa is just on an inconvenient extended vacation, a luxury others can't afford. Trinity, who witnessed the state of her when Giorgio found her, who saw the result of what they did, what she had become.

What she wants to tell Trinity is that there is ultimately no justice except for the one you take for yourself, that no court on earth, certainly not one in Zimbabwe, can give her that justice she craves, that Danika is right, it is the justice that comes from the barrel of a gun and the power it gives you when you stand at the foot of a bed where a hyena snores, after having his fill.

She looks down at the card that Giorgio has given her, reads the doctor's name.

Psychotherapist.

She gets up from the step, the card in her hand.

She could not help Danika.

But, perhaps, she can help herself. And before she can have any second thoughts, she goes inside and makes the phone call.

PART NINE

The Giving of Aid

50

'The only thing you can change about the past is the impact it has on you now. That's the only power you have over it.'

The doctor's words come to her as they drive through the wasteland that is Matabeleland. The doctor was saying a version of what she had told herself a thousand times. The past is the past, you can't change it. You just have to move on. But perhaps it was the way the doctor had said the words, how she had put them together, that seemed to have suddenly opened up possibilities for Gabrielle.

It seems to her that for the longest time, she has been waiting for just these exact words, this configuration of purpose. She has power.

What would it mean if she simply let go, stopped resisting, if she accepted this part of her life with Giorgio and Leah, and let go of the rest, of the past, of Ben?

After months of weekly one-hour sessions that began, like a New Year's Resolution, at the beginning of the year, she and the doctor had finally got round to Ben. Ben, in his third year in Iraq, who had wanted her to come to New Haven again. And she had said no. Christmas and New Year she spent with her family, Giorgio and Leah, in Italy, where she slept in Giorgio's old room and he slept in Marella's room (Marella was away in India) with Leah. She wondered what kind of conversation Giorgio had had, if any, with his parents. In those nights in Rome she imagined Christmas and New Year with Ben, in that big house, waking up to snow, in his arms.

298 • IRENE SABATINI

The last session.

'You have not seen him for three years?'

'Yes.'

'You talk?'

'Yes.'

'On the phone?'

'Yes.'

Four months into his tour of duty she woke up to find a text message on her phone from him. *I'm fine. In Jordan.* She immediately turned on the news. A rocket had hit the US Embassy compound in the Green Zone. Two people were killed, four injured.

'Via Skype?'

'Yes.'

She braced herself for the next question but the doctor fell silent, and she let the silence grow and settle between them. And Gabrielle, even though she knew this was a trap, fell into it. She opened her mouth and spoke.

'I know you think it's crazy. That we can't even call what we have a relationship because a relationship is—'

And here she faltered. She looked over at the calendar on the wall. So many years had passed. And, in all that time, they had been together, physically, in each other's presence, for, at the most, two and a half months. That was all. What did that mean?

She waited for the doctor to give her the words but the silence was left untouched until she broke it again.

'Giorgio says I'm not present with him. I'm elsewhere.'

But that was the Giorgio of some time ago, the Giorgio who gave her the doctor, the Giorgio who wanted her to get better for him, the Giorgio who slept in their bedroom again. She was afraid to say it out loud, how in the past weeks she had felt something come untethered with Giorgio, something of himself coming loose from her. How he had stopped asking her how she was feeling. How he had stopped phoning her during the day just to say hello. How he had stopped touching her. Everything he did which annoyed her had stopped.

They had stopped fighting about Ben's calls, the shut door when she disappeared to talk to him.

They have stopped fighting because Giorgio doesn't care anymore what she does. He's had enough of her. He can't compete with someone who is not there, who is always somewhere else.

And then, in the closing moments of the session, the doctor stunned her.

'Gabrielle, in your present, in your present self, who can you do without?'

Not do *with*, but *without*.

She looks at Giorgio again and thinks if the power she has is to choose this. This life. This present. This future.

But the answer that leapt immediately to her back there at the doctor's office shocked her with its furious certainty. The without could not be Ben. It just could not be. No matter how much sense it did not make. It just could not be Ben.

And why is that? Because she loves him. She does not love Giorgio. And, what's more, this time she does not run from the other truth but says it out loud to herself in her head. The love she has for Ben is stronger than that of her own child, Leah.

'It's bad,' says Giorgio.

Startled, she looks at him.

'They've chopped down so many trees. Not a crop in sight.'

She looks out again. The remnants of commercial farmland can be seen through the ripped fencing. The once-irrigated fields are now either dust bowls or thickets of grass. Rusted frames of tractors lie on the road verges, one in a ditch. Some children sit listlessly scratching the ground with sticks. They no longer chase after cars calling out, 'mukiwa, mukiwa'. They are looking for food.

Giorgio has to check what's happening down here in Matabeleland. In Gwanda, there have been terrible stories coming out, of food aid being taken out of the hands of starving, displaced children by Party militia. The District Commissioner there is someone they know: her father. Giorgio told her how difficult it was to get any information from out there, how desperate the situation was. She insisted on coming with him, perhaps her presence might, however far-fetched the idea, soften her father. Leah is having a sleepover with Patrick.

In Kadoma, they stop at the motel to stretch their legs and for refreshments. They are the only customers.

'Business is so poor,' says the manager. 'The buses don't stop any more, even when they are running, which is seldom – no fuel – and who can afford their prices nowadays?'

She remembers that trip with Giorgio to Bulawayo when she was pregnant and she had thought that her father would somehow surprise her. On their way back to Harare they stopped here to eat something and ended up booking a room for the afternoon; she was so tired.

In Bulawayo, they check in at the Selborne Hotel, its colonial facade still giving off an aura of faded majesty. While Giorgio is having his meeting she goes for a walk across town to the Dominican School.

She looks across the road to the brick facades of the secondary school, up at their white apexes inlaid with the tall glass crosses bearing the school motto, *Veritas*; wonders at the nature of truth she learnt in there. She walks further down the pavement, and there it is, the boarding block, the steps leading to that heavy wooden door where she stood, heartbroken, with her father. It's chilly outside and for a moment she stands on the pavement looking up and down the quiet street. There is a woman crossing the road wrapped in blankets, thick woollen socks tucked into gumboots. She crosses the road too, walks over to OK Bazaars, passes the empty stalls and the ones with bits and pieces lying stranded there, a spool of ribbon, a shoe brush . . . no prices on the shelves because hyper-hyperinflation means prices change by the minute. Clumps of dust are lodged in the jars that used to be stuffed with candies. Down at the supermarket, the fridges and freezers have been switched off, nothing in them.

At the City Hall, the few vendors pounce on her with soapstone sculptures, wooden animal figurines, some beads and painted gourds.

'Good price, good price.'

She is surrounded, the vendors jostling and shoving each other to get to her.

'Sister, sister, you are one of us,' she hears one say. 'You will help us sell our wares. Life is hard here in Matabeleland. We are hungry.'

She picks out a beaded Ndebele necklace and a small, classical stone sculpture of mother and child, a wooden hippopotamus (for Leah), and a ring made of wire with a blue marble. The whole lot costs just over one US dollar; she pays in clumps of zimdollars. She watches two policemen bearing truncheons shouting at the vendors, who scatter. She is followed everywhere by street children, the smell of glue.

She hurries back to the sanctuary of the hotel.

In the morning, Giorgio refills the Land Cruiser at the UN Depot and they set off. A land cruiser from Save the Children is following them, the petite English woman called Sara at the wheel. There was a clumsy introduction at the depot when Giorgio said, 'Gabrielle, this is Sara.'

'So, you're Sara,' she said lightly. 'Giorgio keeps talking about you and all the brilliant work you're doing with orphans.'

.Sara did a funny thing then: looked up at Giorgio and then at her, Giorgio's partner, and there was a silence, which Gabrielle took as Sara's embarrassment at her effusive praise. This awesome Sara was nothing like the fervent missionary type, badly dressed and completely committed to their work, that she had envisioned. Giorgio had not let on how intelligently pretty she was.

This is the dust bowl, drought-prone part of Matabeleland. Deep gullies line the road. The land, completely stripped of trees, has given itself up to wind, erosion. Before, this road was very busy with lorry traffic going to South Africa or coming from South Africa with goods. Theirs are the only two cars on the road. It's like driving through a desert, the land so dry and arid. It is in this very place that some of the worst atrocities of Gukurahundi took place, whole villages razed. She thinks of the old methods being deployed again by the government, the rumoured mineshafts being used to dump the bodies of opposition activists. And she thinks of barns, barns that could lie out there in the dry grass, the smell of animals, and bodies huddled in terror, waiting. They drive on and on; the road, a seemingly endless stretch. They might be swallowed up in it, disappear.

Her father is supposed to meet them at the bottle store which sits abandoned and crumbling at the turn-off. Giorgio gets out, takes a walk around the store. She watches Sara getting out of the Land Cruiser, following him. She thinks of doing the same, but doesn't.

'Empty,' he says when he comes back.

They have been waiting for an hour or so when they catch sight of a vehicle moving towards them. Two youths sit sullenly in the back on sacks of maize or stock feed. They are wearing torn Party shirts. One of the youths looks at Gabrielle and she feels the tremor in her hand. Her father struggles out from the driver's side, his belly knocking against the wheel. He is wearing a safari suit and on his head, a suede farmer's hat. One of the youths leaps out of the truck, walks up to the bottle store and starts rattling the door. Then he kicks it open. The other youth follows.

'Hello, Mr Langa,' Giorgio says, stepping forwards, his hand outstretched.

Gabrielle's father ignores the hand, takes off his hat and starts brushing it with his hand.

'I would like to see the villagers. I have been told that they are being kept in camps.'

Her father puts his hat back on and, looking at the barren landscape, he asks, 'And who has been giving out that information? Nobody is being herded anywhere. And who is that one?' he says, pointing at Sara, who is standing next to Giorgio. Looking at them, a thought flickers in Gabrielle and is then gone in an instant.

Gabrielle looks at this man, her father. She feels so far away from him and yet, what he is, what he has fashioned himself to be, she knows too well. She would like to get back in the Land Cruiser, turn round, drive away, forget this.

'She is a colleague, Mr Langa.'

'The problem with you people, you come here and start making all kinds of false accusations with your reports. The villagers are in feeding centres. The government is looking after them.'

'Yes, yes, I'm very sorry, sometimes my English fails me, feeding centres. Could you please take me to one, Mr Langa?'

'To do what? You UN people, nothing but trouble. The president is right about you white people, the only ones you can trust are the dead ones.'

She watches her father spit into the ground and then look about him as if he is searching for an audience to agree with him. And then he looks directly at her, scowls, mutters something in Ndebele, under his breath.

'I'm sorry to hear that you have had a bad experience,' says unflappable Giorgio. 'I can set matters straight internationally. I see that your truck is full of sacks of maize and that they are stamped WFP. You must be on your way to a *feeding centre*, so I—'

Her father looks up sharply and starts shouting towards the bottle store.

'Boys! Boys!'

The boys come shuffling out. Her father shouts in Ndebele that they should pull the canvas over the bags. The boys grunt as they struggle with the canvas.

'The villagers have been fed already,' her father says. 'You can come with me to the ranch.'

'No, that's fine,' Gabrielle says. 'We have to get back.'

'So why did you bring me out here then?'

Her father is looking over her and she turns round. There is some movement in the bushes. Already the boys have gone in and they come out dragging an old woman, trailed by two children. Gabrielle can see that they are on the verge of collapse, the old woman looks close to death.

'You said you have to go, so go.'

'What, what about these people, Mr Langa, you will—'

'Which people, oh these things? Didn't I tell you that they have already been fed? They are here trying to pretend that they are starving. These are opposition. Go and ask your leader for food.'

'Mr Langa—'

'You are still here, do you need an escort?'

'Mr Langa,' says Sara, 'We can give them a lift. We can come to the feeding centre later.'

Gabrielle is startled by Sara's voice. The resoluteness of it. Shame grows and deepens in her.

'A lift, where? This is Zimbabwe, young lady. Nobody is giving lifts. Go now.'

'Mr Langa—'

'But, are you deaf? Go, and don't write any nonsense. These people are nobodies.'

This is her father, she tells herself. This man who is standing here, making these unconscionable utterances, is her father.

'Baba, give them food, okay, give them a sack of maize.'

'What sack? I came here to welcome you even though your behaviour over the years has been a source of pain for me, and now you come with this boy of yours again to cause problems. Did he even pay damages for your pregnancy? Just come on and get out of my sight. I have work to do.'

Gabrielle breathes in the scent of all that is dying, dead around her.

'Baba, if you have any love left for me, any at all, you will let us take these three to Bulawayo. If you have any love for Mummy, if you remember her soul, you will not let this woman die at your feet. I am begging you. You want me to tell you what happened to me? You want me to expose what your Party, your youths, did to me, what these boys of yours . . .'

She is shaking. Her father looks at her. 'I've already wasted a day for this nonsense. I'm going. A piece of advice, be careful what you say when you open your mouth. Do you see any opposition in these parts?'

She watches him get into the truck. The two youths look confused at the woman and the children. Her father calls out to the youths. They scramble to the back and lie down on the sacks of maize.

Giorgio carries the old woman, who is breathing faintly, to Sara's Land Cruiser. She watches Giorgio say a few words to Sara, put his hand on her shoulder and then watches him walk back to their car, where she sits at the back with the two children. She holds their tiny bodies, they could be one, two, four, six, it's hard to tell from their emaciated limbs, their sunken faces.

In Mpilo hospital there are people lying along the corridors moaning, dying, unattended. When a doctor appears he takes a cursory look at the old woman and the children. The old woman will die, he says. They will have to wait for beds for the children.

'Go and get some rest,' Giorgio says, as if she's an invalid or incapacitated, somehow unable to cope with the scope and scale of the humanitarian disaster unfolding. She should leave it to the professionals. One child is in Giorgio's arms, the other in Sara's. The old woman is lying lifeless on the floor.

She takes the Land Cruiser and drives back to the hotel. Sara will give Giorgio a lift back.

He stays in the hospital overnight, and when he comes to the hotel room late in the afternoon he lies on the bed and falls straight to sleep. After a couple of hours, his phone rings. It's Sara. He is off again to the hospital; one of the children has developed severe diarrhoea.

She sees Giorgio in the evening. The old woman is dead. The boy is on a saline solution. Sara used the emergency kit she had. She has asked for a delivery of further medical supplies from her office. Throughout the morning the child's body convulsed until there was nothing more for his wasting body to give.

The boy dies. The other child appears to be making a recovery. Sara has been there all the time, Giorgio tells her. She hasn't left the hospital at all; she feeds the child slowly, gently, from a spoon with a water, salt and sugar solution, the water boiled three times.

. . .

On the drive back to Harare, Gabrielle thinks of the child left behind. She will be placed in an orphanage; Sara has made the arrangements.

She looks at Giorgio, seems to see him for the first time in a long while, remembers him back then when she was a student. He had sunburn on his nose, cheeks and forehead, at that very first meeting of theirs. He smelled of sweat and dust and smoke. Giorgio, who gave up smoking as soon as Leah was born. I need those extra ten years, he said, cradling the baby. Giorgio who had waited for her, all those years ago when she was so young; she had leaned over and kissed him.

And something unlocks in her, a truth forever known.

She leans in to him and says, 'Thank you. Thank you, Giorgio.'

He looks at her, says not a word. But he understands. He knows.

Two days later he moves out. There is no drama, just the simple sight of him packing his clothes, until Leah sees him. There are tears and heartbreak then. Weeks later, he moves in with Sara.

51

Six months after the Bulawayo trip, Giorgio tells her the news that should not be a surprise, given her father's threats: the government has had enough of him. They are getting rid of NGOs, the foreign press, anything that might cause trouble for the elections. And now, Giorgio.

'Somebody in the office passed on an internal memorandum to the CIO. I've been telling headquarters for months that the office is full of spies. I have twenty-four hours.'

But she can't fully digest what his expulsion means or, more likely, she is afraid of everything it means. How diminished he looks. She's never seen him look so defeated, as if, after all these years of trying to save it, the world is not what he thought it was.

'They can't do it,' she says.

'They're doing it, Gabrielle.'

'We, you, can go to court. They can't just throw you out.'

'They can. I'm here at the invitation of the Zimbabwean government. I have overstayed my welcome.'

'They can't, you have a daughter. We have a case. I'll—'

'Gabrielle. I'm a diplomat. Diplomats get expelled. I'm getting expelled.'

His BlackBerry rings; he has a heated conversation with someone from Geneva about protocol.

She lifts her left index finger, bites into it, gnaws at it until she tastes blood in her mouth.

'They're moving me to the regional office for the Americas, in Washington.'

He stands there and she sees that she has to help him, somehow make it easier for him.

'She'll be okay, Giorgio. Leah will be okay. I'll — '

He grasps her shoulders, pulls her to him. 'Gabrielle,' he says, 'she is coming with me.'

She has heard his words but it is as if she cannot, for a moment, assemble them in the right shape, configuration.

'Gabrielle, she has an Italian passport. Things are a mess here. Anything could happen. The government is out of control. She needs—'

'No, she—'

'Gabrielle, listen, she's not even a Zimbabwean according to the new citizenship laws. Her father's a foreigner, have you thought about that?'

'You want to take her, Giorgio, that's it. You and Sara. You, you don't trust me with her.'

'Gabrielle, it's not safe here. They're moving their campaign into the suburbs. That's the latest information. Truckloads of youths, re-education . . .'

He stands there, the weight of his words between them, the past slamming against her. The youths, the youths, it is always the youths.

'I'm sorry, Gabrielle. I can't leave her here.'

There is steel there, a threat, a love so great it will demolish her.

A love that should be hers, but isn't.

She knows that he is right.

She finds her daughter in her bedroom facing the mirror, trying on her clothes as if they were so many personas that she can so easily put on, take off.

She stands still by the door until Leah stops mid-song. The Leah in the mirror sticks her tongue out, *out, out* as far as it will go and she is watching this Leah, unable to take her eyes off her, then the real Leah spins round and, hands on hip, shouts, 'Stop looking! It's rude.' But she can't help it. The looking, looking. As if to remember.

PART TEN

Beginnings

52

Gabrielle steps out of the South African Airways plane, breathes in the hot, clammy air. She cannot quite believe that she is here, walking into Kotoka International Airport, that she has passed through immigration, customs, collected her one bag and is now at the Arrivals Hall, panicked for a moment that she does not see him, but then he steps out from behind a pillar and there he is. Ben. Here she is, looking up at him and, here he is, bending down, lifting her off the ground, kissing, kissing her.

Her feet touch the ground again. She breathes. He picks up her bag, takes her hand, and she lets him lead her to this new place, her heart beating with an exquisite joy. The two of them, dislocated into this space, neutral territory, as it were. They can be something here together, something they create for themselves. She squeezes his hand; he puts the bag down and kisses her again.

He has rented a car and she watches as he effortlessly navigates the gridlock out of the city, checking now and then the map he has on his lap. Her hand is on his thigh. He is, she sees, well, and her shock at this tells her how much she feared, all the news out of Iraq, Baghdad, Fallujah, the growing insurgency, the contractors killed and burnt, their bodies dragged through the streets, hung on a bridge, the car bombings, the suicide bombings, all of it, shocking. The State Department has kept him in Iraq far longer than was planned, as he is one of the very few Americans there who speak Arabic and who gets on with the Iraqi officials.

'What are you smiling at?' he asks her, changing gear, lanes.

'You're a very, very handsome man,' she says. 'I'm happy, happy to be here, with you.'

He rubs her thigh with his thumb.

They drive west, along the coastal road, navigating the streams of roadside vendors and tuck shops and people darting on the road selling top-up cards, iced water, single cigarettes, food . . . through villages set in so much tropical vegetation, children chasing the car and waving to them as they drive by, cows and goats slowing their progress.

She looks out at the sea, at the fishermen with their boats. The boats are shabby and colourful, more canoes than boats, nothing like those in Cape Town or New England. Most of them with long flagpoles sticking out at the stern end, the pieces of cloth snapping in the breeze – *the red, yellow and green stripes, black star of Ghana, the sombre Union Jack, the US stars and stripes, the blue and yellow of Sweden, the Rastafarian lion of Judah*. As if this was some kind of unorthodox international fleet.

They find the guest house he's rented on the beach, a rondavel, and for a while they lie on the bed listening to the waves breaking, their own breathing.

'God, it's good to have you back, Gabrielle,' he says.

He lifts her hands, turns over her wrists, and she sees what he sees, the faded scars. 'You've lost weight, Gabrielle,' he says.

It's true. She hasn't been eating well at all.

The loss of Leah. Those early days when a blinding fury would overtake her, when she ravaged the house, broke everything in sight, hurling and tearing, crashing, her palms turning blue. The days of loathing and regret when the things of death called to her. Days of Leah's voice screaming in her head. *Mummy bad. Mummy bad.* Days of silence, her hand on the phone receiver, waiting for Leah's voice, Giorgio trying to coax it out of her – *Leah, Leah, it's Mummy.* Silence. And pictures, pictures, pictures. Leah smiling, Leah laughing, Leah waving, not at her, not at her. Leah in the new world. A happy Leah.

Sara's Leah. Giorgio and Sara's Leah. Giorgio wed. Leah, their flower girl, blossoming. Days of longing, and relief, for this was the gift she gave the child.

And Trinity gone, too. It came without warning. One minute Trinity was there, the other not. A rushed call from South Africa, and then, weeks later, from London. I've been detained, she said. An asylum detention centre, near Heathrow Airport, with Patrick.

Godfrey surprised her at the office weeks ago. The last time she had seen him, before then, must have been a year ago when he came to Giorgio's office asking for funding for a magazine he was trying to set up. He was unemployed. The *Daily News* printing presses had been petrol-bombed and when it continued operating, the newspaper was banned by the government. He seemed so diminished as he stood there in her office; he had lost a lot of weight and when she looked down at his hands she saw that he was wearing thick, green-knitted gloves. She had heard about the fingers put through rat traps.

'Gabrielle. It is so good to see you.'

She drew a chair out, watched him sit slowly down, the wince of pain.

The youths, war veterans, police, CIO, take a morbid pleasure in lacerating buttocks, in flaying the flesh there.

'Can I make you some tea, Godfrey?'

'No, no, I'm fine. Maybe a glass of water.'

She had an urge to run out, abandon the room, Godfrey, but she picked up the pitcher of water and poured a glass for him.

'These people have long memories,' said Godfrey. 'They came two weeks ago. They dragged me out of the house, in front of my wife, children. I was not even dressed.'

And the images of Trinity, who was deemed not good enough, and of his son, Patrick, settled there between them. Trinity was not his wife. Patrick was not one of the children.

'Anyway, everyone has their problems. I came to say goodbye. I'm hoping to seek refuge in South Africa. They burnt my opposition card but they can't burn my commitment. They are getting very serious now, for the elections. The Old Man is worried.'

She realized in an instant that he needed money. Hard currency, that's why he'd taken this risk.

Later, she drove him to an address, a safe house in Mount Pleasant, the envelope of rands in his bag.

And there was the visit of youths to the agency when she was out which had badly shaken Isobel. Isobel had taken out a bottle of gin from her drawer and poured herself a drink.

'Dear God, Gabrielle,' she told her. 'They were two thirds evil, one third comedy. They swung so easily from one extreme to the other. I'm thinking one minute, this is some scary shit, and then the next, I'll laugh them out of the office. They're so bloody unpredictable. They could have set the whole place up in smoke, just because.'

The whole mess that is Zimbabwe. The abductions, the killings, starting again. Yesterday, as she was packing with the TV on, there was news on CNN of an opposition activist's wife burnt alive in her hut, when her husband could not be found.

A re-education camp has sprouted up in the parking lot of Sam Levy's Village, the militia moving in at night. The maids and gardeners have been rounded up, made to chant all night long. When she had switched off the TV she could hear them from the house, the drums beating, the whistling.

'Gabrielle, what are you think—?'

'Do you remember that barbecue you took me to in Chisipite?'

She doesn't want him to worry, she doesn't want to be taken care of. She is a grown woman. She can make decisions, has made them. She is here now with Ben.

'Of course I do. Our first date.'

Looking back, that *was* their first date. Sitting in his red car while he leaned over the open door, she had felt like a giddy teenage girl in the movies.

'The food was incredible,' she says. 'That rice, jollof rice, the chicken . . . all of it.'

'Yes,' he says. 'And I've heard good things about the fish stew here and the roadside barbecues at night . . . but maybe we can wait a bit.'

He leans in, kisses her.

Yes, they can wait.

After a meal of grilled fish with peanut sauce and yam balls, they stand now in the shade of palm trees, watching fishermen hauling their nets off the boats, twenty, thirty of them per net, singing and chanting as they drag the nets along the sand. Walking along the beach, they have had to fend off little boys asking them, in high-pitched voices, for some *cedis, please sista, please good brotha, six, five, four, three, even just two,* so they can act as their personal tour guides to the Castle. Ben has charmed them with his easy smile and thumbs up while somehow making it clear that he isn't buying any of their offers, at least not today, so that, in the end, they scoot off, waving merrily back at him, scampering and splashing in the water, running after other American *brothas* and *sistas*, and she remembers him in Harare, this knack he has of never seeming to feel out of place, never seeming to need to be anyone other than who he is.

She looks out along the beach to the whitewashed walls of the Castle, the cannons up on the fort, useless now. She has read about the Castle's history. One of forty slave castles along the west coast, the Gold coast. First built by the Swedes for trade in timber and gold, then taken over by the British who renovated it by adding dungeons.

They go down to the dungeons, to the cells which held so many men, so many women, children, too, babies, the unborn, four, five hundred at a time in the small, dark, airless space, mere holes, high in the walls for patches of light, air – the smell of damp and rot, evil. They walk through the Door of No Return, stand awhile watching the cram of fishing boats and canoes; the sound of casual conversation and laughter, the young men lounging about on the boats, the young girls walking along, tin dishes full of fish on their heads, the slam of dominoes on a wooden board, the harried bark of a stray dog, startling. A muted relief in the bright sunlight, the open space, breathing in the salty air, the waves battering the castle walls, the wind picking up, the waves rising, rising.

She thinks of the captives, the villagers and warriors, the young and very young, the strong and not so strong, hunted down, stolen in their sleep, betrayed, hands bound, shoved and dragged, beaten, thrown into canoes, taken to the ships waiting out at sea for their cargo. She thinks of the monument in New Haven of the Amistad slaves, how they too languished in cells such as those below, how they too must have scratched their terror on the walls, washed the stones with their blood, flesh, penetrated them with their moans and screams; Sierra Leone, not Ghana, the Spanish, not the British, only the beginning of the horrors upon horrors they were to face.

She starts retching on the beach, thin streams of bile leaving her body, onto the sand. She goes into the water, splashes it over her face, the salt stinging her eyes, mouth.

She slumps down on the wet sand. He sits next to her, draws her to him, her head on his arm.

'I'm sorry,' she says. 'It's the heat, tiredness, too much . . .'

She cannot find the words to articulate what there is too much of.

'There're whole branches of my family,' he says, 'on both of my parents' sides, I don't know. My cousins, nephews, nieces . . . nothing. They're here in Ghana . . . I, I don't even know if it's Ghana, or Nigeria, the Ivory Coast, Sierra Leone, Senegal . . . but they're here . . .'

He has saved the coming to this place for her. This too is now part of their shared history, their story.

'I'm going to join the Democratic campaign, as a volunteer. This is one of those moments, Gabrielle. Historic.' He smiles. 'Yes, I know, cheesy, but it is.'

They are sitting on the terrace of a bar, watching boys play football on the beach. After the years in Baghdad, he is going to be in a place where she can imagine him safe, whole.

'Do you really think he can win?'

'Yes, he can.'

'Then fingers crossed at our end, too,' she tells him.

She sees that he wants to say something, that he is stopping himself from saying things.

'I'm going to vote, Ben. It probably means nothing, but I'm going to do it.'

There is talk of an upset. Except this time, unlike during the referendum, there will be no complacency. People were burnt once by their naivety, this time they are ready to put up a fight.

'Gabrielle, if at any time you need, I'm—'

'Yes,' she says.

53

Like others, many, many others, she takes her place in the line. She waits the whole day and still she is nowhere near the polling booth. She sleeps out in the open, huddled with other bodies, together in the damp air. There are youths in a nearby field whistling, chanting. There is no protection should they descend with God knows what in their hands. But the people remain, they remain. And so does she. If she has done nothing, she will do this.

In the morning, when the youths have left their field and now swarm among them, raising fists, chanting slogans, threats, slashing the air with sticks, Gabrielle sees them, hears them but she does not let them overcome her. She remembers what came to her in therapy: the fear will always be with her but the shame, the shame is theirs alone.

She puts her finger in the blue ink, a safeguard against voting more than once, and she parts the curtain and puts down her X for the opposition leader. There has been talk of minute cameras in the booths that will identify where voters put their Xs, and a pulse of panic beats for a moment, *what now?* But that passes and she thinks I have done it. I have done it. She steps outside. She thinks of Ben that bright day in February when they had just begun to know each other, how she longs for him now, standing there, a bag of croissants in his hand, a grin for her.

.   .   .

The wait is long for the results. Rumours. The government is trying to massage them. The opposition has won outright. No need for a second ballot. The army chiefs will never allow this. Never.

The government concedes that the president has lost, but only just. A second round of voting will take place. The election has been stolen. Stolen. Why be shocked? It is the same old story. The Revolution continues.

It has been eight years since it happened. Eight years. She thinks of that girl in her early twenties, newly qualified, so full of fight and hope, and now, here she is, in her thirties, a woman, a mother, a lover. A survivor. Yes, she can call herself that. A survivor. Whatever happens or does not happen to those youths, she has survived. She has lived, continues to live. She has done her best, and yes, perhaps her best was not enough, but she has tried. With Giorgio. With Leah. And even with Danika. She has tried.

Ben sends her a message on the day of their historic win in November.

Change! Yes We Can! Yes, we did!

And she writes back.

Chinja!

She watches the pictures of the crowds in Washington and New York in celebration, the long, mean years over.

But, not here.

Dysentery and cholera in the capital while The Old Man wages his 'Final Battle for Total Control'. After he wins the second round of voting he magnanimously decides to 'negotiate with the little boys of the opposition'. The Old Man's latest rant: cholera as germ warfare by the West.

The final insult: in any deal, every single torturer in the land will be granted immunity from prosecution.

When she looks up at the screen again, it's frozen on a face, a hand lifted in a fist.

'The newly elected Youth Brigade Leader has threatened . . .'

And the nausea rises in her. He is there, breathing his hate into the room.

Coloured, time is short.

This one she knows.

She has felt his hand on her, his breath on her face, her body.

He lay on the bed after his fill. He lay on the bed, snoring.

And now he is here.

The rising of a ghost from its slumber.

Squeeze and release.

She stands by the bed, the gun in her hands, no longer a foreign object but part of her, who she is, who she has become. The man snores. She puts her finger on the trigger like she has seen it on TV, in the movies. She will squeeze, release, and it will be done. Blood and flesh will be her just reward. She is so close. She can do it. Just squeeze and release. But the gun grows heavy again. She feels its weight in her hands. It is a foreign object, no longer who she is, who she has become. She drops it. It clatters on the floor. The man snores. Lives.

54

There is Christmas, New Year with Ben. Days in that little town, in the cabin in the woods, days of rest, days of plenty. He takes her up the mountain and shows her how to ski. The cold is like nothing she has ever felt, it seems to go deep into her bones; the thermals help. She planned to see Leah in Washington but they have gone to England to be with Sara's family and then on to Italy. So she stays for longer with Ben. And they are there at the National Mall in Washington, crushed against thousands of jubilant Americans as their 44th President walks up to the podium and takes his oath. *Change* (Yes, they did it!) finally come. This is her country's dream too, unfulfilled.

They drive on to New York where they will stay for two days, and then she will go back home. Although, when she says that to herself, *go back home*, the words seem stripped of any essential truth, empty and hollow. There is no one waiting for her *back home*. Only good, faithful Mawara.

In a tiny bistro in Soho he mischievously orders a kale dish. It turns out to be a bowl of barely cooked choumoellier, the leaves dark green, glossy, drizzled with olive oil and garnished with an assorted mixture of dried fruit. This is choumoellier like she has never seen. She gamely cuts a piece of a leaf and tries to chew it but is defeated by its toughness and how bitter it is, despite all the camouflage. She discreetly spits it out on a tissue, Ben all the while laughing and teasing her.

And then, over coffee, he says, it seems to her, everything that he has been holding back.

'Gabrielle, this, this isn't working for me.'

And she thinks of something she must have seen in some movie, *break up in a public space so that she won't make a scene*.

'I love you,' he says. 'I want you and me together, in one place, for as long as we breathe, in this life.'

He is looking at her so intently, willing her to say something, something that would make his words true. She doesn't know what to say. She loves him. He knows that. But she doesn't know what living with him would mean.

'I don't want to look after you, Gabrielle,' he says.

He understands her fear.

'I want us to be together, to live a life together.'

She can't find the words to ask him about the practicalities of it all. Where would they live? Does he mean that she would follow him around? What would she do?

'Gabrielle,' he says. 'Say something.'

She leaps into the void.

'I can't leave Zimbabwe,' she says. 'I can't leave.'

He doesn't ask her why, why not.

'Remember, Ben, when you teased me about being an activist?'

'I don't think I was teasing. I was awed.'

'Well, I was doing something that mattered. And I . . . I think I've now come to this place where I feel like I can do something again, I mean not activist work or politics or even law, but, I don't know, something. Maybe it's like you and this election. You had to become part of it.'

The saying of it all makes her feel light-headed.

He cups her face in his hands. 'I love you, Gabrielle Busisiwa Langa. I love you.'

At the airport he gives her such a long, hard kiss as if it is a final goodbye, his letting her go.

.   .   .

Back home, there is the work at the agency. Phone calls with a distracted, fractious Leah. The long nights at home. The Youth Brigade leader is in the news, daily. Her dreams are of Danika, encircled by spirits, their might, the spirits breathing on her, vengeful, one day, she knows, they will unleash their wrath. She thinks of why she told Ben that she could not leave Zimbabwe. She *had* begun to think of doing something, something new. She looks at the university catalogue, even ponders medicine – that would mean going back to school, doing her A levels in Science – too much, but why even consider that? And then she remembers Ben's words. *I had you down as a doctor, that's all.* So, not medicine. She keeps coming back to The Centre. That last place of call for the truly desperate, which no longer exists. She looks about her at this large house, its big grounds, too much for her. The memory of her father's words.

You could have beautiful offices in Borrowdale. What is such an intelligent girl like you doing down here in Hatfield with these people? I can set you up in some smart offices; they can even build it from scratch at Borrowdale Brooke.

Well, perhaps he can get his wish now, in a manner of speaking. Couldn't this become something? A place of refuge. But not only refuge, something else, too, and she struggles to find the word that can encapsulate the idea that is taking shape. *Transformation.* Yes, that's it. A place of transformation. And she thinks that this is perhaps a word she has heard first in the good doctor's office. Not only will there be refuge but also, there will be training facilities and a school, yes, literacy classes, something like that. A place where there can be learning. The idea is breathtaking to her. It is bold. It is dangerous. It will put her out there again. She will become visible. *The only thing you can change about the past is the impact it has on you now.* This is it. This is the moment, the now.

She goes outside, stands on the verandah, looks at all that space, the cottage beyond. She thinks of that morning when she stood here with Giorgio, Leah growing inside her. I can live here, she thought, meaning the cottage. She could manage that. She would pay rent to Giorgio, she thought. She would be independent. She was so lost. And then she sees Danika in the cottage, how she let her go. She failed Danika then, but now perhaps she can do something for the others.

There will be many obstacles. Will the City Council, for one, even give her a licence for any kind of office, centre here? But still . . . there is the voice of Trinity urging her, willing her to snap out of her fear-fuelled inertia and *do* something.

Yes, she will try.

In the middle of March, a phone call from Ben.

'I have some news, Gabrielle,' he says.

'What is it?'

'I'm back with the State Department—'

'That's great, Ben.'

She fears what he will tell her next, what danger zone he is about to go back to.

'And I've made Cultural Attaché!'

She laughs, relieved.

'But that's not the real news.'

Here it comes, she thinks, bracing herself. Here it comes.

'My next posting is in the Republic of Namibia.'

A weight falls from her. She knows that this is not a coincidence, mere luck. If she cannot come to him, he will come to her.

'So, I'll be seeing you, Gabrielle. A lot.'

She has news of her own to give him.

She has, in spite of her doubts, been given permission to open a hospice. That is the term she used in her applications: *hospice* could stretch to mean many things, her lawyer self at work there. She has written countless letters to aid organizations asking for funding, has had plans drawn up for the reorganization of the house and the grounds. She has attended so many meetings that she wouldn't blame Isobel for firing her, for never being in the office.

As she sits on a bench in Africa Unity Square, she takes it all in, this leap she is making, the hard work, the challenges that lie ahead.

She is undeterred.

She is ready.

At last.

23 December 2017

Seventeen years after he first set foot in Zimbabwe, Ben waits impatiently in his seat. He has been travelling for just over a day. He was in Washington when news broke of *the coup that was not a coup*; Gabrielle sent him shaky, WhatsApp videos of the rapturous crowds in Harare clambering up on military tanks embracing and high-fiving soldiers, the images of the placard-waving crowds – *Gucci Grace STOP It* – thronging the streets, all over the front pages of the *Washington Post, New York Times* – and now, a month later, the dust has somewhat settled, The Old Man, banished to his blue mansion in Borrowdale with a generous 'retirement' package and the leader of the *new dispensation, the Crocodile*, promising elections soon which he says will be *free and fair*. Gabrielle: 'Yes well, we've heard that before, Ben.'

He comes to her with news of his own. He is no longer an employee of the State Department. He handed in his resignation yesterday, together with thirty other senior diplomats serving around the world. After a year, his position as Deputy Ambassador had become untenable – he could no longer serve under his country's own *new dispensation*.

As he walks down the stairs, he thinks of Gabrielle who is waiting for him; he thinks of that incredibly strong woman who has stood her ground through it all. If she will have him, he is here to stay. He has ideas of setting up a gallery, getting serious about painting.

But, before she sees him, she will see Leah first – with her bright pink hair, Doc Marten boots, and BLACK LIVES MATTER t-shirt – who is just in front of him. He is holding the folder with the temporary guardianship letter signed by Giorgio, her birth certificate and her passport. She has been his responsibility on this long journey. This is the third Christmas and New Year the three of them will spend together; the first two have both been in New Haven. Once on the tarmac, Leah shoots out ahead and he imagines Gabrielle watching her, smiling. He hopes Leah will show Gabrielle the clipping she has in a notebook – Gabrielle Busisiwa Langa receiving a Human Rights Award in Sweden. Her mother is a hero, more than worthy of her love, forgiveness.

'Welcome to Zimbabwe, sir,' says the immigration officer as he gives him back his passport. 'Thank you, it's good to be back.' For a moment he thinks he may have blown it. If *it's good to be back* it must mean that he was here once before and now the immigration officer will demand his passport back and check for his name against the expelled persons list. He thinks all this even though he was assured by the embassy he was free to come. The immigration officer makes no demand for his passport; he is free to go with Leah.

And then there is that moment when his eyes find her.

Gabrielle.

He doesn't know what it is, perhaps it is something in the air of the new Zimbabwe, but the years seem to spool backwards and he is the oh so young diplomat in the vet's surgery who turns on his heels to find a beautiful girl sitting, a restless dog at her feet.

They walk out into the blazing sunshine, Leah just ahead, pushing the trolley, Gabrielle's hand firmly in his.

AUTHOR'S NOTE

The Criminal Law Amendment Act referenced has been modified in the novel. The full law is: *Criminal Law Amendment Act: Chapter 9:05, Section 3. Unlawful Carnal Knowledge of a young girl or idiot.*

The sections of the law pertaining to 'idiot' have been omitted in the novel.

The Sexual Offences Act [Chapter 9:21] came into effect in 2002.

ACKNOWLEDGEMENTS

My deepest thanks to the following:

Ellah Wakatama Allfrey
Susie Nicklin
Alex Spears
Vimbai Shire
Iain Maloney
Tendai Huchu
and (as ever),
Fabio.

ABOUT THE AUTHOR

Irene Sabatini spent her childhood in Bulawayo in Zimbabwe. After attending the University of Zimbabwe in Harare, she moved to Colombia, where she worked as a teacher. She has a master's degree in child development from the Institute of Education at University College London. Irene is the author of two previous novels; her debut novel, *The Boy Next Door*, won the 2010 Orange Award for New Writers. She divides her time between New York, Geneva and Bulawayo.

THE

INDIGO

PRESS

Sign up for our newsletter and receive exclusive updates, including extracts, podcasts, event notifications, competitions and more.

www.theindigopress.com/newsletter

Follow The Indigo Press:

@PressIndigoThe
@TheIndigoPress
@TheIndigoPress